The Awakening of Dr Amelia Leighton

Vernon Coleman

GW00503532

Books by Vernon Coleman include:

Medical
The Medicine Men
Paper Doctors
Everything You Want To Know About Ageing
The Home Pharmacy
Aspirin or Ambulance
Face Values
Stress and Your Stomach
A Guide to Child Health
Guilt
The Good Medicine Guide
An A to Z of Women's Problems
Bodypower
Bodysense
Taking Care of Your Skin
Life without Tranquillisers
High Blood Pressure
Diabetes
Arthritis
Eczema and Dermatitis
The Story of Medicine
Natural Pain Control
Mindpower
Addicts and Addictions
Dr Vernon Coleman's Guide to Alternative Medicine
Stress Management Techniques
Overcoming Stress
The Health Scandal
The 20 Minute Health Check
Sex for Everyone
Mind over Body
Eat Green Lose Weight
Why Doctors Do More Harm Than Good
The Drugs Myth

Complete Guide to Sex
How to Conquer Backache
How to Conquer Pain
Betrayal of Trust
Know Your Drugs
Food for Thought
The Traditional Home Doctor
Relief from IBS
The Parent's Handbook
Men in Bras, Panties and Dresses
Power over Cancer
How to Conquer Arthritis
How to Stop Your Doctor Killing You
Superbody
Stomach Problems – Relief at Last
How to Overcome Guilt
How to Live Longer
Coleman's Laws
Millions of Alzheimer Patients Have Been Misdiagnosed
Climbing Trees at 112
Is Your Health Written in the Stars?
The Kick-Ass A–Z for over 60s
Briefs Encounter
The Benzos Story
Dementia Myth
Waiting

Psychology/Sociology
Stress Control
How to Overcome Toxic Stress
Know Yourself (1988)
Stress and Relaxation
People Watching
Spiritpower
Toxic Stress
I Hope Your Penis Shrivels Up
Oral Sex: Bad Taste and Hard To Swallow
Other People's Problems

The 100 Sexiest, Craziest, Most Outrageous Agony Column
Questions (and Answers) Of All Time
How to Relax and Overcome Stress
Too Sexy To Print
Psychiatry
Are You Living With a Psychopath?

Politics and General
England Our England
Rogue Nation
Confronting the Global Bully
Saving England
Why Everything Is Going To Get Worse Before It Gets Better
The Truth They Won't Tell You...About The EU
Living In a Fascist Country
How to Protect & Preserve Your Freedom, Identity & Privacy
Oil Apocalypse
Gordon is a Moron
The OFPIS File
What Happens Next?
Bloodless Revolution
2020
Stuffed
The Shocking History of the EU
Coming Apocalypse
Covid-19: The Greatest Hoax in History
Old Man in a Chair
Endgame
Proof that Masks do more Harm than Good
Covid-19: The Fraud Continues
Covid-19: Exposing the Lies
Social Credit: Nightmare on your Street
NHS: What's wrong and how to put it right
They want your money and your life.

Diaries and Autobiographies
Diary of a Disgruntled Man
Just another Bloody Year

Bugger off and Leave Me Alone
Return of the Disgruntled Man
Life on the Edge
The Game's Afoot
Tickety Tonk
Memories 1
Memories 2
Memories 3
My Favourite Books

Animals
Why Animal Experiments Must Stop
Fighting For Animals
Alice and Other Friends
Animal Rights – Human Wrongs
Animal Experiments – Simple Truths

General Non Fiction
How to Publish Your Own Book
How to Make Money While Watching TV
Strange but True
Daily Inspirations
Why Is Public Hair Curly
People Push Bottles Up Peaceniks
Secrets of Paris
Moneypower
101 Things I Have Learned
100 Greatest Englishmen and Englishwomen
Cheese Rolling, Shin Kicking and Ugly Tattoos
One Thing after Another

Novels (General)
Mrs Caldicot's Cabbage War
Mrs Caldicot's Knickerbocker Glory
Mrs Caldicot's Oyster Parade
Mrs Caldicot's Turkish Delight
Deadline
Second Chance

Tunnel
Mr Henry Mulligan
The Truth Kills
Revolt
My Secret Years with Elvis
Balancing the Books
Doctor in Paris
Stories with a Twist in the Tale (short stories)
Dr Bullock's Annals
The Awakening of Dr Amelia Leighton

The Young Country Doctor Series
Bilbury Chronicles
Bilbury Grange
Bilbury Revels
Bilbury Country
Bilbury Village
Bilbury Pie (short stories)
Bilbury Pudding (short stories)
Bilbury Tonic
Bilbury Relish
Bilbury Mixture
Bilbury Delights
Bilbury Joys
Bilbury Tales
Bilbury Days
Bilbury Memories

Novels (Sport)
Thomas Winsden's Cricketing Almanack
Diary of a Cricket Lover
The Village Cricket Tour
The Man Who Inherited a Golf Course
Around the Wicket
Too Many Clubs and Not Enough Balls

Cat books
Alice's Diary

Alice's Adventures
We Love Cats
Cats Own Annual
The Secret Lives of Cats
Cat Basket
The Cataholics' Handbook
Cat Fables
Cat Tales
Catoons from Catland

As Edward Vernon
Practice Makes Perfect
Practise What You Preach
Getting Into Practice
Aphrodisiacs – An Owner's Manual
The Complete Guide to Life

Written with Donna Antoinette Coleman
How to Conquer Health Problems between Ages 50 & 120
Health Secrets Doctors Share With Their Families
Animal Miscellany
England's Glory
Wisdom of Animals

Copyright Vernon Coleman May 2023
The right of Vernon Coleman to be identified as the author of this work has been asserted in accordance with the Copyright, Designs and Patents Act 1988.

The Awakening of Dr Amelia Leighton

Vernon Coleman

Dedication

To Antoinette, the kindest, gentlest, brightest and most beautiful of God's stars: thank you for being you and for everything you do. You make every season, every month, every hour worthwhile.

Chapter One

There are many different kinds of parties.

There are parties organised as celebrations. There are parties organised to promote something or someone. There are parties where the guests wear funny hats and play games. There are parties where people stand around, drink wine and nibble at finger food. There are parties where people sit down and eat endless courses of food served by smartly attired waiters. There are parties which people attend in the hope of meeting new people, and there are parties which people attend in the hope that they will meet people they know but haven't seen for a long time. There are parties where at least some of the people who are there fervently wish they were somewhere else, and parties where at least some of the guests spend at least some of their time trying to avoid people they don't want to see.

There are almost as many different kinds of party as there are different kinds of guests, and the slim girl standing beside the roaring log fire, currently the origin of a cloud of rather sweet smelling smoke, courtesy of a sudden change in the wind, disliked them all. Slightly shorter than average height and attractive in a classic sort of way, rather than extravagantly beautiful or fashionably pretty, she wore her blonde hair cut short, in the sort of style that Clara Bow had first made popular in the 1920s (not that anyone remembered Clara Bow any more) and she wore a simple black dress (which was six-years-old but would never go out of fashion, largely because it had a hem which could quite easily be raised or lowered according to the dictates of the merry band of gay frock designers in Paris who decide these things – it was, for those whose role in life it is to take note of such things, currently just above knee level), simple black shoes (in court style – also unlikely to go out of fashion), a classic pearl necklace (fake, but good enough to fool anyone not equipped with a loupe and a professional eye) and classic pearl earrings (fake and ditto). She also wore the old Rolex that had once been her paternal grandfather's, had been worn by her father and which was now hers because she no longer had a father and didn't have any brothers. (She didn't have any sisters either.) She'd had the watch's classic two tone band altered to fit her wrist, which was (inevitably and rather happily) several links smaller than her late father's had been.

The young woman looked around her, thinking that she really should make more of an effort. After all, the party had been arranged in her honour. Still, she thought, the other guests seemed to be managing quite well without her.

The room she was in, clearly a drawing room, was over-furnished in the way the Victorians used to favour, with ornaments on every flat surface and pictures decorating just about every square inch of wall; it was crowded and warm, though not uncomfortably so. And books! There were books everywhere. There were three glass fronted walnut bookcases and two open shelved bookshelves and there were books piled high on the floor. Virtually none of the books had dust wrappers.

Outside it was an agreeable day, the first really warm few hours of spring, and the log fire, crackling and spluttering in the huge fireplace, wasn't necessary, though it gave the room a focal point. There was a huge basket of logs to one side of the hearth and a huge set of fire irons on the other. People in London ranted angrily about log fires, complaining that they were destroying the quality of the air and contributing to global warming, but she liked the smell and the look and the sound. Was that shallow, she wondered? Probably. Did she care? No, she didn't. There were two leather armchairs, one each side of the fireplace, their leather cracked and split open in places, and one leather sofa, facing the fireplace, also showing signs of having been sat upon a great deal, an oak writing desk with an old ladder back dining chair, a mahogany table covered in books, of course, six chairs, five of which matched. It was a large room. The young woman looked around and realised that although there were at least twenty people in the room, it wasn't the people who made the room look crowded but the furniture.

She didn't hate parties in the same way that she hated long, dull meetings, cauliflower cheese or car parks that won't let you park unless you have a smart phone equipped with the correct app, but she'd never really grown to like them. The party for her 14th birthday was perhaps the most recently memorable and thoroughly enjoyable one that she could remember, and, although that had been

15 years ago, she vividly remembered that she had eaten too much cake and suffered a probably well-deserved stomach ache that kept her awake for hours. She hadn't dared complain because her mother had repeatedly warned her about eating too much of the cake. But her grandmother, who had been a baker by trade and a cake-maker by inclination, had made the cake especially for her and it had her name written on the top in pink icing. Under those very special circumstances it had seemed quite reasonable to eat as much of the cake as she'd been able to manage. She could remember everything about that party. All her friends and acquaintances had turned up with presents, and her parents had hired a conjuror who wasn't very good and who told terrible jokes, the sort of gags you usually found only in crackers. Dr Leighton had been mortified to start with. Only small children had conjurors at their birthday parties. But everyone had laughed (more 'at' than 'with' the performer) until their stomachs ached.

Remembering the party brought sadness to her heart, as it always did. Five months later the world had slipped off its axis when her father had suffered a massive heart attack and had died at his desk. He'd gone off to work that morning, cheery and looking forward to a football match on the television that evening, but he had never come home. There hadn't been any more parties or holidays or day trips to the seaside or the wildlife park. Her mother, overcome with grief, had started drinking to make the evenings bearable. And then the afternoons had needed blotting out, and finally the mornings too.

She had long ago realised that the bit of her that might have enabled her to enjoy dressing up, abandoning her daily anxieties and letting herself go in the way that her contemporaries seemed able to do, was under-developed or missing altogether and she found herself wondering why this was. Maybe it was because she was too conscious of the behaviour of the other guests. Maybe she was too inhibited. Maybe she was just too shy. Too often, she thought, too many of the participants at parties she'd attended had been trying too hard to be witty, wise, bright and beautiful while other guests, wrapped in their insecurities, were busy studying books in a bookcase, looking for ones they'd read or even heard of, or trying to look desperately interested in the curtains or the glass they were holding. ('It looks like crystal but I don't like to do that 'ping' test.') Parties, she thought, were like alcohol: they made some people become more like themselves, or more like the 'themselves' they thought they were, or more like the people they thought people expected them to be, or wanted them to be.

Tired and bored by her own introspection, she decided to make yet another effort to stop herself thinking, and to try to just start enjoying.

And that was another thing, she thought straight away. She'd never mastered the art of just allowing herself to relax completely. She'd never been able to just 'go with the flow', as her ex-husband used to say. Peter had gone with the flow many times and eventually flown off with an advertising executive who insisted on being called Waldo but whose real name was Philip. Waldo, or Philip, had flown away himself a month later but Peter hadn't returned and for that she was grateful. She wondered if she ever would be capable of relaxing and going with the flow. On the whole, she thought it was rather unlikely.

She suddenly became aware that Dr Hill, the host of the party and now her new employer, was saying something. Dr Hill was very softly spoken and she couldn't always hear what he said. She didn't like to keep saying 'Pardon?' so she just tried to guess what he was saying. She wondered if she were going deaf. It didn't seem very likely at twenty nine but you could never tell. Maybe she had an acoustic neuroma. Like most doctors, and all medical students, she was very good at thinking up rare and often deadly disorders with which to label even the most commonplace of signs and symptoms. Or maybe Dr Hill just didn't speak very loudly.

She'd only met Dr Hill once before, when she'd been interviewed for the job, and he had seemed taller than he now appeared to be. He was remarkably thin, almost skeletal, and wore a linen jacket, that was creased in that expensive way that linen always seems to be creased, and a pair of corduroy trousers that were bald on the knees and around the pockets. She couldn't help noticing that he needed a haircut too, although there wasn't all that much hair to cut. He was clearly not a man who spent a good deal of money or time on his appearance. She wondered if he had always been a bachelor or if he had ever had a wife. He certainly didn't look like a man who'd have ever had a wife or, for that matter, ever been a husband. Even at her age she felt she could tell, somehow. Mind you, things had changed a lot in the last few years. Today, in London just about every other man she met delighted in talking about his husband doing this, his husband doing that, his husband being wonderful, his husband being very caring, very good looking, very everything. She was just old enough, and old-fashioned enough, to still find this rather strange. Not uncomfortable, just strange.

'This is Dr Amelia Leighton, who will be working with me in our practice,' said Dr Hill, introducing her to a middle aged man with no hair at all on his head but, as though in generous compensation, a generous growth of the stuff sprouting from both ears, both nostrils and his upper lip. Dr Leighton didn't quite catch the man's name and didn't like to ask Dr Hill to repeat it. The man, who appeared to have no neck at all, was quite round and looked, she thought, a little like one of those dolls that can't be pushed over because they always bounce back and become upright again. Dr Leighton wondered which of the man's cervical vertebrae were missing and whether he found having no neck an inconvenience. The hair decorating his upper lip had been groomed in the shape of an old-fashioned toothbrush moustache, the sort which the Grandfather she had never met had worn in the sepia pictures which had been her only memory of him, though this moustache looked as though it hadn't been trimmed for a while and her Grandfather's moustache had been manicured perfectly, though perhaps just for the photograph. The spherical man's moustache was lopsided too, one side being notably longer than the other. She wondered, idly, if it were possible to tell if a man were right handed or left handed simply by looking at the irregularity in his moustache. It was the sort of query that a postgraduate student in search of a PhD would leap on as a suitable subject of enquiry. Several crumbs of what looked like some sort of pastry were clinging to the growth, and Dr Leighton wondered if the man ever combed them out or just brushed them onto his tongue if he suddenly felt peckish. He wore a three piece suit in a very loud tweed check which made him look like a bookmaker. He was holding a food-laden plate in one hand and a wine glass in the other, and he somehow managed to transfer the wine glass to the hand holding the plate so that they could shake hands. She tried not to wince. Someone had obviously told him that if a man has a firm handshake it means that he is solid, reliable and trustworthy. She wondered if anyone had ever done any research into whether a firm handshake meant anything at all. She couldn't help noticing that the plate he was holding was laden with pastry covered brown food; there looked to be plenty of fats and carbohydrates but very little in the way of protein or vitamins. She wondered what his coronary arteries looked like; she imagined she could see them silting up.

'What do you do? In what way will you be assisting?' asked the man with the moustache, putting a good deal of emphasis on the last word as though he'd just said something remarkably clever and funny. He had a remarkably patronising way about him. It's not easy to be patronising in two short sentences but he managed it with plenty of words to spare.

Dr Leighton stared at him, bemused, not quite sure how to answer. He looked, she thought to herself, like the sort of man who has expensive luggage and wraps it in protective covers and then, when he arrives at his expensive hotel, removes the covers so that the porters and reception staff can admire his expensive luggage.

'Dr Hill is here to work with me,' explained Dr Leighton. 'In the practice.'

'Oh, you're a doctor!' said the man with the moustache, the iron grip and the almost certainly narrowing arteries. 'I thought you were here to help out with the housework and the laundry – a bit of cooking and dusting and stuff like that.' He laughed merrily at what he clearly thought was a jovial remark. 'Are you really a proper doctor? You've very short for a doctor. Are you going to look after the women with their special problems?'

'I didn't know there was a size requirement for doctors,' Dr Leighton replied, thinking that three insults in a single breath were pretty good going. 'I think that used to be the case with policemen, but I think I heard that they'd abandoned that rule now.' She decided that if the man wore a hat he would probably protect it with a plastic cover if there were any threat of rain. She disliked him quite intensely. Unconsciously, she tried to stand a little straighter, caught herself doing it and slumped back to her more normal posture. But she did wish she'd worn shoes with a bigger heel. She was five foot three inches tall. That, she thought, wasn't small at all. Even in quite flat heels she was five foot four inches tall and that's nearly five foot five inches. That was quite a decent height for a woman. Why, she wondered, did people feel it so easy to criticise others for their appearance. You were too small or too tall, too thin or too fat. Her red shoes, the ones from Jimmy Choo, had three and a half inch heels and they would have made her over five feet seven inches tall. She felt herself reddening with anger. She wanted to say something cutting but her brain let her down. She never thought of witty things to say until she was in bed, or in the bath, and wherever it was, the bon mot always arrived a few hours too late. She thought most people were probably much the same but she did envy those who were quick witted. Her former husband, Peter, would have skewered the pompous, little man with a sentence or two and left him deflated like an old balloon. She wondered why she kept remembering Peter and hoped it wouldn't be long before she didn't. She hadn't worn the Jimmy Choo shoes, she tried to convince herself, because they just didn't go with the dress she'd chosen. But she knew that wasn't true. She hadn't worn the Jimmy Choo shoes because Peter had bought them for her as a birthday present and she didn't like to wear anything he'd bought her. Actually, he hadn't paid for them. He'd been broke and she'd had to pay. But she always thought of them as shoes he had bought her. She would have given them to a charity shop but they cost a fortune and she'd have to work her way up to giving them away. She'd never have paid that much for a pair of shoes herself. And she'd always thought 'Jimmy Choo' a rather silly, childish name for a pair of shoes anyway. She wondered if there had ever actually been anyone called Choo. It seemed unlikely. And she was furious about the crack about patients with women's problems. Did Dr Hill only deal with prostate difficulties?

'Have another vol au vent,' said Dr Hill to the pompous man with the moustache. Dr Hill had picked up a plate laden with the things, and he now offered him the plate, or, rather, his choice from the plate's contents.

'Oh yes. Rather like those,' said the man with the moustache, bending over the plate with a greedy gleam in his eyes, even though the plate he was holding was already piled high with brown food.

'Well, take two. They look home-made but we got them from the village shop. They have an excellent bakery display just next to their Post Office counter.'

'I've never been in the village shop,' said the man with the moustache. He said this as though he were complimenting himself.

'Oh you should,' said Dr Hill. 'It's run by Mick and Doreen; a lovely couple who come from Middlesbrough.' He stopped and thought for a moment. 'It might have been Marlborough. Or even

Scarborough. It's almost certainly somewhere ending in borough. He was an accountant and she did something or other with income tax and they'd both always wanted to run a village shop. Isn't that strange? I wonder if it was a dream they shared or a dream one of them had and then the other acquired later?'

The man with the moustache, whose name Dr Leighton hadn't quite caught, took two, bit the first one in half and sprayed flaky pastry everywhere. 'So you can buy buns and stamps at the same shop?'

'Oh yes, village shops have to do a bit of everything to survive. I can't see how they make a living to be honest but they always seem happy and welcoming. They do deliveries in a very old Citroen van. The one they used to advertise as having such a good suspension that you could drive over a ploughed field without breaking the eggs you had piled on the back seat.'

Dr Hill, sensing that Dr Leighton, was about to explode and wanting to introduce her to the other guests, gave her a glass of wine and led her away.

The wine, as Dr Leighton already knew, was white, cold and quite delicious. At the last reception held by her previous practice the wine had always been warm and sharply acidic, the sort that would have given a car battery a severe bout of indigestion. The glasses, she noticed looking around the room, were all different – some were proper wine glasses, some were tumblers and some were whisky glasses. Hers was an old-fashioned champagne glass, one of the ones with a big bowl that allowed the bubbles to escape too quickly. You really could tell Dr Hill was a bachelor, she thought. He was in his mid to late 60s she thought, and she remembered, with a smile she didn't show, that he had told her earlier that he had organised the catering himself. It was clear that organising the catering meant calling in at the bakery, pointing to things and taking out his wallet. She wondered where on earth he'd found the wine and strongly suspected that it wasn't on a shelf in the village shop.

'His name is Scrymgeour Wallace and he invited himself,' whispered Dr Hill, as he moved her away. 'He hasn't lived in the village long, but he bought himself a house here a few months ago. It was one of those houses that gives the owner the right to describe himself as Lord of the Manor and he likes people to address him as 'Your Lordship'. I always forget I'm afraid. He had a coat of arms drawn up by those people in London who do those things and had it put on his notepaper.'

'Do you have parties very often?' asked Dr Leighton, who was pretty sure she knew the answer to her question before she asked it.

'To be honest with you, no, not very often,' replied Dr Hill. 'I'm afraid I am not what you city folk would call a party person. I had one to celebrate the moon landings, I was very young then, of course, just an assistant to my predecessor, and I think the last party I organised was held to celebrate young Charles's wedding. The one when he got married to that young girl who died so tragically. We didn't have a party for the other wedding, though I've nothing against the new woman despite the fact that she seems a little determinedly horsey. And we certainly didn't bother when the sons got married. We thought about a celebration party when Queen Elizabeth died but it didn't seem appropriate to have a party, even though it would have been a celebration for her life, not her death, of course. I just thought it would be nice to have a little get together to welcome you to the practice and to the area.'

Dr Hill put a hand on Dr Leighton's shoulder, very gently, and for just a brief moment, smiled and nodded. 'I'm not sure it was entirely the most sensible thing to do,' he added softly. 'But it was arranged with the best of intentions.'

Dr Leighton thought he had a very comforting, reassuring manner and was probably an excellent, if perhaps slightly eccentric general practitioner.

Dr Leighton smiled at him, as though what he'd said made sense and muttered something appropriately grateful. She was trying to remember what year the moon landings had taken place. Dr Hill must be older than she thought. And she wondered where the other partner was. She hadn't yet met him, which seemed strange to say the least.

'Is your partner not here?' she asked, looking around.

'Mallory, that's Dr Croft, doesn't socialise much,' explained Dr Hill. 'He sent his abject apologies. He's really not being rude but he finds the world a bit of a trial and doesn't much like having to talk to people.'

'Doesn't that rather make his life as a GP rather difficult?' asked Dr Leighton. 'How does he manage?'

'Well, he doesn't actually see patients,' replied Dr Hill. 'I do the surgeries and any visiting that's necessary. That's why I needed another pair of hands.'

'So what does Dr Croft actually do?'

'He does the paperwork and sorts out the accounts. Believe me, as far as I'm concerned that makes a fair sharing of the workload. We have a small practice, less than a thousand patients, but the paperwork expands every year and Mallory keeps all the bureaucrats off my back. It's amazing how much easier it makes life. Financially, we manage satisfactorily thanks to a few rural practice payments we receive. And we do our own dispensing which brings in a little extra money.'

Just then there was a loud cheer and looking around, Dr Leighton could see that a thin, sharp faced woman had climbed up onto the dining table and was waving for everyone to be quiet. 'I'm going to recite a poem,' she announced.

'That's Miss Jackson,' whispered Dr Hill who was clearly surprised by this development. 'She's a local school teacher and a parish councillor. She's usually very restrained.' He looked a trifle confused. 'She's not usually like this at all. On the whole, I would say she is usually on the dreary side of dull.'

Miss Jackson seemed to have lost all her inhibitions. She recited the first verse of something that Dr Leighton thought was probably by Wordsworth, forgot the next verse, recited a few lines by Burns and then gave up and started to sing a Christmas Carol. As she sang, she kicked off her shoes and then removed a very thick tweed skirt.

'It can't possibly be the wine,' said Dr Hill in a whisper. 'Imelda Jackson is a fervent teetotaller. And even when I need to examine her she's always very reluctant to remove any item of clothing which covers anything above her ankles.'

Miss Jackson then started to remove her blouse, but had trouble with the buttons. Having sung a verse of Hark the Herald Angels sing, she suddenly sat down with a thump and started to hiccup uncontrollably. As she did so a very small man wearing a suit made for a man at least three sizes larger climbed up onto a chair and started to explain why the earth wasn't spherical, as most people apparently believed it to be. He suddenly stopped preaching, sat down on one of the leather armchairs and started to snore very loudly.

'That's the vicar,' said Dr Hill now obviously very confused. 'He's not known to be a heavy drinker either.'

'Well, if it's not the wine…' began Dr Leighton.

'…it must be something in the food,' said Dr Hill, completing the thought for her. 'Come with me. Have you met Martha, my housekeeper and cook?'

'No, I don't think she was here when I came for my interview.'

'Ah, no it was her day off. I remember. You must meet her,' insisted Dr Hill, taking Dr Leighton by the elbow and leading her through a door and into a huge, old kitchen where a plump, red-faced woman who looked to be in her eighties was sitting at a large pine table staring into space.

'Did you by any chance add anything extra to the food?' asked Dr Hill.

Martha, looked up at him and then at Dr Leighton. She seemed rather pleased with herself. 'Well the vol au vents seemed rather dry so I borrowed one of your syringes, doctor, and squirted in something to make them a little moister. I hate a dry vol au vent.'

'What did you squirt into them, Martha?'

'That,' said Martha, nodding towards a half empty bottle standing on a nearby Welsh dresser.

Dr Hill picked it up. 'Sodium amytal,' he said, showing the bottle to Dr Leighton. He turned to his housekeeper. 'How much did you put in each vol au vent?'

'Just a syringe full. It was a small syringe. Very small. And that was all they seemed to need to soften them up a bit.'

'Did you do anything else to the food?' asked Dr Hill, who seemed surprisingly calm.

'Well the trifle looked a bit thin so I added a few dozen stuffed olives and the rest of the gentleman's relish,' said Martha. 'The gentleman's relish had been in the pantry for months because you bought it but don't like it and it seemed a pity to throw it out.'

'Did we have stuffed olives? I didn't think we had any stuffed olives.'

'I stuffed them myself.'

'What did you stuff them with?'

'I found some lovely red, little jellies in the dispensary. I cut them in two and they fitted very nicely into the holes in the olives. They made the olives quite chewy.'

'Which jellies were those?

Martha stood up, found a box on the dresser and showed it to Dr Hill who showed the box to Dr Leighton. 'Pessaries,' he said, unnecessarily.

'Was there anything else?'

'There weren't any of those little sugar things on top of the trifle so I added some.' Martha thought for a moment. 'Hundreds and thousands they call them.'

'And we didn't have any of those, did we?'

'No, we didn't. So I made some. I found some pretty red tablets and some blue ones and ground them up. They look really lovely. Very colourful.'

'So that's the vol au vents and the trifle? Did you add anything to anything else…?'

'Oh no,' said Martha, beaming. 'Everything else seemed fine.'

Dr Hill and Dr Leighton went back out into the drawing room and collected up the plates containing the vol au vents and the two dishes containing the trifle.

'Oh are you taking those away,' said the man with the moustache, pouncing on them as from nowhere. He grabbed three vol au vents and put them onto his plate. Dr Leighton and Dr Hill looked at each other but neither of them said anything. They then took the plates out into the kitchen and quietly emptied them into a waste bin.

'Martha is well into her 80s and suffering from some variety of dementia,' explained Dr Hill. 'She has been with the practice since she was a girl and I could never sack her – it would make her very sad. But perhaps I need to keep more of an eye on her.' He smiled. 'She sometimes gets confused about which is the cooker and which is the fridge but I've got used to drinking cold soup. I don't think anyone will come to lasting harm.'

'Have one of these instead,' said Dr Leighton, when they were back in the drawing room. He offered her a plate which was full of chunks of pineapple and cheddar cheese on little wooden sticks. 'These are fine,' he said, when he sensed her reluctance. I put these together myself. And the doughnuts and mince pies are fine. I was surprised they had mince pies for sale in May but Doreen in the shop, I'm sure it was Marlborough that they came from, assured me that although they were left over from Christmas they were still within their sell-by-date. I did try one, I confess, and found it a trifle chewy.' He paused. 'I could find you a packet of biscuits if you'd prefer. I wouldn't blame you a bit. I think we have some Hobnobs. And there may be some chocolate digestives.' He looked a little embarrassed. 'I eat a lot at the pub,' he explained. 'Or they send something over.'

'I'm not really hungry,' said Dr Leighton.

'Would you like another glass of wine?'

'Oh no, thank you.'

'Well, I think I will,' said Dr Hill.

'Aren't you worried that you could get into trouble?' asked Dr Leighton.

'What on earth for?' enquired Dr Hill, who seemed genuinely puzzled by the suggestion.

'For inadvertently drugging your guests,' explained Dr Leighton.

'Oh no, I don't think that'll be a problem. I always keep the key to the dangerous drugs cupboard in my pocket,' he said, taking a small key out of his waistcoat pocket'. 'And in future I'll keep the dispensary door locked too. There's no point in worrying about these things. No great harm has been done.' He saw the rather startled look on Dr Leighton's face. 'I promise you we are usually a pretty dull crowd.'

Dr Leighton found it difficult to believe that just a month earlier she had been in a London suburb, sitting, bored to tears, in a practice meeting where the participants had, with great seriousness, been discussing the advisability of making gender neutral loos available for the patients.

Chapter Two

Dr Amelia Leighton had been working in a large, multi-partner general practice in London. That had been the beginning of a journey which had brought her to Dr Hill's drawing room and a world in which serving vol au vents laced with a barbiturate had somehow seemed to her new employer to be of little real consequence.

She remembered sitting behind her large, soulless desk and looking at the large clock on the wall opposite her. The clock had been carefully positioned, behind the chair where each patient routinely sat, fixed high on the wall in such a spot that only she could see it. The position of the clock had been selected by time and motion experts who had been brought in when the practice building was designed. It was there to remind her that allotted time for each consultation was five minutes. Dr Leighton was booked to see ten patients in each hour, with the extra ten minutes allocated for typing in additions to each patient's medical notes (on a special software programme installed on the computer on her desk) and adding suggestions, where appropriate, for referrals to the local hospital.

And since, Mrs Tapley, the current occupant of the patient's chair had been there for three and a half minutes. Dr Leighton had just ninety seconds left in which to bring the consultation to a conclusion, to offer advice and to tell the patient what, if anything, she intended to do to arrange further help. She couldn't remember when she had last had time to examine a patient. There was an examination room down the corridor, equipped with a couch and a sink, but she hadn't used it for weeks. There simply wasn't the time for such day-consuming niceties. The time and motion person had deliberately installed the examination room in an inconvenient position so that it would be rarely used. The practice building and organisation had been designed, in its entirety, to maximise the number of patients who could be seen and the profit that could be squeezed from their care.

But no one had told Mrs Tapley that her allotted time was running out and she was still alternately talking and crying. She'd already used up two of the paper tissues from the box which was conveniently positioned on the patient's side of the desk.

'I bought one of those blood pressure machines from the chemist,' said Mrs Tapley. 'Just as Dr Chester suggested. She said that if my Reg wanted to be seen by a doctor he had to come to the health centre. But he hasn't been out of the house for six months. He sleeps in a chair in the living room and hardly moves from it. We did try to get a taxi to bring him here but the taxi driver said they couldn't bring him. Our flat is on the first floor and we have no way to get him down the stairs.' She dabbed at her eyes. 'I bought the best blood pressure machine I could afford. They're quite expensive, aren't they?'

Dr Leighton, listening to this, felt deeply ashamed of her profession, her practice and, indeed, herself. It was by no means the first time she had felt embarrassed and ashamed. She sometimes couldn't understand what had happened to medicine. Dr Chester was another of the doctors working in the practice. Dr Leighton, who found her colleague cold and supercilious, had never got on with her.

The notes on the computer confirmed that Dr Chester, who was one of Dr Leighton's colleagues, had seen Mrs Tapley on her last visit. The practice's highly efficient appointment system did not allow patients to choose which doctor they saw and it was, indeed, quite rare for patients to see the same doctor twice in a row. Scrolling through the screen in front of her, Dr Leighton could see that on Mrs Tapley's last seven visits she had been seen by four different doctors and three different nurses.

'I'm afraid they are expensive,' said Dr Leighton, who privately thought it dreadful that patients were now expected to do almost everything themselves. Patients of the practice were told to take their own blood pressure, to test their own urine, to take their own pin prick blood samples, to inject themselves and to do just about everything shy of open heart surgery at home and by themselves, under only the loosest of medical supervision. She glanced at the clock which was still ticking away mercilessly; it was equipped with a large, red second hand which seemed to take special delight in catching her eye and holding her attention away from her patient.

Mrs Tapley had not come to the health centre for herself but on behalf of her husband, who was a few years older than her, and although still only in his mid-sixties already had heart failure, diabetes mellitus and high blood pressure. Old age can, and usually does, bring a variety of inglorious afflictions. The list sometimes is literally endless: angina, valve troubles, myocarditis, high blood pressure, deafness, joint troubles, backache, cataracts, glaucoma, macular degeneration, incontinence, a smorgasbord of different types of dementia, impotence in men, bowel disorders, sciatica – oh the diseases circle like buzzards as the elderly become weaker and less resistant. Some of them arrive singly while others seem to hunt in packs. It isn't always easy to see where one problem ends and another begins. And diagnosing all these problems can be like doing a puzzle; with clues appearing and then disappearing and then reappearing, and with prescribed medications smothering some symptoms and causing others.

Over the years, different doctors (most of whom had never actually seen Mr Tapley, let alone examined him, had prescribed a variety of powerful drugs for him to take) and as a result he was, each day, swallowing a complex cocktail of medicaments. Most of the drugs, thought Dr Leighton, had probably been prescribed to deal with side effects caused by some of the other drugs on the list. Some of the pills needed to be taken every three hours, some were prescribed to be taken four hourly, two were recommended to be taken twice a day and there were three tablets and capsules which, it said clearly on the computer, were designed to be taken once a day. It did not say on the screen whether they should be taken in the morning or in the evening, though the consequences of getting this wrong could be calamitous. Dr Leighton had lost track of the number of patients she had seen who had complained of drowsiness in the day time and insomnia and incontinence at night, and whom she had discovered were taking their sleeping tablet in the morning and their diuretic last thing at night.

'We tried to take his blood pressure but couldn't find it,' said Mrs Tapley. 'Our neighbour came in to help. She used to work as an orderly at the hospital so she's got some medical training but not even she could use the machine. The instructions weren't very easy to understand. I think they were in Japanese.' She dabbed at her eyes again. 'It could have been in Chinese,' she said after a moment's thought. 'I hope this doesn't sound racist but I'm afraid I can't really tell the difference.' She paused. 'I expect they can themselves, though,' she added.

'Would you like me to come and visit him at your home,' said Dr Leighton suddenly, after glancing at Mrs Tapley's address. 'I could pop in later this afternoon, after I finish the next clinic.' When she'd spoken, she suddenly felt apprehensive. Doctors in the practice weren't allowed to visit patients at home. She wasn't quite sure why but there had been a directive from the British Medical Association or the Royal College of General Practitioners or some other body. She wasn't quite sure what the thinking was behind the ban but seemed to remember it was something to do with protecting the planet from climate change. Nevertheless, she didn't see how stopping her car on her way home could be a serious threat to polar bears or glaciers.

'Oh would you?' said Mrs Tapley, eagerly. 'Are you allowed to do that? Oh that would be a great relief if you could.'

'Well, if you don't tell anyone I won't get into trouble,' said Dr Leighton with a small smile. 'Would about five o'clock be alright with you?'

Mrs Tapley said that would give her plenty of time to get home on the bus and that it would be very fine indeed.

Chapter Three

And so it was that at just after five that evening Dr Leighton parked her Lotus sports car in the small car park provided for the block of privately owned and operated flats where the Tapleys had lived for over thirty years.

Acton Court was not, she thought, the sort of place where the flats were likely to be featured or advertised in magazines such as *Country Life* or *My Beautiful Home*. Three of the six available car parking spaces were occupied by burnt out hulks, two of them without wheels and balanced rather precariously on piles of bricks, and the grassy patch that had presumably once featured prominently in promotional photographs, was now almost entirely grey with occasional flashes of worn-out green where there had been grass. The whole area was decorated with surprisingly generous monuments to the canine bowel.

Dr Leighton looked around, hoping not to see the over-sized beast which must have been responsible for the monuments. She took her handbag and a plastic bag containing a sphygmomanometer and a print out of Mr Tapley's medical records from the passenger side front seat and locked her car. This she did rather more, it has to be said, in hope rather than expectation that the lock would protect her pride and joy. The Lotus was the first brand new car she'd ever owned and she was very proud of it. It had been, and still was, her only expensive, self-indulgent purchase.

As she moved towards the front door of the flats, tip toeing between the souvenirs left behind by the beast, the broken beer bottles and the empty cola cans, she regretted the fact that she had never acquired a black medical bag. It would have made a better weapon than a plastic shopping bag.

She remembered that her own GP had, on the solitary occasion when he had visited her (she had been suffering from the chickenpox) had carried with him a large, black Gladstone bag (so named because a former British Prime Minister had hardly ever been seen without a similar valise) from which he removed a seemingly endless variety of instruments: she remembered a stethoscope, an auriscope and a thermometer. And there had been (she knew because she'd peeped) lots of small bottles and packets of pills.

These days GPs didn't do home visits at all (not even for emergencies) and so there was no need for a GP to own let alone to fill a black bag. It was, she thought, a pity. She'd have enjoyed selecting a proper, old-fashioned sort of bag and fitting it out with suitable equipment.

As she climbed the crumbling concrete stairs to the first floor, she found herself wondering what Gladstone had kept in his bag and why he was always pictured carrying it. The stairs stank, and there was clear evidence that they had been used for more than climbing. Fluid stains, condoms, broken bottles, and evidence left behind by the anonymous dog all made it vital to tread carefully. A light bulb, hidden behind a rusty metal grill, was still shining but it didn't give out much light and Dr Leighton didn't think that sensitive, ailing, frail or nervous residents would want to be out and returning home after dark.

It occurred to Dr Leighton that she had never before been into the home of someone she didn't really know. It was true that as a young girl she'd visited friends in their homes. And she had visited Peter's parents once or twice, but that had been very different. This seemed strange, intrusive in a way. She wanted to turn round and run away. She could always tell Mrs Tapley that she'd discovered that the doctors weren't allowed to visit patients at home. She could say there was a law about it. She could say she got lost. She could say she had a family emergency or that her car broke down. She could, she thought, smiling to herself at last, say that the dog had eaten the address.

Promising to visit Mr Tapley at home had been easy when she'd been sitting in her consulting room, with the patient's wife sat opposite her, on the other side of the desk. But now she felt nervous. No, she thought, she felt terrified. When she'd worked as a doctor in hospital, the patients had been seen on her terms. The hospital gave her the home ground advantage that sports teams regard as so significant. And seeing patients at the health centre wasn't very different. The health centre was, again, her home ground and an alien, frightening place for patients. Her own GP, when she'd been a child, had worked in the front room of his own home. What was clearly the family's dining room doubled as a waiting room. The family's best crockery could be seen in a glass fronted cupboard and there were family photographs on the walls. The dining table was covered with magazines, most of them dog eared and years out of date, but it was obviously a dining table. And instead of being tucked neatly under the table, the six dining chairs were, with a dozen other assorted chairs, old and battered, arranged around the table. On busy days, if the doctor was running behind time, additional patients stood in the hallway or sat on the stairs. The receptionist sat on a chair behind a moveable trestle table, with two filing cabinets behind her and a telephone and a large diary in front of her.

Eventually, Dr Leighton found the front door to the flat she was looking for and rang the bell. Moments later she was admitted to a narrow hallway that smelt of a strange mixture of furniture polish and some sort of antiseptic, though less attractive and rather more pungent odours lingered irresistibly in the background. She was then led into a small sitting room, roughly the size of the rarely used examination room at the health centre premises. There was just enough room for two armchairs, both covered in a nauseating orange fabric which Dr Leighton thought must have been commissioned in error or purchased at a special knock-down sale price, a rather elderly looking television set, balanced on top of a rickety looking table and a sideboard, upon which were arrayed bottles and packets of pills and a clipboard upon which was fastened a chart of the pills for the day. The date was written on the first sheet and it was clear that underneath it lay a sheaf of similarly sheets, all ready to be brought into use. It was, it seemed to Dr Leighton, a simple but effective way of dealing with an overload of medications and it occurred to her that with so many drugs to sort, to remember and to swallow there can have hardly been time for Mr Tapley and Mrs Tapley to do anything else with their lives.

'My grandson Jorge made the charts for us,' said Mrs Tapley, having noticed the direction in which the doctor's eye had roamed. 'They help us keep track of Reg's pills. Jorge is eleven and his teacher says he is very bright. I asked him the other day what he wanted to do when he left school and he said he either wanted to be a plumber or a hospital administrator.'

Dr Leighton, who thought that Jorge was indeed as bright as his teacher had suggested and that these were sensible career choices, assumed, not without good reason, that Reg, Mrs Tapley's husband and the reason for the visit, was the extremely large man wearing the half of a pair of garish heliotrope pyjamas and a pair of grey Y fronts and sitting in, and over-filling, one of the easy chairs. He looked, thought Dr Leighton, like a hen's egg balanced on a thimble. His ankles were so swollen that the bones had been swallowed up in a continent of white, oedematous flesh and he was wheezing and coughing alternately. He did not look like a man you'd want to commission to carry a message from Marathon to Athens for you. Actually, he didn't look like a man you'd expect to be able to cross the room. A glass urine bottle and a bed pan, both apparently freshly washed, were positioned almost out of sight on the floor and gave some clue as to the nature of the unattractive odours lingering in the background.

Mrs Tapley introduced the doctor to her husband and her husband to the doctor.

'It says in your records that you have a serious hearing impairment,' said Dr Leighton, enunciating each word with particular care and making sure that Mr Tapley could see her face.

'Oh, I don't know about that, doctor,' said Mr Tapley. 'But I am a bit deaf. I worked in a car factory for years. There was a lot of noise. They didn't tell us to wear ear defenders in those days. Everyone who worked there went deaf.' He spoke slightly louder than most people, but not extravagantly so.

'How are you feeling?' asked Dr Leighton, immediately regretting the senselessness of the question. Mr Tapley was sitting in a chair from which it was clear that he rarely, if ever, managed to escape. He was having trouble breathing and his legs were the size of tree trunks. It was, she thought to herself, like asking a man on death row what plans he'd got for the future.

'Quite well today, thank you,' replied Mr Tapley entirely unexpectedly. It was, the young doctor thought, a very English sort of answer. She suspected that an American or a Frenchman might have recited a litany of complaints in response to such a query. But a man like Mr Tapley would never readily confess to feeling anything more than slightly under the weather.

'Can you roll your sleeve up?' asked Dr Leighton, taking the sphygmomanometer out of the plastic bag she was carrying.

Mr Tapley tried, but after he had succumbed to a rather alarming flurry of coughing and wheezing, his wife moved forward, took over and rolled up his pyjama sleeve. His whole arm was a mass of bruises or, rather, it seemed to be just one very large bruise.

'What on earth has happened to your arm?' asked Dr Leighton, staring in horror at the multi-coloured skin.

'He had some blood taken,' explained Mrs Tapley.

'Who on earth took the blood?' asked Dr Leighton, without thinking.

'One of the doctors at your health centre,' answered Mrs Tapley. 'It was four months ago. We'd asked for a repeat of the prescriptions and we got a phone call from a receptionist telling us that Reg needed to have a blood test before his prescriptions could be renewed. Reg was a bit more mobile then, though we had quite a job to get him to the health centre and back. It took us a whole day and the taxi there and back cost £70. We had to ask a neighbour to help carry Mr Tapley down the stairs because the taxi driver couldn't manage by himself. When we got back from the health centre the neighbour had gone to work so we had to sit on the bottom step for two hours and wait for him to come home.'

'Who was the doctor you saw?'

'I think his name was Dr Keith,' said Mrs Tapley. 'That's what he told us we could call him.'

'A thin, young man with red hair?'

'That's right,' beamed Mrs Tapley.

Dr Leighton nodded sadly and wrapped the cuff of her sphygmomanometer around Mr Tapley's arm. Keith, she knew, was certainly not a doctor and had no medical qualifications whatsoever. His solitary examination success had been in obtaining two GCSE certificates: one in basic golf course management and the other in gymnastics. He was one of the care assistants and some sort of relation of Mrs Fuller, the practice manager, a woman with firm opinions and an unbridled enthusiasm for red tape which she openly regarded as an essential means of constraining such dangerous emotions as imagination and hope.

Although he wore a similar white coat to those worn by the receptionists and nurses, and sometimes liked to try to pass himself off as a doctor, the practice manager's relation had absolutely no medical or nursing training and shouldn't have been taking blood samples. He was employed to help the maintenance man and was supposed to hold ladders and carry the maintenance man's bag of tools. Mind you, thought Dr Leighton, the practice phlebotomist wasn't much better than Keith was. Her blood taking always seemed to lead to a large bruise, and Dr Leighton suspected that this was because instead of approaching the vein from an angle close to the horizontal, she attacked the vein from the vertical – with the result that she was inevitably doomed to go straight through the vein, puncturing the back of the vessel as well as the front, producing copious internal bleeding and, subsequently marking all her patients with large and painful bruises.

The practice manager allowed her relative to do whatever he liked and Dr Leighton wouldn't have been surprised to have turned up one day to find him examining patients. The ones chosen for examination would, she suspected, have all looked like the sort of women who pose for the type of calendars which ended up hanging on the office wall in garages and workshops. She had a rumour that Keith sometimes asked the best endowed female patients to pose nude for photographs which, he apparently and falsely claimed were for inclusion in their computerised medical records.

'Have you been feeling dizzy?' she asked Mr Tapley, when she'd taken his blood pressure.

'I have,' he agreed. 'If I try to stand up I have to hold onto something. If I don't I'd fall over.'

'Your blood pressure is very low,' said Dr Leighton. The systolic pressure, the higher of the two numbers, had been considerably below 100 mm of mercury when she'd have expected it to be at least 20 mm higher. She started to sort through the bottles and packets of pills. 'Why do take these?' she asked him, picking up one bottle.

'To lower my blood pressure,' replied Mr Tapley.

'And these?' she asked, showing him another bottle.

'What's the name on the bottle?'

Dr Leighton told him.

'I think those are also to lower my blood pressure.' He closed his eyes in contemplation. 'Or the doctor may have given me those for the itchy spots I had last summer.'

Dr Leighton, who had vaguely heard of the name on the bottle (and with, literally thousands of drugs on the market who could possibly have heard of them all) looked up the drug in the pharmacopeia which she'd wisely brought with her. 'You were right the second time,' she said. 'They were prescribed last summer when you had an itchy rash. You were only supposed to take them for a week or two at most.' She plucked another bottle from the display. 'And these?' she asked, holding up a bottle of dark red pills.

'I'm pretty sure that those are to stop my blood clotting.'

'And these?' She held up a bottle of small, blue tablets.

'I was given those because my blood was too thin. The doctor who gave me those thought I needed something to thicken my blood.'

Dr Leighton smiled and nodded but felt like screaming. The blue tablets had been prescribed to oppose the action of the red tablets. She wondered why no one had thought of simply reducing the dose of the dark red pills. She took another bottle off the sideboard and showed it to Mr Tapley.

'The doctor said those are to help me pass urine,' said Mr Tapley with confidence. 'I have to take them last thing at night.'

'Are you sure you are supposed to take them at night?' asked Dr Leighton. 'Diuretics, designed to increase urinary outflow are usually prescribed to be taken in the morning.'

'Oh, I think so,' said Mr Tapley, now not quite so sure. 'Would those pills make me wake up and pass urine several times during the night?'

Dr Leighton said they would. She looked at the label on the bottle. It contained no information about when the pills needed to be taken.

And so it went on. Those tablets are for my heart. Those capsules are for my chest. Those pills are for my legs. Those pills are to get rid of fluid. Those tablets are to lower my blood pressure. Those capsules are to relieve the dizziness I get if I try to stand up. Those are for my kidneys or my bowels. Those are to help me sleep. Those are to wake me up. Those are to stop the itching caused by these. Those are to stop the diarrhoea which these capsules cause. Those are to help with my constipation. Those are for pain, though to be honest I don't have much pain. Those are also for my blood pressure – though I'm not sure whether they're to bring it down or push it up. Those are in case in I get a severe pain in my chest. Those are for anxiety. Those are for the depression which I've developed since I started taking all these other tablets.

'And what do you do with these?' asked Dr Leighton, picking up a box of suppositories.

'Oh I take those every morning and every evening,' said Mr Tapley. 'They're a bit rubbery, very chewy, and they taste pretty terrible. I can't remember what they're for.'

Dr Leighton explained that the suppositories contained a painkiller. 'But you're supposed to put them into the hole at the other end of your intestinal tract!'

'I told you so!' said Mrs Tapley to her husband with glee. 'They're like pessaries.'

'What are pessaries?' asked Mr Tapley.

'You don't need to worry about that, dear,' said Mrs Tapley, patting him on the shoulder, looking at Dr Leighton and nodding conspiratorially. Dr Leighton smiled back. It had long ago occurred to her that although suppositories are an excellent way to give drugs and reduce the side effects (and are immensely popular with the French) they aren't well suited to the British patient.

Arrayed upon the sideboard there were 32 different bottles of pills, capsules and tablets and two bottles of medicine and the box containing the suppositories which carried a very small label, printed in minute print suitable only for someone equipped with a microscope, warning that the contents should be kept in the fridge.

As the months and years had gone by, the various practice doctors had each added new remedies to the toxic cocktail taken every day by Mr Tapley and, as Dr Leighton had suspected, one half of the drugs seemed to have been prescribed to combat the side effects caused by the other half. It wasn't the most chaotic collection of prescriptions Dr Leighton had ever seen, but it wasn't the most logical either. The tragedy was, she knew, compounded by the fact that the situation in front of her was repeated in millions of homes because the medical establishment had created a system which excluded common sense and promoted mayhem; the system denied patients access to the same doctor but in large practices allowed doctor after doctor to add their signature to the chaos, without anyone ever trying to make sense of the whole.

And two factors made things worse.

First, the habit of providing repeat prescriptions, largely on demand and largely without end, meant that once a patient had begun a course of treatment, they were likely to stay on it until they died – whether or not they still needed the treatment. (In practice it was not uncommon for prescriptions to be issued, quite automatically, long after a patient had died.)

And second, the establishment's decision to prohibit all home visits meant that the sickest patients, the ones most desperately in need of some thought and the ones who were physically unable to travel to the doctor's consulting room, were never seen or assessed by a doctor at all.

'Your blood pressure is a little low,' said Dr Leighton. She spoke directly to Mr Tapley, since he was the patient and she thought a doctor should always address the patient directly rather than via the relatives, the nurses or the maintenance man changing a light bulb (as she had once seen happen in a hospital where she'd worked) but from time to time she also addressed Mrs Tapley because Mrs Tapley was half of what was clearly a very close marriage, and it was because of Mrs Tapley that she was there with Mr Tapley and because in her heart Dr Leighton believed, or perhaps wanted to believe, that when two people have been together as long as Mr Tapley and Mrs Tapley had been together then they become as close to being one person as it is possible for two people to be.

'I think you are taking too many tablets,' she added. 'I think we can cut down what you need to take.' And so Dr Leighton patiently went through the pills and the tablets and the capsules one by one and looked at the medical records she had brought with her, and she accessed a formulary on her smart phone and checked out all the side effects and found out which drugs could be stopped because they were duplications or dangerous or old and now known not to do what they had originally been thought to do (because drug companies keep making old drugs which no longer work, since older doctors often just keep prescribing them without ever bothering to check out what has been shown to be as useless and as out of date as blood-letting and arsenic tablets).

All this took her an hour and a half but it was time well spent because she knew it would change Mr Tapley's life for the better. She was, at last, practising real medicine. She was, she thought, making a difference.

'These are the only medicines you need take,' she eventually said to Mr Tapley. She turned to Mrs Tapley. 'Do you have a plastic shopping bag I could have please?' She looked at the pile of pills she had to take with her.

Mrs Tapley went into the kitchen and came back with a plastic bag. Dr Leighton swept all the superfluous pills and tablets and capsules off the sideboard and into the bag. 'I'll amend your medical records to show that when you need a new prescription these are the only drugs you need.'

And when she was ready to leave, Mr Tapley insisted on shaking her hand and Mrs Tapley was in tears and kept asking if she was sure she wouldn't have a cup of tea and something to eat because it would be absolutely no trouble at all to make something and even if she didn't want a proper meal, wouldn't she just have a piece of cake because they had some which was fresh and everyone said it was very nice because it had coffee cream in it and walnuts on the top, and Dr Leighton gave her a hug and it was the first time she'd hugged a patient since she'd become a GP though she remembered that once when she'd been a medical student she'd hugged a patient whose six-year-old son had died when he'd been knocked off his bicycle by a lorry, and then she remembered that when she had been doing her first job as a house officer in hospital she'd hugged a woman whose husband had died at just 42 years of age after a heart attack.

And eventually Dr Leighton left carrying three bags. The first bag, the one she'd brought with her, contained her sphygmomanometer and that part of Mr Tapley's medical records which she had printed out. The second bag contained all the pills and tablets and capsules that weren't needed. And the third bag contained a large piece of home-made cake and six home-made scones, which Mrs Tapley said would taste much better if they were spread with a little butter and possibly some jam. And Mr Tapley said his favourite was strawberry jam but just about anything would do and he had to be careful because of his diabetes but, he said, Dr Leighton didn't have to worry and should smother the scone with jam and clotted cream as they did in the cafes in Devon and Cornwall in the West of England.

It was dusk when Dr Leighton walked down the staircase and back to her car. Because it was becoming dark, she felt nervous and she was pleased when she was settled back in the Lotus and on the road again. She was also relieved that her motor car still had all four wheels.

But she was glad she'd been to see the Tapleys. It had been the most professionally satisfying time that she could remember since she'd started in general practice.

Chapter Four

Dr Leighton looked at her watch. She had been in the Wednesday morning edition of the Practice Participatory and Planning Meeting for six minutes but it seemed more like six months. For the last five of those six minutes she had been bored and daydreaming.

The practice manager, Mrs Fuller, who always chaired these three times a week meetings had been droning on, yet again, about waste, explaining that if lights were switched off when not necessary, emails used instead of sending letters which required postage, the central heating turned off in rooms which weren't being used and tap water used instead of bottled water there would not only be a considerable saving in fiscal terms but the environment and the planet would benefit enormously from the saving in otherwise wasted energy and resources. She gave the same lecture once a week and although it was doubtless well-intended, it was rather losing its effectiveness since very few of those listening to it were hearing what she said.

The practice held these meetings on Mondays, Wednesdays and Fridays and attendance was compulsory. Even the senior partner, and the four other partners in the practice, always attended.

Dr Leighton looked around. The conference room was huge and for these meetings the chairs were arranged in a circle, presumably, she thought, to give the proceedings an air of democratic informality. She counted the number of people in the room, and after three attempts had produced three different results. She concluded that there were 41, 42 or 43 people present. If everyone employed by the practice had been present, there would have been 54 people in the room and they'd have had to bring in chairs from the waiting room. Several members of staff were on holiday, three who had just given birth were taking their twelve months maternity leave, one of the salaried GPs was on sick leave and she had no idea what had happened to the rest or where they were. The front door of the health centre was locked and so there was no one manning (or, more properly, womanning) the reception disk, and an answering machine was telling any callers that the practice cared about their welfare very much and would they please visit the website if they wished to order a repeat prescription or make an appointment. Those without access to the website were advised to ring back another time. Those with urgent problems were advised to ring for an ambulance or make their way to the local hospital.

Dr Leighton did not think any of this was the way to run a practice but she didn't know what to do about it. Her suggestions that they change things, or at least discuss the possibility of changing the way the practice was run, had always been met with negativity.

And so, by managerial consent, the health centre premises were open from 9 am until 11 am and 2 pm until 5 pm on Mondays, Wednesdays and Fridays and from 9 am until 1 pm and 2 pm until 5 pm on Tuesdays and Thursdays. After 5 pm, and at weekends and on bank holidays, the telephone answering machine told callers to contact the number of an emergency doctor. Theoretically, this meant that the practice offered patients a 24 hour, seven day a week service but unfortunately the emergency doctor was responsible for an area which contained nine million patients. The duty emergency doctors never left the telephone they were paid to answer, and all they ever did was tell callers who needed medical help to visit the Accident and Emergency Department attached to their nearest major hospital. An answering machine would have been just as useful but then neither the practice nor the NHS would have been able to claim that there was a doctor available 24 hours a day.

It was hardly surprising that the A&E department couldn't cope and that patients usually had to wait at least 12 hours (and sometimes much more) to be seen, and even then they would usually be seen by a nurse or lightly trained health assistant.

Years before, hospitals had been instructed that patients who visited casualty departments had to be seen within four hours but no one took this seriously now. The local hospitals got round this woefully unambitious casualty waiting time target by employing what was called a 'hello' nurse. The nurse just says 'hello' but didn't offer any treatment. She wrote down the patient's name, and what appeared to be wrong with them, but that was all. But she was officially the end of the waiting time. Struggle into a casualty department with a leg hanging off, and a nurse will totter over and say 'hello'. That's it. Hello. You can sit there and bleed to death. No one cares. You've been seen within four hours. Everyone knew it was deceitful and dishonest, but it satisfied the regulations and it fit the Government's style like a rubber glove. Of course, broken bones would eventually be plastered, gaping wounds would eventually be stitched but patients suffering from heart attacks or strokes would be lucky to live and patients whose problems or concerns could have been sorted out by a GP in five minutes would wait most of a day and then be told, brusquely and without sympathy, to go back home and make an appointment to see their GP. Dr Leighton was painfully aware that the system had broken down and no one, least of all the GPs whose changing working practices had caused the breakdown, seemed interested in mending it.

When she'd been a small girl, Dr Leighton's family doctor had worked alone, with his wife, a former nurse, serving as his receptionist and secretary. How things had changed.

The practice in which she was employed had five GP partners, two junior partners, eight salaried GPs (of which Dr Leighton was one, and one of three on the shortlist for promotion to junior partner), four registered nurses (one of whom had a certificate entitling her to prescribe drugs), two health care assistants (whose duties she had never really understood), a phlebotomist (who did nothing all day but take blood samples), a Health and Safety Officer, a Human Resources Manager (together with an assistant), the practice manager (who was pretty much in charge of everything including, it sometimes seemed, the doctors and who had her own personal assistant as well as her own secretary), a quality and performance manager (whatever that was), a diversity manager (whose main job seemed to be to ensure that all racial, religious and sexual inclinations were properly respected), two reception managers, five dispensers, twelve receptionists, a senior administrator who dealt with all the paperwork (all computer records not relating directly to patient care were printed out at the end of each day and stored in a row of twelve filing cabinets with one cabinet being emptied every three months and sent off to a secure storage facility three hundred miles away), five ordinary administrators, two prescription clerks, a medical records summariser (who had for three months been arguing that she needed an assistant), four medical secretaries and a full-time maintenance man who had an assistant to help him (this meant to hold the ladder if the maintenance man had to replace a light bulb and to hold the tool bag if a dripping tap needed attention). There were, in addition, three attached social workers (who always attended all the practice meetings and were constantly campaigning for them to be held daily, rather than merely three times a week) and two attached nurses who were supposed to travel around the district attending to bandages and so on but who seemed to spend most if not all of their time drinking coffee and eating biscuits in the reception area. Amazingly, the practice where she worked was not the largest in the area. She didn't know of any single-handed GPs still in practice, and the smallest practice in the area had six doctors and an appropriate number of administrative staff.

The chairs were distributed in two rows and Dr Leighton always tried to sit on the outer row so that she could hide away as much as possible. She never, or hardly ever, spoke at these meetings. She examined the head of the man sitting in front of her. Dr Henderson was in his early 40s, still a salaried GP and rather bitter about the fact that he hadn't been put onto the shortlist for promotion. He had a bald spot on the back of his head which Dr Leighton thought was noticeably bigger than it had been a fortnight ago when she'd last examined it. She wondered if he knew but then realised that he could not possibly know unless someone told him. Did he care, she wondered. Some men cared enormously about going bald. Maybe his hairdresser told him and offered him some sort of ointment or salve to encourage hair growth. Her hairdresser always held up a mirror behind her so that she could check the back of her head. She wondered if barbers did that for male customers. It was strange, she thought (her attention now wandering freely and quite untethered from the proceedings to which she was supposed to be devoting her attention) that barber surgeons were the forerunners of surgeons. They used to cut hair, remove legs and chop out bits of anatomy which were regarded as, for some reason superfluous or dysfunctional. She had read somewhere that barber surgeons, or surgeons as they eventually became known, were regarded as the lowest of the low – well beneath apothecaries and doctors who were members of the Royal College of Physicians.

All this inconsequential trivia passed through Dr Leighton's mind as she avoided listening to the droning voice of Mrs Fuller. And when the practice manager had finished, it was the turn of Dr

Partridge, one of the partners and the only one who always spoke at all these meetings. Dr Partridge was second in line to become the senior partner and she was painfully aware that time was running out if she were to achieve her ambition and move into the permanently allocated corner consulting room that went with the post of 'senior partner'. She was constantly heard encouraging the man who stood in her way, and who was just two years older than her, to think of the joys of retirement and the limitless joy of endless rounds of golf.

Dr Partridge spoke quietly, and with an adopted mid-Atlantic drawl which she felt gave her an air of worldliness which her natural voice, bred in the west midlands, would have almost certainly denied her. And she always spoke on the same topics: keeping down prescribing costs and limiting the number of investigations (blood tests, X-rays and so on) which were ordered. Somehow, she always managed to find yet more evidence to support her favoured hobby horses. One week she argued that generic drugs offered a huge cost saving over branded drugs, and the next week she argued that too many investigations were ordered. Her argument was not that patients were unnecessary inconvenienced, or put at risk, but that the costs of unnecessary investigations were an unsupportable burden and a danger to the environment and to global health. These two speeches alternated interminably and the assembled staff listened, or pretended to listen, and nodded or shook their heads as when they thought it most appropriate. Dr Partridge usually concluded her advice with the suggestion that all patients who needed blood tests or X-ray examinations should simply be referred to a hospital consultant on the unarguable grounds that this would reduce the time the practice spent in ordering, receiving and filing the inevitable results.

The next speaker, Mrs Rogers was one of the receptionists who had a complaint to make about the new white coats with which they had been issued as compulsory wear.

'There's a very real problem with these coats,' she said defiantly and with great confidence. 'It's a potential transparency issue. I accidentally spilt some coffee on mine so I washed it off straight away with water and a little soap only to find that the material became quite diaphanous. If I had been wearing black underwear under the coat the underwear would have been very visible to patients.'

'Do you only wear underwear under your white coat?' asked Dr Quentin, who seemed genuinely startled by Mrs Rogers's complaint. 'And would it not be possible to wear white or skin coloured underwear in order to prepare yourself for any such unlikely eventuality?'

'Under what circumstances do you think it possible that your white coat might become wet?' asked the practice manager, steaming into the conversation. 'We spent £2,500 buying this new supply of coats. I don't want us to consider replacing them so soon.'

'Well, if one of us was out in the rain for any period of time,' suggested Mrs Rogers, after some thought.

'You shouldn't be going out in the rain in your white coat,' said Mrs Fuller firmly and immediately. 'It's a simple question of avoiding damage to the coats. These coats are to be worn in the reception area and to and from your locker in the mixed gender conveniences.'

Dr Leighton, who had now woken from her reverie about barber surgeons, was surprised that the practice manager did not seem concerned about the question of hygiene. She had read some discussion in one of the journals of the risk of staff taking antibiotic resistant infections out from hospitals and health centres and into the community. She thought about mentioning this and then decided, as she usually did, to keep quiet rather than introduce another element into the discussion.

'If there were a fire in the building then we'd have to go outside,' pointed out another receptionist, who was hidden from Dr Leighton's view. 'And if the fire brigade were called there would be bound to be water around.'

There was a pause as this thought was assimilated.

'I don't think it appropriate for the practice to tell us what colour underwear we can wear,' said Miss Norman, who hadn't been listening to the whole of the conversation but had been told by Miss Vincent, who was sitting next to her, that Dr Quentin had suggested that receptionists should wear white brassieres. The remark, made rather offhand, had been misinterpreted, as Dr Quentin should have realised it would be, and Dr Leighton thought that this might at least take the meeting into new and possibly revealing areas for discussion.

There were murmurs of surprise from those members of the staff who had completely missed the previous parts of the conversation. Encouraged by what she thought of as signs of support, Miss Norman extended her theme. 'Are there going to be rules about the colour of underwear that male members of staff should wear?' she demanded. Miss Norman who was a militant feminist and lesbian always had to be taken seriously lest she initiate a formal complaint against the practice. To date she had initiated five formal complaints, all of which had taken a good deal of time to resolve.

'I think we're straying off the point,' said the practice manager, endeavouring to rescue the discussion from what she realised could soon become a tabloid scandal. 'I think maybe we do need to ask the supplier of the white coats to confirm that the coats do not become unduly transparent if they become wet.'

'Or clingy,' said Miss Norman. 'We don't want them to become too clingy. We don't want to look as if we're taking part in a wet T-shirt competition.' She visibly shuddered at the thought of this.

'I've just started to go through the menopause,' said Mrs Hughes, in a very loud voice. Mrs Hughes, a receptionist, was slightly deaf and a specialist in sharing non sequiturs.

No one quite understand the relevance or the significance of this revelation but it was genuinely felt, by those in attendance, that the best way to deal with what could have proved to be both something of a red herring and a side issue, was to express sympathy and solidarity and to move on and so this was done.

'I think we should consider refusing to wear these coats until all this is sorted out,' said Miss Wilson, the phlebotomist who had also been issued with one of the white coats. When she spoke, everyone in senior management listened very carefully because her husband was a reporter on the local newspaper and was, moreover, believed to have been the source of a story about an unfortunate incident which had taken place when the ceiling based fire extinguishers in the gender neutral cloakroom had inexplicably turned themselves on, severely embarrassing Mrs Smithson who had been using the facilities at the time and who lived on her nerves at the best of times. She had emerged, drenched, and hysterical and had had to be driven home, wrapped in two towels and Dr Tavistock's Burberry raincoat, by Dr Tavistock himself. The story, embellished with four quotes, two allegations and a threat, all of which had later been denied by everyone concerned, had appeared in the national press and had even merited a 30 second 'funny piece' on the local television news. The practice manager had, as a result, insisted that everyone undergo a two hour symposium on Gender Awareness Training conducted by an American woman who had a rather sparse beard and a very hectoring style. The result of that was a confused and confusing period during which Miss Norman announced that she would in future prefer to be known as 'him' while Ms Siddows, who had been known as 'her' for a two week trial period would go back to being 'him' but keep the name Violet.

It was perhaps the memory of this unfortunate experience which brought Dr Bishop into the conversation.

'I think we should perhaps take another look at our gender neutral loos,' he said. 'Not the ones for staff, obviously they are a splendid idea and must be retained. The space saved has enabled us to provide a small meeting room for the visiting social workers.' This confidential assertion was met with silence. No one liked the gender neutral staff loos and most people, except Dr Quentin, had privately expressed reservations to the practice manager. 'I am however, still slightly concerned about the gender neutral loos for patients,' he continued. 'The removal of urinals means that there are always long queues and there have been a number of problems with teenage boys hanging around and on at least two occasions trying to peep under the cubicle doors.'

'The doors are only six inches above the floor,' pointed out Mrs Fuller.

'I am aware of that,' said Dr Bishop. 'But on two occasions teenagers have been found lying flat on the floor, using a mirror to try to see inside the cubicles.'

This was met with more silence, since one of the teenage boys involved was the younger son of one of the social workers attached to the practice and it had been agreed, particularly by the social workers, that these incidents should be forgotten and never mentioned again.

'I'd like to mention the biscuits,' said Mrs Jones, leaping into the silence. Mrs Jones liked to remind everyone at least once an hour that she was a member of the Green Party and had attended four of the last conferences to discuss global warming. She regularly defied Mrs Fuller's instructions that white coats should not be decorated with badges of any kind by attaching to hers several badges advertising the wonders of the Green Party and the perils of global warming. 'I think we should endeavour to source locally produced biscuits. Some of the biscuits we have purchased are imported.'

This suggestion was greeted with total silence. An entire meeting, just a month earlier, had been spent discussing the type of biscuits which should be bought and the prospect of having to revisit the issue was not one which was generally welcomed.

'And I think we should also purchase only locally grown tea,' she added.

'Is there any tea grown in Britain?' asked Dr Quentin. 'I thought all tea came from Ceylon.'

'I think you'll find that Ceylon has been known as Sri Lanka for some time,' said Mrs Perkins.

Dr Quentin publicly apologised to the meeting and to the people of Sri Lanka and quietly hoped that his faux pas would be forgotten and not end up as a page lead in the *Daily Mail* newspaper.

'Maybe we could organise a sub-committee to look into this,' suggested Mrs Perkins. 'If necessary we could make a suitable donation to a responsible fair trade supporting charity.'

No one was excited by this suggestion and in the silence which ensued, Mrs Jones pointed out, not for the first time it has to be said, that she felt that all letter headed notepaper and all the practice leaflets (of which there were many) should be printed in Welsh as well as English.

'I think we looked into this and found that the practice did not have any patients who are exclusively Welsh speakers,' said the Practice Manager.

'If we take that attitude then the Welsh language could die,' argued Mrs Jones.

'I don't think that is a burden which we could be expected to take upon our shoulders,' said the Practice Manager. 'If we print our headed notepaper in Welsh as well as English there will be very little room left for any communication and we will end up using twice as much notepaper.'

'Printing all our leaflets in Welsh as well as English will adversely affect everyone's end of year Christmas bonus,' pointed out the senior partner. This was the equivalent of solving a playground fight with a nuclear bomb, and Mrs Jones's suggestion was immediately forgotten.

'Talking of the annual bonus, I would finally like to add one more recommendation that I found in the suggestion box,' said the Practice Manager. 'The person who wrote it, anonymously of course, suggested that we could increase our throughput of patients if allotted appointment times were reduced from five minutes to four minutes. This would improve the practice productivity by 20% at a stroke and enable the practice to obtain a regional health authority productivity award. And the productivity award would allow us to improve the annual Christmas bonus by a commensurate amount. I'd like to hear the meeting's views on this suggestion.'

Suddenly there was what sounded like a scream of pain. It was only when she realised that everyone was staring at her that Dr Leighton realised that she had been the source of the scream.

'I do apologise,' she said, feeling herself redden with embarrassment. 'I think it was a little touch of hay-fever.' She looked around at a sea of curious and disbelieving faces. 'It seems to start earlier and earlier,' she said, now very red faced and apologetic. She did not, in truth, feel in the slightest bit apologetic for her outburst.

Dr Leighton was not just bored. It was more than that, although boredom itself can be an under-rated pain. The extreme boredom she felt had led her down its usual back-roads and by-roads into annoyance, frustration and weariness. She felt angry, though she wasn't entirely sure why, and she wasn't entirely sure with whom or with what she felt angry.

She would have rather spent her time dealing with patients, for that was why she'd become a doctor, but it seemed to her that neither she nor any of the other doctors spent much time looking after patients these days. The practice seemed committed to looking after itself, more than to looking after patients. There was much talk of cutting costs, maximising income, avoiding lawsuits and practising defensive medicine and very little attention was paid to the needs of patients or to solving clinical problems. She couldn't remember when she had last had a clinical discussion with one of her colleagues. Patients who were regarded as in some way 'ill' were immediately referred to a specialist at the local hospital. Their problems would then be regarded as having been 'solved' though the patients would invariably wait many months for a primary appointment , wait more months for investigations to be performed, wait months more to receive the results of their investigations, wait months for a second appointment to discuss those results and then, if they were still alive and regarded as well enough to manage the rigours of the recommended treatment process, wait months again for an appointment for whatever remedy had been considered appropriate. She felt that, in many cases, opportunities were missed for helping to get patients better without sending them to hospital.

Like most of the other doctors she knew she spent three quarters of her time filling in forms (the General Medical Council, which controlled doctors' licences and which, like all bureaucracies, was devoted to acquiring more power and money, required registered and licensed doctors to fill in a filing cabinet full of forms every year and took licences away from those who failed to do so or who were, for some reason, unable to do so with satisfactory speed and comprehensiveness) and she sometimes wondered how the profession had allowed itself to be bullied into such a woeful state.

She was, in short, dispirited and out of love with medicine. She was not yet 30-years-old and already she felt burnt out. The idea of spending the best working years of her life doing what she was doing now filled her with a deep, dark depression. She was, like all her colleagues, very well paid but she envied acquaintances who had simpler jobs and earned far less money but who seemed more content. Whenever she had her hair cut she found herself envying the hairdresser, and she had more than once considered abandoning medicine and taking up some other profession.

It suddenly occurred to her (and she had no idea where this thought came from) that her life had made her increasingly isolated and that although she had plenty of acquaintances (mostly people at work for whom she signed birthday cards, congratulatory cards and leaving cards) but apart from Jasmine, a doctor who worked as a medical researcher in London and who was, in truth, more of an acquaintance than the sort of person you could ask for help at three in the morning, she didn't have a single friend in the world. There was no one with whom she could share the way she felt. She looked around the room and realised that she knew very little (a synonym for 'next to nothing') about the outside lives of the people she regarded as acquaintances. People left, to take a year off for a pregnancy or a wife's pregnancy, and she often didn't even notice they'd gone until they suddenly returned.

And her problems were not confined to her work. Dr Leighton had once heard it said that we are all susceptible to emotional, mental and physical changes in three separate areas of our lives – relationships, home and work – and that we should endeavour to avoid changes which affect more than one of those at a time.

Dr Leighton had problems in all three of those areas.

She was, as we have seen, deeply unsatisfied at work.

Her last serious personal relationship had dissolved just four months earlier, when she and her former husband had divorced. The divorce had, according to her solicitor, been only moderately acrimonious by some modern standards but she had felt, at the time and for a month or so afterwards, seemed that the word 'moderate' was woefully misplaced. Her erstwhile husband, an ambitious cosmetic surgeon who worked in a London hospital (and was building up a large and remunerative private practice) had suddenly moved out of their shared flat and into a flat occupied by a male fashion model and former patient of his. Dr Leighton could not remember now just why she had married him but when she thought about it (which she tried not to do) she reckoned it probably had something to do with the fact that he had been applying (unsuccessfully) to be adopted as a Parliamentary Candidate for the Conservative Party and had been told that in order to be successful he needed a wife. And so he'd asked her to marry him and she, not quite knowing why, but not wanting to spoil his chances at becoming an MP, had said 'yes'. She wondered if there had ever been a feebler excuse for getting married. That had been two years earlier and the political landscape had changed. Today, he would, she thought, take along his male boyfriend and be welcomed. Indeed, the selection committee would probably be more impressed by his turning up with an a la mode husband (in designer, painted on jeans and a pink sweater) rather than with a boring, old-fashioned, wife in a little black dress and pearls. He would, she thought, make a successful politician. It occurred to her that the most daring thing he'd ever done in his life had probably been to remove the Do Not Remove tog rating tag from a duvet.

When he had moved out (without warning of any kind) the surgeon, now out of a closet she didn't ever know he'd been in, had stripped the flat of just about everything of any value (including a wardrobe full of £4,000 suits and £800 shirts and silk socks which cost as much if not more than her best frock) and, proving himself greedier than she had ever suspected, had pretty well emptied their joint account (leaving just enough in to keep the account alive and so to ensure that the bank didn't write to Dr Leighton to tell her that the account had been closed). He knew her well enough to know that she'd never complain and would let him get away with it. She thought it was sad that he had so carelessly destroyed all the good memories she'd once treasured though there hadn't been many of those. She searched her memory and came up with the time, when they first met, when he had looked at her, examined her as though he were an antique dealer and she a prize piece of 18th century furniture, looking at her from this angle and then from that angle, and then told her that she bore an uncanny resemblance to Audrey Hepburn, the film actress, famous for such classics as 'Roman Holiday' and 'My Fair Lady'. (The knowledge, acquired later, that he routinely compared women he met to film stars had only slightly affected the delight of that moment.) There was the time, on their honeymoon in Italy, when their rented car had broken down and they'd had to walk five miles in a thunderstorm. The car, a convertible without a hood, had been of no use as shelter and they'd had no coats or umbrellas. They'd eventually arrived at a small village, both soaked to the skin, and in the first café they came to, shivering in their wet clothes, had ordered huge bowls of steaming hot fish soup, containing something neither of them could identify (nor particularly wanted to identify) and a litre of local red wine. The proprietor had wrapped huge towels around them and suddenly, for no reason at all, they had both looked up, seen each other draped in colourful, striped beach towels and had spontaneously burst out laughing. Out of that adversity had come glorious memories.

But the happier memories had been submerged in more recent and less joyful memories.

Dr Leighton had arrived home early one Thursday evening to find that the only furniture left in the flat was their bed, a kitchen table made by IKEA and a solitary armchair. Just as concerning was the fact that the flat, which they had rented together, cost far too much for her to continue to occupy by herself.

And thereby lay the third problem, though here there had been a modicum of good fortune.

When Dr Leighton telephoned the owner of the block of flats, she was told that she need give only one month's notice since there was a queue of prospective tenants, all prepared to pay considerably more in rent than she and her husband had been paying. She had escaped the embarrassment of living in accommodation she could not afford but in just a month she would be homeless.

So, that was her life. She had no real friendships, no husband and no home and her work life was unbearably unsatisfying. She tried hard not to feel sorry for herself but found it difficult.

Eventually, the morning's meeting finished and the participants broke up and went their separate ways – some heading home for lunch, some heading for the staff lounge where they would invariably sit alone, eat their packed lunches alone, heat soup on the stove or use the microwave oven to warm up a ready prepared meal. Some headed into town to have lunch in a café or one of the few remaining pubs, and maybe find time for a little light shopping.

Dr Leighton always thought it odd, and rather sad, that in the staff lounge people mostly sat alone. Occasionally, two receptionists would sit together, but mostly people ate by themselves, constantly looking at their smart phone screens, constantly scrolling upwards and downwards, occasionally tapping the keyboard. Time and time again she had been shocked to see people using their mobile phones to communicate with each other without talking. Someone had once told her that teenagers on nights out would, while sitting opposite one another in a café, communicate exclusively by text or email. It seemed strange but it was true. In the staff lounge, as in the health centre as a whole, conversation was rare, friendship non-existent and gossip unheard of. Dr Leighton had wondered why this was, at first, and had eventually realised that everyone was afraid of saying the wrong thing, being overheard and being reported to the practice manager, who very much believed in the value of snitching and sneaking and who felt that whenever two or three were gathered together, betrayal could only ever have a positive effect. She positively encouraged and rewarded those who went to her with small pieces of evidence of disloyalty.

'Could I see you for a moment, Dr Leighton,' called the unmistakeable voice of the Practice Manager.

Dr Leighton's heart sank. Appointments with the practice manager were, like tax audits and blocked drains, rarely a source of merriment or celebration.

Chapter Five

The Practice Manager (who had made it clear on numerous occasions that when her job title appeared in written communications, it should be dignified with initial capital letters) worked in a corner office which was exactly the same size as that of the senior partner, and decorated with the same IKEA furniture that had been used everywhere in equipping the building. The emphasis was on economy and functionality rather than on style. The pictures, all of which were screwed to the walls, were modern art prints in rather dull, washed out colours which made them look faded. Someone, probably the Practice Manager herself, had read that pictures on the walls make people feel more at home and more comfortable. Traditionally (which is to say a few thousand years ago) it had been proven that patients benefitted enormously if music were played and wards decorated with pictures and bunches of flowers. And so a machine played music in the waiting room, the reception area and the gender free loos. It was the sort of mind-numbing music usually played in lifts and supermarkets. The music was played in a loop so after a while no one really noticed it was there. It was, like the slightly nauseating smell of mint air freshener (which came out of dispensers plugged into every fifth wall socket) just present. Still, thought Dr Leighton, it was marginally better than the alternative: the smell of illness, urine, disinfectant and bowels that usually pervades all medical establishments – except hospitals where there is also the awful smell of over-cooked food to contend with. There were no flowers in the building because a sub-committee of the medical staff had decreed that there might be a risk of hay-fever but everyone knew that was merely an excuse. The real reason for not having flowers was that it had been impossible to decide which member of staff would change the water in the vases, nor which budget the flower bill should be taken from. The sub-committee had decreed that artificial flowers might be considered at some future date but that future date had not arrived and nor did it seem likely to do so.

Mrs Fuller, the Practice Manager, ruled everyone and everything like a feudal lord overseeing her domain in another, earlier England. Even the partners listened to her, took instructions from her, accepted her admonitions and read her weekly, neatly prepared and printed leaflet of Administrative Notes with more care than they ever gave to their weekly issues of the *British Medical Journal* (which, it must be admitted, in most cases, lay unopened in the recipient's in-tray for a week before being replaced by the next week's issue, also destined for its place in the green, plastic recycling box labelled 'newspapers, magazines and journals only'). It was rumoured that the Practice Manager's annual remuneration exceeded that of the Senior Partner.

As she made her way to the corner office, Dr Leighton felt as though she were climbing the stairs up to the dock at the Old Bailey. Was this how condemned prisoners felt when walking to the gallows or the courtyard where the firing squad was waiting?

That was all nonsense, of course.

What was the worst that could happen?

Could the Practice Manager fire her without asking the partners? Actually, she almost certainly could. More importantly, thought Dr Leighton, did she care?

Suddenly, and to her own surprise, Dr Leighton realised that she didn't give a damn whether they fired her or not. This wasn't the sort of medicine for which she'd spent six years studying. No, she realised, it was longer than six years. There were all those years at school, studying and passing examinations to satisfy the entrance requirements for medical school.

'You were seven minutes late for this morning's meeting, doctor,' said the Practice Manager, looking at the electronic notepad which she carried with her at all times. She used the word 'doctor' in the same way that a policeman uses the word 'sir' when addressing a member of the public whom he has discovered lying in a gutter outside a public house.

'I do apologise,' began Dr Leighton. 'I was with a patient. I'd just had to tell her that the laboratory results showed that her father's condition was deteriorating. He has dementia, heart disease and prostate cancer which had metastasised. She was, not surprisingly, in tears and needed a little support. Sympathy was all I could give.'

Dr Leighton suddenly remembered reading that if you ever found yourself facing someone in authority you should try to imagine them sitting there naked. Or imagine them sitting on the loo. No, that last thought was too much. She tried to imagine the Practice Manager sitting there in her underwear and found herself having to suppress a giggle. What would the Practice Manager wear under her blue scrubs? (And why on earth did she wear scrubs, as though she were ready to perform a heart transplant? None of the doctors wore scrubs.) She'd doubtless wear something white and sensible underneath, thought Dr Leighton. No ribbons or lace but lots of elastic and straps and heavy duty buckles. She'd be trussed not dressed. Dr Leighton had to fight hard to suppress the giggle that wanted to escape.

'It's the third time this month,' said the Practice Manager, glancing at her computer. She seemed uninterested in Dr Leighton's explanation and seemingly unaware of the effort Dr Leighton was having to make to keep a straight face. 'Our regular meetings are the backbone of the practice structure. As one of the doctors, albeit a junior one, it is your role in the practice to act as an example to other members of staff.'

'My patient and her father had always been close. She was in tears and I felt I couldn't just rush away for a meeting.'

'Our Practice Participatory and Planning Meetings are the basis of our community and they unite us in our common purpose,' continued the Practice Manager, sounding for all the world as if she were reading from a training manual printed by the Chinese Communist Party. 'They provide us with an opportunity to share our essential sense of diversity and to draw together the lessons we learn about the need for on-going sustainability in an increasingly fragile eco-system.'

Dr Leighton had suddenly noticed that the Practice Manager had a clearly defined moustache and, with her short hair parted to one side in a manly sort of way, she bore an uncanny and slightly alarming resemblance to the unlamented leader of the Third Reich. Meanwhile, obviously unaware of this imagery, the Practice Manager droned on about management practices and administrative responsibilities.

'The important thing which we all have to remember is that we must all follow the guidelines,' she said. 'We have to follow the rules that define our common purpose and these regular meetings are an integral part of our path towards that end.'

Dr Leighton wanted to say something but couldn't put what she was thinking into words. She had always thought that her primary responsibility was, put simply, to provide her patients with the best care she could offer. She hadn't really thought about it very much but she thought that the administration which lay behind or underneath that responsibility was of secondary importance. She wondered how long this harangue was going to last and found herself thinking that she'd really prefer it if the Practice Manager simply gave her lines to write out. 'Write out five hundred times: 'I must not be late for the practice meetings.' It would be less painful if the practice manger told her to hold out her hand to be caned. Or ordered her to hoist up her skirt, bend over and take six of the best on her bottom.

'I don't think this is anything to smirk about,' snapped the Practice Manager, now fully into headmistress mode.

'I wasn't smirking,' protested Dr Leighton, who most definitely had been smirking.

The Practice Manager scowled and glowered at Dr Leighton. And then after a moment or two she continued.

'Do you have friends or relatives living in Acton Court?' she asked.

'Acton Court?' repeated Dr Leighton. 'No, I don't.' She didn't know why but she went cold inside.

'I didn't think it likely,' said the Practice Manager, who was nothing if not a snob. 'But I have to drive past Acton Court on my way home and I saw your car parked outside in that little car park they have there. You do have a green sports car, don't you?'

'Yes, I have a Lotus and it's green.'

'I was so concerned by what I'd seen that an hour later I drove back past Acton Court and I was astonished to see that your car was still parked outside.'

'I visited someone at Acton Court,' said Dr Leighton, feeling herself turning bright red with a mixture of anger and indignation. 'I'm not sure why…'

'I checked on the computer and noted that the Tapleys live in Acton Court. Mrs Tapley was one of the patients you saw in your clinic two days ago. Do you deny that?'

'Of course I don't!'

'And I see from the computer that you made changes to Mr Tapley's prescription schedule.'

'I did,' agreed Dr Leighton. 'He was receiving far too many prescriptions and I believe some of the drugs he was taking were making him ill. I think he'll feel better if he takes fewer drugs.' Dr Leighton felt her heart beating faster. 'Are you questioning my clinical judgement?'

'But Mr Tapley's name does not appear on any of your clinic schedules,' said the Practice Manager, ignoring Dr Leighton's question.

'No, he's not been well enough to leave his flat. Actually, he's not been well enough to leave his chair.'

'So you visited him at home?'

'Yes. I did. He needed to see a doctor. He couldn't get to the health centre. So I visited him at home. It seemed the sensible, decent thing to do. And I went there on my own time.'

'Do you not realise that this practice policy is that doctors do not visit patients at home? We do not do night calls, we do not visit patients at weekends or on bank holidays. We provide telephone consultations and we provide two-way video consultations for patients who are unable to travel to the health centre,' said the Practice Manager.

'But a lot of our patients, particularly the older ones don't have computers or access to zoom technology,' said Dr Leighton. 'And they feel uncomfortable trying to explain all their symptoms on the telephone.'

'The BMA and the RCGP both support distance consultations,' pointed out the Practice Manager, as though this settled the matter.

'I know they do,' said Dr Leighton. 'But I'm afraid they're wrong. It is impossible for a doctor to make accurate diagnoses through consultations over the phone, even with a video link. The doctor can't touch the patient, can't look down their throats or into their ears. From a distance you can't smell anything either.'

'I'd have thought that was a distinct advantage!' sneered the Practice Manager, wrinkling her nose to make clear what she meant. 'I'm surprised at your arrogance in suggesting that you know better than the BMA and the RCGP.'

'They're not infallible,' said Dr Leighton.

'It is this practice policy always to follow the advice of all the relevant bodies. It has been decreed by the senior partner and myself, and agreed by the staff, that visiting patients at home is a poor use of a doctor's time, as well as being bad for the environment and a notable contributor to global warming. Moreover, it could leave us with legal liabilities for which our insurance would not be valid. If you were to fall while making a visit, or to be attacked by a patient, it is highly doubtful that our insurance would cover you, and if you were to damage someone's property while visiting a patient, the practice would almost certainly be held liable. Most practices around the country have adopted the same policy.'

'Oh I wouldn't expect the practice to take responsibility if I had an accident,' said Dr Leighton.

'That is as may be,' said the Practice Manager. 'But we have to look at the broader picture and consider the environment. If doctors drive around in motor cars they will be contributing to air pollution and to climate change.'

'But surely,' said Dr Leighton, 'more energy will be consumed if our patients all drive themselves to the health centre.'

'I don't think there is any point in continuing this discussion further,' said the Practice Manager. 'The official policy of this practice is the same as that of the Government, the British Medical Association and the Royal College of General Practitioners who are all agreed that home visiting is wasteful and unnecessary and that if patients cannot make their way to the health centre then consultations should be conducted by a video link or over the telephone.'

'A lot of experts think the same as I do and there's good evidence that many mistakes are made if doctors try to make diagnoses at a distance. You can't examine an abdomen over the phone. How do you perform a rectal examination over the phone? You can't do a vaginal examination. You can't take a blood pressure. There are some conditions which produce tell-tale smells,' said Dr Leighton. 'Diabetes mellitus, for example. The smell of ketones is pathognomic for diabetes.'

'Ketones?'

'Ketones smell like nail varnish remover,' explained Dr Leighton. 'They accumulate in the body when the pancreas isn't functioning properly. Instead of burning glucose the body burns a good deal of fat. And the result is that ketones are produced. You can't use your sense of smell if you try to make a diagnosis over the telephone.'

The Practice Manager, clearly unimpressed, sniffed and persisted. 'It is our policy that we can provide patients with the best possible care by insisting that all clinical confrontations take place within these walls. A lot of patients have their own blood pressure measuring devices with which they can take their own blood pressure readings. If a patient needs any treatment which cannot be provided here then it is our policy that we send them to hospital. And if patients cannot leave their home for any reason then it is practice policy, agreed by the senior partner, that they need to be undergoing institutional care of some kind.'

'Even those patients who have sphygmomanometers have difficulty with them,' said Dr Leighton. 'And when I see a patient I don't see it as a confrontation!'

'It's just a word,' snapped the Practice Manager. 'Anyway, I'm not going to discuss these things with you. The senior partner has asked me to give you an official warning about your behaviour.' She opened a folder in front of her, removed a letter and slid it across her desk to Dr Leighton.

'What's this? Are you firing me?' asked Dr Leighton, picking up and examining the letter.

The practice manager paused for dramatic effect, in the way that television quiz show hosts are trained to do so that the tension builds up and is dragged out in an excruciating way before they eventually tell the contestant whether or not he or she had been correct in claiming that Louis XIV was the King of England who came before Henry the VIII. 'No, I'm not firing you at this stage. But I'm giving you an official warning, which will go onto your employment records. If you break practice rules again then your employment with us will be in peril. If you feel unable to obey our very simple requirements then perhaps you would be happier working in a more solitary capacity. Maybe as a doctor working on one of those tramp steamers which make a little extra money by taking passengers on board when transporting cargo around the world.' The Practice Manager leant back and managed to look like a cat who'd just eaten a couple of canaries.

Suddenly, the clouds parted and everything was surprisingly and unexpectedly clear.

Dr Leighton's mood changed as she realised that she could not possibly spend the next 30 to 40 years of her life practising medicine in such a way. She had no pride in what she was doing.

As a student she'd had such high hopes. Now, she felt like an artist condemned to spend the whole of her life painting by numbers: filling in numbered areas on a painting with pre-ordained colours from an allocated palette.

'I'd like to resign,' said Dr Leighton. 'Could you please tell me the correct procedure? I've never resigned before. I expect there are some forms for me to complete.'

The Practice Manager stared at her, with her mouth slightly open, clearly shocked.

'Oh, I don't think that will be necessary, doctor,' she said, suddenly backpedalling. Dr Leighton was, she knew, quite popular and always turned up for the surgeries she was supposed to do. 'It's just a small thing. But it would be very much appreciated if you could perhaps make a little more of an effort to come to the meetings on time in future.'

'I don't want to work here any longer,' said Dr Leighton very firmly. 'I want to leave. How soon can I go?'

'Is there something wrong? Something worrying you?' asked the Practice Manager, pasting on her very best patronising smile and human resources manner.

'No, not really,' said Dr Leighton brightly. 'But I don't want to work here anymore. How soon can I leave?'

The Practice Manager, now blushing a rather deep and unbecoming shade of red, pressed some buttons on her keyboard and studied her screen carefully.

'Well, according to your contract you are required to give four weeks' notice, but I see that you have five weeks' holiday due and also a three month sabbatical vocational break. I think we could let you take the four months straight away if you feel stressed and need a break.'

'That would be splendid,' said Dr Leighton. 'Do I get paid while I'm on a sabbatical?'

'Yes, that was agreed when the current contracts were compiled.'

'Splendid! Would you please ask the accounts department to just put what I'm owed into my account.' Dr Leighton stood up. She felt strange; as though she had just been released from prison. 'And if possible I'd like to leave straight away,' she added with her very best, syrupy smile. She paused on her way to the door and turned back. 'I shan't want a leaving party, thank you.'

The Practice Manager, clearly in a state of shock, said nothing whatsoever but, as Dr Leighton opened the door and left, fiddled with her smart phone as though she had something important to do.

Dr Leighton went to her locker and collected her coat, handbag and a pile of personal mail (including that week's copy of the *British Medical Journal* which was still in its wrapper). Apart from the senior partner, none of the doctors had a personal office – they just worked in whichever consulting room they were allocated – so there were no personal photographs, pot plants or other bits and pieces to collect. She'd always thought that rather sad for it meant that the consulting rooms were all stark, cold and impersonal. It had also occurred to her, on several occasions, that if there had been no conference room it would have been possible for the practice to provide each doctor with a decent sized consulting room of their own. She was old-fashioned enough to think it added a touch of humanity to what could be a sterile environment if a doctor added photographs, flowers, bits of sculpture and even pot plants to the area where they worked. She thought it would make it easier for them to have a proper relationship with their patients.

No one said goodbye as she left but then no one knew that she wouldn't be coming back.

Dr Leighton knew that within a day, or less, it would be as though she'd never been there.

Outside it was raining. It seemed appropriate. It was one of those misleading, light showers that soaks you while you're trying to decide whether it's raining hard enough to bother putting on your coat or put up your umbrella. Dr Leighton, who had never carried an umbrella, didn't notice the rain.

Carrying her bag, coat and a carrier bag containing her belongings, she had walked nearly a mile into town before she remembered that she had left her car parked in the health centre car park. Instead of going straight back to fetch it, she slipped into a nearby café, ordered a black coffee, a salad sandwich and a large slice of chocolate cake and took them over to an empty table. She felt numb and wondered if she had been rash or reckless. She was no martyr; she was not, she knew, the stuff of which missionaries are made. She didn't want to rush off and practise medicine in the wilds of Africa. She liked having a nice car and a warm home and a constant supply of clean water and electricity. But in her heart she knew that medicine had gone much too far in search of something she found quite alien. All the caring had been taken out of medicine and had been replaced with cold, depersonalised bureaucracy.

She was reminded of two furniture salesmen whom she knew. One sold IKEA kitchen furniture (and had helped her choose the kitchen table which was one of the few items of furniture which she owned) and the other sold genuine antique furniture made by Chippendale and Sheraton. The first had no great love for what he did, no sense of vocation, and readily admitted that he would have just as happily sold curtains, motor cars, life insurance or refrigerators. The other, the fellow who sold antiques, was, as he put it, in for the long haul. He loved what he did and cherished the things he sold.

She was, she realised, working in the medical equivalent of IKEA and, without wishing for a minute to be elitist or superior, she didn't like it very much.

When she'd finished the sandwich (chicken, beetroot and asparagus tips on rye bread with a special ten herb seasoning – it was the 'speciality of the day' and all they had left) she took her copy of the *British Medical Journal* out of the carrier bag, opened the wrapper and turned to the back pages of the journal where jobs were advertised.

She had four months' worth of salary due to her but she wanted to start looking for a job straight away. She wanted to find a less sanitised version of medicine; something with more humanity and less bureaucracy; something she could be proud to do. She knew that she wasn't entirely alone in the way she felt. At least two of her erstwhile partners had hobbies which took up far more of their time and energy than medicine. One was a keen golfer, the other dealt in antiques. Their hobbies, more than medicine, defined how they thought of themselves and how other people saw them. She knew that she wanted her job to be a vocation; the activity which defined who she was and who she was to become as the years went by.

She felt strangely invigorated; she had no idea what she was going to do but she was excited by the future.

Before she started looking at the jobs which were available, she took a notebook and a pen out of her handbag and started making a list of what sort of new job she wanted. Ever since she'd been a little girl she'd felt that making lists gave her an illusion of having an analytical mind and a feeling of being in control. She knew it was illusory but she still did it; especially when there was a decision to be made. She'd acquired the habit from her father. He was an inveterate list maker. He had a list of things to do at work, a list of things to do around the house, a list of things to do in the garden and a list of personal things to do. Naturally, he also had a list of his lists. He used to keep all these lists in an old, blue backed notebook which he described as his brain.

After ten minutes of hard thinking she had written down just one word: 'satisfying'.

Chapter Six

For two weeks Dr Leighton had done nothing but consider job prospects. The first three practices she contacted had been looking for trainees and didn't want anyone with her experience. 'I'm afraid that you're far too well qualified. We're looking for someone just out of medical school.' The next two practices were looking only for locum doctors – one to stand in for a partner who was pregnant and taking a year off work, as was her statutory right, and one to stand in for a partner who was recovering from a heart attack.

She'd found a shipping line that was looking for doctors to work on board their cruise ships and ready, it seemed, to take on anyone with a licence and a pulse, but she'd belatedly remembered that she'd always got sick even when just crossing the English Channel. The human resources director at the shipping company assured her that no one ever felt even slightly nauseous on their modern liners – something about gyroscopes was mentioned – but Dr Leighton decided that, after all, she didn't want to be imprisoned on a ship where she would be confined to treating endless bouts of sunburn and indigestion and providing hangover remedies and morning after pills.

To her surprise, she'd had a telephone call from the senior partner of the practice from which she'd resigned so recently. After five minutes of gossipy chit chat he'd asked why she had resigned, said the practice would be sad to lose her and wondered if she would reconsider and think about coming back when her extended sabbatical was over. She'd thanked him and graciously declined.

She'd been offered a job at a private clinic in central London. They wanted someone to deal with patients walking in off the street and, if things were quiet, to offer advice on a computer as part of their online doctor service. But that wasn't what Dr Leighton wanted either. She wanted some continuity. She wanted to be able to diagnose patients and then see them through their treatment. She wanted to get to know her patients, and for them to think of her as 'their' doctor. She wanted to practise in the sort of way that her GP had practised when she'd been a young girl; the sort of medical practice that had excited her and drawn her into a career in medicine.

At the job she'd left, she had rarely seen the same patients twice. Patients were not allocated to individual doctors but to the practice as a whole, and with so many doctors and so many patients this meant that everything was very 'clinical' and impersonal. She was, like all the doctors in the practice expected to work for 24 hours a week (to her own surprise this was around the national average for GPs in the United Kingdom) and she dutifully did her allocated number of surgeries and that was that. She was contracted to work for 12 sessions, each lasting for two hours. In six of those sessions she was expected to hold a clinic and see whatever patients were booked in for her. In the other six sessions she would do essential paperwork and administration. If she said to a patient 'Come back and see me next week' there was little or no chance that she would ever see that patient again because the receptionists did not give the doctor's name when handing out appointments. It was, thought Dr Leighton, about as personal and as satisfying as working in a tax office or on an old-fashioned production line in a 1950s factory.

And then Dr Leighton spotted a rather unusual advertisement in the personal columns at the back of the *British Medical Journal*.

'Doctor required. Village practice. Ageing partners need new blood.'

That was it. There was no website, no email address and no mobile phone to ring. There was just a landline telephone number. She rang the number, spoke to a man who said he was one of the partners and made an appointment for an interview to be held on the following day.

'Do you have any forms for me to complete?' she asked.

'Forms?'

'Application forms for the job. Do you want me to download anything?'

'Good heavens, no. Just bring yourself. I don't do anything online I'm afraid. Oh, if you could bring a copy of your licence to practice that would be a good idea.'

'If I give you my licence number you can check it out on the General Medical Council's website.'

'Oh, that would involve a computer wouldn't it?'

'Yes, it would.'

'I don't have one of those, I'm afraid. I did think of getting one but I've never got round to it.' He paused and then lowered his voice as though airing a seditious thought. 'They do seem to take up an awful lot of time. I'm a little old-fashioned, I'm afraid.'

'Have there been many other applicants?'

'No, not yet. Yours is the only application.'

'Could you email me the address of the practice and directions, please?'

'Oh, I'm afraid I don't do email,' said the doctor. 'I know people who swear by it, of course.' He gave her the name of the village, Stratford Peverell, the practice address and some rather vague directions which involved the village pub. 'Come for luncheon,' he said. 'If you're here by about one o'clock I should have finished the morning visits by then.' Dr Leighton thanked him and wrote down the details. The two doctors said they were looking forward to seeing each other. When she'd put down the telephone, Dr Leighton looked up the village. It was some distance from London and some miles from anywhere that could call itself a town. It would, she thought take around three hours to get there.

Only then did she remember what he'd said.

'I should have finished the morning visits by then.'

It sounded as though she might have found a practice with a difference.

Dr Leighton, not realising that the mobile phone service in the area to which she was headed was no better than it had been just before the First World War, put the address of the practice into her smart phone in order to plan her route and, she innocently believed, provide her with detailed advice as she travelled.

Chapter Seven

'A small problem has developed with finalising your divorce,' Dr Leighton's solicitor told her. 'I've spoken to Peter's solicitor and, unusually, we both agree that this might be something you could sort out together.'

'Must I?' Dr Leighton replied with a sigh. 'I really don't want to see him. What's it about?'

'It's about the house your mother left you,' explained her solicitor. 'Peter is apparently suggesting that the proceeds from the sale of the house should be regarded as common property and shared between you.'

'But my mother died after our divorce,' said Dr Leighton. She reminded the solicitor that her mother had suffered from dementia and had lived in a private nursing home for the last nine months of her life. The nursing home fees, which Dr Leighton thought outrageous, had eaten up every penny of her mother's pension, including both State pension and the private pension she'd inherited from Dr Leighton's father, plus all the money in a savings account which was the extent of her mother's modest wealth. But, the house in which she and Dr Leighton's father had lived for all their married life, had survived by the finest of margins. Dr Leighton had fond memories of the house but had never considered keeping it for herself. (Whenever she thought of the house she remembered Christmas. The house had always been decorated with crepe paper streamers and balloons, and her parents, who had been rather stuck in their ways, had always lit their tree (always a real one, selected and cut by her father and herself from a Christmas tree plantation) with real candles; small coloured ones stuck into tiny candle holders on the tree's branches. The candle holders, which had been inherited from her mother's parents, had been rather unstable and at least once every Christmas one would topple and the flaming candle would set fire to a crepe streamer or the tree itself. Her parents kept a bucket of water under the tree for such eventualities. Once they had bought small electric candles but they too had caught fire and her father, worried about whether or not it was safe to throw a bucket of water over electric candles, had discarded them and gone back to the candles with real flames.)

'Peter's threatening to reopen the divorce,' said her solicitor. 'He claims that since you had power of attorney over your mother's estate, and knew what was in your mother's will, the proceeds from the sale of the house should have been regarded as common property.'

'Can he do that?'

'I'd have to take advice,' said the solicitor. 'It's a rather grey area. Your husband is also suggesting that your mother's death predates your separation if not your divorce – I gather there is some confusion about the dates and under the circumstances, with the power of attorney, there are certainly some issues to resolve. But your husband's solicitor has suggested that the two of you talk about things. It would certainly be a lot quicker and considerably less expensive than asking counsel for an opinion.'

'My ex-husband.'

'I beg your pardon?'

'Peter is my ex-husband. I thought we were divorced and that everything had been sorted out. He emptied our bank account and took all the furniture worth taking. He left me my clothes and I think I was probably lucky they weren't his size.'

The solicitor made a strange, croaky sort of noise which Dr Leighton assumed was a laugh.

'Peter suggests that the two of you have lunch together sometime this week. Can you manage that?'

'I suppose so – if I must.'

'Good. I think that would be easier and quicker than going back to court. Peter's solicitor says that Peter has provisionally booked a table for two at the restaurant at the Savoy Hotel.'

'I hope he's paying!'

Again, the solicitor made the strange croaky noise. This time he bared his teeth in which he probably thought was a smile. Dr Leighton thought it made him look as though he were about to take a bite out of her neck. She felt a pain in her stomach. She wondered if her main memento of their marriage was going to be an ulcer or an on-going irritable bowel syndrome.

Chapter Eight

Dr Leighton knew as she walked to the table, where Peter was already sitting sipping an aperitif, that she was going to roll over and give him whatever he demanded.

She knew, in her heart, that she owed him nothing. But she no longer had any fight left in her. The last few months had exhausted and depressed her.

'I hear that you quit your job,' said Peter, the minute she sat down. There were no social niceties. No 'You're looking good', 'That's a nice outfit' or 'Your hair looks lovely'.

They hadn't even ordered any food. Two menus sat on the table before them, unopened.

'Yes.'

Her ex-husband was wearing a grey, silk suit with a pink shirt and a blue tie. The suit jacket was hanging open and she could see the Christian Dior label inside. She wondered how much a suit made by Christian Dior cost. A black leather handbag, the sort usually carried by women was lying on the table.

'Why on earth did you do that? It was a damned good job. Short hours, good pay. What more can you possibly want?'

'I hated working there. It was like working in a factory. Someone pushed patients through the door and we fed them pills or, if we couldn't think of any pills that would mend them, we fixed them up with a hospital appointment, knowing that they wouldn't be seen for six months and wouldn't be treated for twelve. It wasn't medicine. I don't know what it was but it wasn't the medicine I want to practice.'

Peter laughed. 'What the hell else did you expect from general practice?'

'Something more.'

'If you'd wanted more money you should have made one of those YouTube videos. I know a GP who is making a fortune. He's recorded a series of videos promising mysterious wonder cures for common ailments. The videos are free to watch but YouTube plasters them with adverts and he makes thousands every week. I heard he was making £800,000 a year from YouTube alone. Then at the end of each video comes the kicker. There's a secret remedy for each of the ailments he talks about. He sells a herbal remedy used for thousands of years by some South American tribesmen and a special type of yoghurt made from cows fed solely on daisies and buttercups. Punters pay $40 a month. They just click a button, hand over the money from their PayPal account and he's another $20 richer. A company in Guernsey designs, sources and packs up the remedies. All he has to do is sit back and wait to get ever richer. He works one half day a week in general practice so that he can say he's a practising GP, and spends a day a month recording new videos. He's got a Ferrari and one of those new Bentleys and he's buying a chateau in the South of France. As the quality of care in general practice gets worse so he gets richer. Every time a punter leaves their GP feeling short changed, the chances are great that they go home and, in despair and desperation, watch one of his videos. The funny thing is that although he's one of the richest people I know he is also one of the thickest. I don't think he's ever read a book he didn't have to read and he only got through medical school because his uncle was one of the examiners. He has absolutely no sense of style or taste. The noise they play in lifts is his favourite type of music and when they eventually invite him on Desert Island Discs to ask him about his knighthood he'll ask them to play eight LPs full of supermarket music.'

'He sounds a disgusting person!' said Dr Leighton.

Peter laughed in delight. 'But he's gloriously rich! If he can do it I'm damned sure I can. Kevin is setting up a YouTube channel for me. He's got some great ideas. We're setting up a studio in our spare bedroom. He can operate the camera and the lighting and we're going to make it look like a small operating theatre. I'll put on some scrubs, park my bum on the edge of an operating table and talk straight to the camera. Brilliant! We should make an absolute fortune. Each video will describe a different surgical procedure. I'll explain what the surgery involves. Then if the viewer wants a personally recommended surgeon I go all confidential and reassuring and tell them to key in their zip code or their postcode – anywhere in the world. Our software automatically emails them the name and address of the nearest recommended surgeon. We've invited surgeons all over the world to pay to join our list of preferred professionals. They pay $1,000 to join and then kickback $200 for every patient they get from us. All I have to do is make the videos. We reckon we can easily make two videos an hour. And Kevin reckons that with the YouTube advertising fees and the surgical referrals we'll gross at least £1,000,000 a year. Once we've got that up and running we'll start a weekly podcast. A friend of Kevin's says we can charge subscribers at least $20 a month but the big money will come from sponsors and advertisers. The drug companies will pay a fortune for me to recommend their products.'

'That's so utterly dishonest!' cried Dr Leighton in horror and disbelief. 'You don't even know that the surgeons you are recommending are any good! And how are you going to know that the products you recommend really work? How will you know they're safe?'

Peter shrugged and shook his head, as though with disbelief at Dr Leighton's simple-minded naivety. He opened his menu, thought for a moment and then looked across at Dr Leighton. 'I think I'll have the Dover sole. What about you?'

'Just a salad. I'm not hungry. What on earth have you got in that bag?'

Peter looked down at the bag, as though he'd noticed it for the first time. He reached out and touched it. 'Just the usual things – phone, wallet, change purse, house keys, car keys. If you carry all those in your suit pockets you ruin the line and the material gets baggy. Kevin bought it for me. Everyone has one of these nowadays. What sort of salad? You can't just have two lettuce leaves and a slice of tomato.'

Dr Leighton looked at the menu again. 'Lobster,' she said. It was the first thing she saw. She didn't want lobster, salmon or anything else. She just wanted to get out of there as quickly and as painlessly as possible.

Peter waved his menu and gave their orders to a waiter. 'And a bottle of Chateau Mouton Rothschild Aile d'Argent,' he added. He had, Dr Leighton remembered, always been fussy about wine. He looked across at her. 'It's a white Bordeaux,' he explained, patronisingly. For a moment she regretted having chosen a dish that would go with the wine she knew he'd order to go with his Dover sole.

'My mother's house was left to me after she died,' said Dr Leighton.

'I thought we'd wait until we'd eaten to get down to business. Isn't that the civilised thing to do?'

'I don't feel terribly civilised.'

'OK, if that's how you feel about it,' sighed Peter, as though humouring a child. 'But you had power of attorney over your mother and her estate. My solicitor says he thinks I would have a good case if I asked for half.'

'The lawyers' fees would eat up every penny,' said Dr Leighton. 'It was a semi-detached house in Portsmouth. I've accepted an offer for £350,000.'

'It's still a sizeable tax free sum.'

'What do you want?'

'My fiancé says I'm entitled to half.'

'Is that Kevin?'

'Yes. Kevin is my fiancé.'

'You're engaged then?'

'Yes. I thought you knew.'

Dr Leighton found it difficult to believe that her former husband was now about to acquire a husband of his own. She had no prejudices about homosexuality but she just found it strange.

'No, I didn't.

'It was in *The Times*.'

'I don't read *The Times*. Is Kevin a lawyer? I thought he made YouTube videos.'

'He isn't a lawyer. But his previous boyfriend is a barrister and he says that I have a case.'

'Why can't you just forget the past and let me get on with my life?'

'I've got expenses. Setting up the studio is going to cost an arm and a leg. And Kevin thinks I've got a good chance at the next election. I have to buy a house in the constituency and that won't be cheap. I can hardly buy a terraced cottage, can I, even if I'm never going to be there? And I need to set up a constituency office with staff. These things cost bags of money.'

'I'm not giving you half.'

'I'll take a third.'

'I'm not giving you a third and I'm not haggling as if we were negotiating over buying a fake Rolex from a street trader.'

'So, what do you suggest? You agreed to meet. You really don't want to take this to court. The legal expenses would finish you.'

The wine waiter came, opened the bottle and poured a little into Peter's glass. He tasted it, swirled it around his mouth, thought for a moment and then nodded. The wine waiter bowed slightly in acknowledgement, poured wine into both glasses and backed away.

'I'll give you £50,000 to go away and leave me alone and promise never to ask for anything else,' said Dr Leighton. It wasn't a sum she'd thought about. She'd plucked the figure out of the air. 'If you won't take that then we'll battle it out in court and the whole £350,000 will go to the lawyers.'

Peter looked at her for a long moment. 'You would do that, wouldn't you?'

'I would.'

There was a pause in the hostilities as the waiter came with their food.

Peter sighed. 'You always were rather greedy and selfish,' he said when their food lay before them. He looked at the fish on his plate and prodded it gently with his fork, as though checking that it was dead.

'So, what do you want? £50,000 or nothing?'

'I'll take the £50,000,' said Peter at last. 'But I want a cheque this week. And you can pick up the bill for lunch.'

'I didn't expect you to pay for lunch,' said Dr Leighton. 'You always manage to land someone else with the bill. But before you get the cheque I want a legal acknowledgement that you won't ever ask for anything else.'

She found her mind wandering. Had her husband changed as much as she thought he had. Or had she been so very, very blind when she'd been married to him? Had her perception of him changed?

'OK,' said Peter with a little sigh, as though he were being pressured into accepting something very unfair. 'I'll speak to my solicitor this afternoon. You can send the cheque direct to me. There's no point in letting the solicitor put it through his account.' He looked petulant, like a small boy who has been told he can't go to the circus.

For a while they sat and ate. Or Peter ate while Dr Leighton, who had no appetite, picked at her salad and occasionally nibbled at a radish or a slice of tomato.

'Does Kevin refer to you as his husband?' she asked. 'What I mean is, are you both called husbands? I've always wanted to know.'

'Yes, he's my husband and I'm his husband.'

'Why isn't one of you called a wife? Wouldn't that make more sense?'

'It would be utterly absurd,' snapped Peter. 'I didn't expect you to be prejudiced.'

'I'm not prejudiced! I just wondered. I've often wondered but I never had the opportunity to ask anyone before.' She ate a piece of lettuce. 'It just seems strange for there to be two husbands in a relationship.'

They ate in silence for a while.

'So what are you going to do now?' asked Peter, now apparently content with the result of their negotiations. He drank some wine. The waiter, noticing that his glass was empty approached and refilled it.

'I've got an interview at another practice.'

'I'm surprised. Won't that be just continuing to do something you decided you didn't like? Or are you having second thoughts? Why not ask if they'll take you back? Where is the practice? Here in London?'

Dr Leighton ignored most of this barrage of questions, answering only the last of the sequence.

'It's in the country,' she said. Not wanting Peter to know where she might be going she didn't give him any more information than that.

'Whereabouts?' demanded Peter.

'It's a small practice in a village. It's miles from anywhere.'

Peter laughed, quite cruelly and patronisingly. 'Some of those old country practices are barbaric. You'll be working with doctors who have probably only just discovered antibiotics!' he sneered. 'You'll be able to teach them all about X-rays and anaesthesia.'

'I'm sure they'll be well up to date,' said Dr Leighton. 'I expect the medical journals reach there.'

'I bet the Wi-Fi creaks,' said Peter rather scornfully. 'Kevin and I went to stay in a country house hotel for the weekend and the Wi-Fi there was intermittent at best and when it did work it was painfully slow. It nearly drove poor Kevin crazy. We had to come back immediately after lunch on the Sunday.'

'It'll be nice to get away from the internet and email,' said Dr Leighton.

'You'll be cut off from the real world. You'll be going back a hundred or two hundred years. I bet country doctors still use leeches. You'd better take yourself a supply. You need to keep them in a special jar. And buy yourself a pestle and mortar so that you grind your own powders!' he laughed. Peter, she could see, was suddenly enjoying himself at her expense.

Dr Leighton felt herself blushing but didn't say anything.

'How far from London is it?'

'Two or three hours in the car.'

'They don't have a railway station?'

'The nearest mainline station is just over 30 miles away,' said Dr Leighton, who had checked.

'And the train stops there just once a week?'

'There's a service every day.'

'Every day, eh?' laughed Peter, who was enjoying himself. Dr Leighton remembered that he had always been like this; had always enjoyed belittling her and sneering at any of her hopes or plans while she had always supported his plans. When he'd told her that he wanted to stand for Parliament she had, she remembered, been excited for him. She'd bought him an armful of books about Parliamentary procedure and history.

'We'll never see you again,' he said. 'You'll probably never find your way out of the village. If a patient needs an operation the hospital, which will probably be an hour and a half away if the ambulance can find you, will offer just two choices: some old duffer who needs an atlas to find the gall bladder and who sharpens his knife on the sole of his shoe and a young flash harry who thinks he is the bees' knees because he attends a surgical conference once a year and who wears tweed suits with a fresh rose in his buttonhole every morning.'

'I'm sure it won't be anything like that,' said Dr Leighton confidently, though secretly she suddenly feared it probably would.

'I bet you it will. There won't be any decent specialists available. If you have a tricky diagnosis to make and you need help, you'll have to send your patient to London anyway. If you need investigations doing you'll be stuck. The local laboratory will probably be pushed to manage a haemoglobin level and the local radiologist will be out of his depth if he's expected to read anything more complicated than a chest X-ray.'

Dr Leighton didn't say anything.

'I think I'll have pancakes for pudding,' said Peter. 'They serve a big pile of them, served with fresh raspberries and two types of ice cream. What are you having?'

Dr Leighton shook her head and took another sip of the expensive wine she'd bought.

'Have the pancakes!' urged Peter.

Dr Leighton shook her head.

'And your country practice will be in the middle of a cultural desert!' continued Peter who had finished his Dover sole. Watching him, Dr Leighton thought how lucky he was to be blessed with a metabolism which meant that however much he ate, he never seemed to become fat, let alone obese. And then, as he bent back for a moment she couldn't help noticing that he had acquired a notable roll of fat. It hung over his trouser belt. This pleased her and she felt slightly guilty that it did.

'You'll be miles from the opera and the British Museum!' he said.

'I've lived in London for years and I've never been to either,' said Dr Leighton. 'How often do you go to the opera?'

'I went last month!' retorted Peter smugly. 'Kevin has a friend in the chorus. He's considered by many experts to be a rising star. He'll probably be given a contract as a principal dancer next year.'

'That's nice.'

'Anyway, it's not just going to these places, it's knowing that they are there and being able to go to them without having to travel on a stage coach for six days.'

Dr Leighton wondered how much longer this trial was going to continue. Peter shut his menu, signalled for a waiter and ordered his pudding, with a cappuccino to follow. Dr Leighton took her purse out of her bag and removed her credit card, ready to pay the bill. Why, she wondered, did she allow herself to be bullied by this awful man. Why did she agree to give him anything? Why did she allow herself to be manipulated into paying for the meal? She didn't need to think about the questions. She knew the answers. She allowed herself to be bullied because she couldn't stand rows. She always wanted the easy way out. She hated confrontations. The meeting with the Practice Manager had exhausted her emotionally and would, she knew, leave her drained for weeks.

'I bet the only restaurant will be the local pub. They'll do steak and kidney pie with chips and mushy pies. And there will be apple pie for afters. And at the weekend they'll push the boat out and offer carrots with the pie and custard with the apple pie.' He laughed. 'And you'll be an eternity away from Harrods and Selfridges and Foyles. How can anyone possibly try to live without Knightsbridge, Regent Street and the Burlington Arcade? I really don't think I'd want to live more than a mile or two away from Hatchard's, Simpson's and Fortnum and Mason.'

'I've never bought anything from any of those,' said Dr Leighton.

'Yes, you have. I went to Hatchard's with you once. And you were with me when I bought beautiful cashmere sweaters from that little shop in the Burlington Arcade.'

Dr Leighton remembered the sweaters. He'd bought three of them. Together they came to well over £1,000. It was nearer to £1,500. She'd had to put them on her credit card and he'd never paid her back for them.

'I read the other day that London has the worst traffic jams in the world. You can't drive your car into the city centre without paying a fortune, parking is an absolute nightmare and the pollution is still as bad as ever.'

Peter shrugged and shook his head at this. 'Nonsense! Utter nonsense.'

The pancakes, together with raspberries and ice cream, came and went and the coffee too appeared and disappeared.

'Aren't you going to tell me where this country practice is situated?'

'I've only got an interview. I haven't got the job.'

'Kevin and I could come down and bring you fresh supplies. We'll get you one of those huge hampers from Fortnum and Mason: three different types of marmalade, four different types of chutney, two tins of caviar, a huge smoked ham, a bottle of claret and two bottles of champagne.' He laughed.

Dr Leighton smiled weakly at him. Peter, she remembered with relief, was always making rash promises which he never kept.

'Anyway, that was splendid, thank you,' said Peter, draining the last of his coffee, as Dr Leighton handed her credit card to the waiter. 'We must do this again.' He called the waiter back and told him to add 20% to the bill. The waiter nodded, thanked him and disappeared.

'I don't think so,' said Dr Leighton, quietly irked by Peter being so lavish with her money.

'No, I don't suppose so. Not with you tucked away down in the country. They're probably all married to their sisters and too busy buggering the sheep to know what day of the week it is. You'll forget how to eat with a knife and fork because I expect they all eat with their fingers.' Peter stood up, threw his napkin down on the table and smiled at Dr Leighton. 'Don't forget the cheque for 50K,' he reminded her. 'You can pop it in the post to the flat or send it to me at the Harley Street rooms.' Peter, she knew, had recently acquired a share in a suite of rooms in Harley Street. She also knew that he rented the rooms, a receptionist and a secretary by the hour.

And with that, he was gone.

It was only when he'd disappeared that Dr Leighton remembered that the sale of her mother's house hadn't yet gone through. She didn't have £50,000, or anything like it, in her bank account. She'd have to grovel to her bank manager and ask for a bridging loan. That would add to the expense, and take up another half a day.

Chapter Nine

Three years earlier Dr Leighton had bought herself a small sports car, a Lotus, in a colour known as British racing green. (British Racing Green, she was informed by the salesman, had a curious history. The 1902 Gordon Bennett Trophy was won by a British driver, Selwyn Edge, in a Napier motor car. Selwyn Edge was unable to defend his title in 1903 because motor racing was illegal in Britain. So the race took place in Ireland and, as a mark of thanks to the Irish the British entrants painted their cars green.)

The Lotus she bought was the cheapest model the company made but it looked wonderful, performed well and was easy to drive and to park. She'd chosen a model with a hard top, partly in deference to the English weather (which wasn't kind to convertible motor cars) and partly because she knew two people who'd had soft top cars in London and both had had their soft tops damaged by vandals. Most of the people she knew who lived and worked in London no longer bothered to own a car. What was the point? Special charges and endless fines meant that running a car in any big city was hugely expensive and once you stopped moving, there was never anywhere to park. Even if you managed to find a garage or a parking space, the chances were big that when you wanted to move again you'd either find that your vehicle had been clamped or blocked in by a selfish motorist. Most people she knew hired a car when they wanted one, used a taxi or an Uber car, rode a bicycle or travelled by Tube. One or two people she knew drove motorcycles but they both wore leathers and helmets and whenever they arrived anywhere it took them an age to disrobe and find somewhere to store their specialist clothing. Bicycle riders weren't much better off – they always arrived at their destination soaked with sweat and filthy dirty. And who wanted to breathe in all those foul and dangerous fumes while exercising?

But Dr Leighton had always wanted a sports car and so when she could afford one she'd bought herself the feisty little Lotus as a treat. It was her one major extravagance. When she'd bought it, her mother had still been alive and fairly well and living in a bungalow on the south coast. Whenever she could, Dr Leighton drove down to see her, often spending the weekend with her or, more recently, in a small hotel nearby. When her mother had died a few months earlier, Dr Leighton had considered selling the car, which she now hardly used, but there was a parking space allocated to the flat she occupied and in the end she never got round to arranging the sale. A salesman at the one garage she'd visited had sniffed, shaken his head a good deal and offered her a derisory price, telling her that electric vehicles were all the rage and that the demand for petrol driven vehicles was shrinking rapidly. He pointed out that the world was changing rapidly and that no one, especially in London, wanted a car with an internal combustion engine. She had decided to keep the car.

The journey to Stratford Peverell had, as she'd expected, taken around three hours. The first part of the journey, the long, dull miles on the motorway, had been as stressful as motorway journeys always seemed to be (with the ever changing speed limits slowing down the traffic for no obvious reason and consequently causing frequent traffic jams) but once Dr Leighton had left the motorway, the little Lotus seemed to purr with delight. And the narrower the lanes became the more she and her car enjoyed themselves. The car's satellite navigation system, usually so reliable, stopped working and when Dr Leighton paused in a farm gate way, she found to her surprise that her mobile phone had no connection. But she had a map in the car and there were still a few old-fashioned finger posts about and all was not lost.

Besides, it was a good day for a drive.

It was April and the blossom was starting to come out. The countryside was waking up after what had been a long, harsh winter and everywhere she looked there were signs of new life: buds on the trees and lambs in the fields.

She'd set off earlier than she thought necessary, allowing time for diversions and hold-ups, and so it was just after twelve when she reached the outskirts of Stratford Peverell and ten past noon when she spotted the The Jolly Roger, an old-fashioned looking village pub with whitewashed walls.

She thought she'd freshen up, and sit for a while before her interview. She hated being early as much as she hated being late. She parked in a small car park which contained an elderly Land Rover, which didn't look as if it had moved for a while, and a rusty trailer.

A traditional, painted pub sign showed a grinning, good natured traditional pirate with a patch over one eye and a parrot settled on one shoulder. The wood of climbing roses, tied neatly to trellis which surrounded the front door promised much for the summer. There were wooden benches and tables outside on a stretch of lawn. A faded and slightly tattered Jolly Roger flag fluttered half-heartedly from a thirty foot tall wooden flagpole. Dr Leighton thought that if she chatted to the barman or barmaid she might learn a little about the village and its inhabitants.

Inside, the pub looked as old fashioned, as original and as inviting as it looked outside. There were half a dozen wooden tables, a couple of dozen wooden chairs and two old leather armchairs positioned beside a roaring log fire. It seemed to Dr Leighton, from her modest experience, that everyone in the country had a log fire blazing. She wondered if they kept them burning throughout the summer.

In one of the chairs sat a man with a sunburned face and shoulder length grey hair. It was a warm, spring day but the man had moved his chair as close to the fire as it was possible to get. He wore scruffy, stained jeans, a jacket that would have been rejected by any self-respecting second-hand clothes emporium and Wellington boots with the tops turned down. Dr Leighton wondered why he had done that and then also wondered if he knew that in London's Bond Street she had seen similarly styled boots, with the tops turned down, and described as 'cavalier' or 'musketeer' boots, selling for £2,000 a pair. And that had been in the sales.

The man had the stub of a pencil in one hand and was studying a newspaper. There was a glass two thirds full of Guinness on the small table beside him and, alongside that, a packet of cigarettes and a box of matches and a cheap pad of paper.

'You'll be the new doctor, then,' said the barmaid, as she'd served Dr Leighton her coffee. She looked about the same age as Dr Leighton but was slightly taller and notably curvier. She wore a dark blue skirt and a white blouse with the top buttons unfastened, in traditional barmaid style. Her long, brown hair was tied back in a ponytail. 'I'm Rosemary. My husband and I run this place. I won't offer you the menu because you're the new doctor and you'll be having lunch with Dr Hill,' she said. 'And you'll need a good appetite!'

Dr Leighton was startled. 'It's just an interview,' said Dr Leighton. 'I might not be offered the job. But, yes. Dr Hill did invite me to have lunch with him.'

The barmaid laughed at Dr Leighton's evident surprise. 'Oh, this is a village; there aren't many secrets here. But don't worry, no one's been gossiping about you. It's just that Dr Hill was in here yesterday evening and he asked me to take round three of our steak and kidney pies and one of our apple pies for him to put in the oven for your lunches. He said you were coming from London. Actually, he said he thought you'd probably pop in here for a coffee and to use our loo. He said he thought you'd allow too much time, arrive here a little early and call here to freshen up. He said that's what he'd have done. We make the steak and kidney pies in special pots. Martha, who is Dr Leighton's housekeeper and cook, has gone over to see her mother. She always goes over on Thursday mornings and comes back on Saturday mornings. There aren't many buses that will get her there and back.' She suddenly grinned. 'You wouldn't want Dr Hill cooking you anything. If we didn't sell food I don't think he would ever have a hot meal inside him on a Thursday and a Friday. I was once there when he was using a toasting fork to try to make toast on an open fire. He must have burnt half a loaf before he produced anything remotely edible. We bought him a toaster for Christmas and he was tickled pink with it.' She paused. 'Besides, I guessed you were the young doctor Dr Hill is expecting because we don't get that many young women calling in here by themselves at this time of day. To be honest with you, most of the people we do see at this time of day are lost – tourists who just stop here for directions. Mind you, I'm not complaining, most of the folk who call in because they are lost usually have a drink and something to eat,' she continued. 'That might be because they feel they ought to buy something while they're here, but I like to think it's because they like the look of the pub!'

'I suspect it's the latter!' said Dr Leighton. 'Most people in towns and cities have a dreamy idea of what a country pub should look like – and this is it!' She sipped at her coffee, which was very good.

The barmaid disappeared for a moment, saying something about needing to bring in another basketful of logs.

Dr Leighton suddenly found herself wondering if she would accept the job if she were offered it. She realised, to her own surprise, that she hadn't even thought about it properly. Did she really want to live and work so far away from what she was used to? The drive from London had been long and tiring and she felt as though she were a good distance from civilisation. It was a little disconcerting; like being in a foreign country.

She remembered what Peter had said about working in the country. She would be cut off from the world she knew. Would she ever see anyone from her old life – even if she wanted to? Or would it be good for her to make a clean break? Was she cut out for a life away from everything that London had to offer? But when she thought about it she couldn't remember when she'd last been to a live theatre, and her evenings out usually meant a fairly ordinary meal in a fairly ordinary café or bottom of the range restaurant. Occasionally, she'd go to a cinema. A man she knew had once taken her to watch a cricket match at Lord's cricket ground. Once had been enough. Another man had taken her to a rugby match at Twickenham. Again, once had been enough. She couldn't really think of anything about the city that she'd really miss.

What would she miss if she weren't in London?

Well, she'd notice the absence of traffic jams and the ever present traffic wardens.

The barmaid (what on earth was her name, wondered Dr Leighton) put a full log basket beside the fire and put the few logs which were left in the old basket onto the fire before taking out the now empty basket and then returning to her position behind the bar.

The barmaid, having returned, nodded towards the man beside the fire.' Jeffrey is always here. He's our Resident Poet and what folk round here usually call a Bit of a Character and believe me, even by local standards he is certainly that. He comes in to borrow our newspaper and study the racing. He never makes a bet but just picks his horses and then sees how they did in the following day's paper. He's been doing it for as long as I've been here and he's £797,000 in debt to a non-existent bookie so far. When he's picked his horses for the day he works on his play. He always seems to be working on a new play. I don't have the foggiest idea what happens to what he writes. I think he probably puts them all in a trunk and forgets about them. He tells extraordinary stories and says they're all true but I don't think they are. Between you and me, I think he makes everything up. But they're entertaining stories so who cares if they're true or not? It doesn't really matter, does it?'

Rosemary, thought Dr Leighton. The barmaid's name is Rosemary.

'It's £798,000,' muttered Jeffrey, who'd obviously been listening but who didn't lift his head from his newspaper. 'I've had a bad week, though I did win £500 on a long shot running at Newbury on Tuesday.' He then looked up and nodded to Dr Leighton. 'Welcome, doctor. I'll be along to see you when you've settled in. You look a damned sight more scenic than dear old Dr Hill, that's for sure. Maybe you'll have a better remedy for piles than he's got on offer.'

'It's only an interview,' protested Dr Leighton. She smiled to herself. At her last practice, the word 'scenic', used as a compliment, would have immediately triggered a sexual harassment inquiry.

'Oh, you'll get the job if you want it,' said Jeffrey. 'Most young folk don't want to live in a village like this and I doubt if doctors are any different.'

'Are you really a poet?'

'I'm a 'limerickist',' replied Jeffrey. 'I write a limerick every week and stick it on the village noticeboard outside the gent's loo.' He held up an empty glass. 'Another glass of Sheep Dip, please darling.'

'Jeffrey's limericks are mostly so rude that I think they should be stuck on the wall inside the gent's loo,' laughed the barmaid, pouring a generous measure of fluid from a bottle she took from the shelf behind her. 'He's written two about me! We pay him with one free pint a month so that he can call himself our resident poet,' said the barmaid. 'If anyone sits in his favourite chair he makes them move.' She carried the glass over to Jeffrey.

'Sheep Dip?' asked Dr Leighton. 'Why on earth is he drinking Sheep Dip?'

'It's a brand of whisky,' explained Rosemary. 'Sheep Dip. Farmers buy it by the crate and put it down as a taxable expense. My husband says it's the biggest scam in the country and tax inspectors still don't seem to have caught on.' She turned, took the bottle from the shelf and showed it to Dr Leighton.

'Is Dr Croft the other partner in the practice?' asked Dr Leighton.

'That's right, he is. But he doesn't see patients these days. I saw him once when I was little. He's lovely. They both are. You'll get on well with them both. Dr Hill does all the surgeries and visits. Two years ago he broke his leg when he fell off a hay rick and had to go to hospital to have a plaster put on. As soon as he came home he started doing surgeries again. Timothy the odd job man took him round to do his visits. Because of the plaster cast Dr Hill couldn't get into his truck so he lay in the back. Dr Croft has been sort of semi-retired for quite a while. I don't rightly know what he does now. I hardly ever see him. He keeps very much to himself. But his name is still on the brass plate on their door.'

'What's Stratford Peverell really like?' asked Dr Leighton.

Rosemary thought for a moment or two. 'Very quiet and old-fashioned,' she said at last. 'The nearest traffic lights are nearly 30 miles away and there are people living here who haven't ever travelled that far. My granddad used to work at a farm six miles away. He walked to work every morning, worked in the fields all day and walked home every evening. He never saw a set of traffic lights in his life. Come to that I don't think he ever saw a street light. We don't have any of those round here – the nearest street lights and zebra crossings are all nearly an hour's drive away. Teenagers round here say that when they want excitement they go into town to watch the traffic lights change colour.'

She paused and looked at Dr Leighton's smart phone which was on the table in front of her. 'By the way, don't expect to be able to make or receive any calls on that while you're here.'

'There's no mobile phone reception?' said Dr Leighton, quietly astonished. She hadn't been anywhere which didn't have mobile phone reception for years.

'Someone did tell me that if you go up to the top of Gibbet Tor you can get some sort of reception – one bar, I think they said it was – but I don't have one of those phones so I've never tried it.'

'No Twitter, Facebook or YouTube?'

'Not unless you happen to find a cottage or a house with good reception,' laughed the barmaid. 'Are you keen on social media?'

'No, not much,' admitted Dr Leighton. 'I use one or two medical apps occasionally but I could manage without them.' She shrugged. 'I used to have a Facebook account but to be honest it's so long since I used it that I don't know if it's still there. My husband was very keen on all social media but I was never all that enthusiastic, and after we got divorced I didn't bother.' She smiled. 'He had custody of our joint social media accounts and I was quite happy to see them go.'

'How long were you married?'

'The quick answer is 'too long',' said Dr Leighton. 'Technically and legally, the marriage lasted two years and a month but although I didn't realise it at the time, it was a marriage of convenience. My husband, who turned out to be gay, was hoping to become an MP and had been told that he needed a wife in order to be taken seriously. I was free and single and not doing anything else…so he married me. I suppose I was what they call a beard. He was several years older than me and considerably more sophisticated. I was flattered and found him rather exciting. Actually, I think I thought I was in love with him.'

'But you weren't?'

'I'm pretty sure I wasn't!' laughed Dr Leighton.

'You make it sound all very casual and flippant but I don't suppose it was.'

'No, it was rather painful. And afterwards I felt bitter, used and just a bit emotionally battered. And when it came to the divorce, he turned out to be greedier and more mercenary than I would have thought. We had a joint account with an online grocer, though the account was actually in my name, and after we parted, his lawyer wrote to me demanding that I pay him for half of the loyalty points we'd acquired. They'd worked out how much they thought I owed. I ended up sending a cheque for £7.49 which I thought was pretty pathetic.'

'The lawyer's bill for working it out must have come to more than that.'

'I'm sure it did,' agreed Dr Leighton. She suddenly felt surprised that she had talked so much about herself. She had never told anyone else so much about her life. She took in a big breath and let it out slowly. 'So, seriously, there's no mobile phone service at all?'

'No, there's no mobile phone service. There's talk about them doing something about it, putting up an aerial or something, but nothing ever happens.'

'What about Wi-Fi and the internet?'

'Oh, some folk get their Wi-Fi through their landline,' said Rosemary. 'But to be honest it's not usually terribly good. The phone lines to the village come through two forests and there are always branches rubbing on the line. They cause a lot of crackling and sometimes you can hardly tell what the other person is saying. To be honest, it's better some days than others but it's never better than hit or miss. If it's snowing or raining there's no reception at all. Gordon, one of the locals who is into computers and does a lot of work with the internet, had a special aerial put up but the parish council complained and said he hadn't applied for planning permission, so he had to have it taken down. It did look awful. Around here you need planning permission if you intend to take a deep breath.' She paused and thought for a moment. 'I've lived here all my life, my parents ran this pub, and I know that most of the people round here don't mind much about being cut off from the outside world. We don't like to rush. We like to consider everything and to weigh up all the options. And while we are considering and weighing up, we always, more or less on principle, oppose anything new. Most people in the village haven't really decided whether the internet is a good thing or not. We've just about accepted that the telephone is useful, as long as it's tethered to a house. Most people aren't keen on telephones that you can carry around with you.'

'Don't you miss social media?'

'I've never seen Facebook or Twitter or any of the others. I've heard of them but I've never seen them and you don't miss what you've never had. Anyway, we don't want to be one of those dull pubs where people spend all evening staring at their little screens. Visitors' kids are the only ones who really complain when they find out that there is no connection to the internet. Some of them start crying and insist that their Mum and Dad take them off somewhere else where they can check that their private little world hasn't vaporised. Kids seem to get genuinely upset if they can't update their Facebook page once an hour. And they worry they might be missing crucial texts – as if any message a child gets is ever really crucial! Still, at that age the world is different, isn't it?'

'Why on earth do they call that hill you mentioned Gibbet Tor? Don't tell me there's a gibbet there!'

'Yes, there is, but the gibbet that's there now is a reproduction of the one that was there in the 18th century. The new gibbet, the one that's there now, which you can see from some of our bedrooms, was put up in the 1920s by a slightly eccentric local land-owner. I've no idea why he did it. It was just one of those follies you read about, I expect. Rich land-owners put up towers, and Greek temples and so on – so why not a gibbet? Some of these follies were built just to provide work for the local stone masons and carpenters so we shouldn't be too critical. It sounds a bit macabre I know but people go up there for a walk on Sundays. The view is amazing. They say you can see four different counties on a clear day. It's only a forty minute walk along the bridle path at the end of the lane.'

'How far is that in miles and inches?'

The barmaid laughed. 'I have no idea. In the country we measure time and distance differently. In a town you'd say somewhere was a mile away. Here people tend to say it's half an hour away on foot or five minutes in a car.'

'What do people do for entertainment?'

'Well, we have a darts tournament, a bar billiards tournament, a skittles league and a pool tournament. The trouble is that we're a bit isolated here so the Stratford Peverell teams aren't in any leagues. We used to be in a darts league but the other teams complained that it took too long to get here and that going back in the dark took forever because they always got lost, so we gradually got squeezed out. There's a village cricket team which plays in a league and two football teams which just play each other because they got fed up with all the travelling. You can't blame them. Some visitors would spend six hours travelling for a ninety minute match and because they play football in the winter, the drive home was always done in the dark. It became a bit of a joke, with people saying that one visiting team was still driving round and round three months after they left. Now the two local teams just play each other in our field behind the pub. It's not quite wide enough for a proper pitch but it's just long enough. And the president of one of the teams bought a silver coloured trophy which is presented every spring to the winner of the League Cup. It's not really silver but it looks quite impressive when it has had its annual polish. The cup was originally awarded to the winner of a Scottish curling tournament but they've covered up the inscription with a sticky label. There were always moans from the losers so the present of the other team bought another trophy – they got them both from a junk shop somewhere – and so the losers have a smaller cup which has a sticky label hiding the fact that it is engraved to the winner of a darts tournament. So each team always get something to celebrate. We keep both cups on the shelf. One year someone bought a pile of horse show rosettes and gave red 'First Place' rosettes to all the members of the winning team and blue 'Second Place' rosettes to the losers. They all wore them all evening. We keep both cups here in the pub.'

The barmaid pointed to a shelf over the fireplace upon which two cups, one large and one small, were positioned. Both cups were severely dented and the paper labels were faded. Rosemary nodded towards the man sitting by the fire. 'Jeffrey is goalkeeper for the One-Legged Limpers,' she said. 'The other team is called the Blind Warriors.'

'In my youth I used to play inside left,' said Jeffrey, who had clearly been listening. 'But that was before I got arthritis in my knees. Playing in goal means I don't have to run about. I keep a chair beside the goal post so I can have a rest if they're playing at the other end. And I get to tidy up the grass near the goal mouth and clear out any cowpats that Clarence has missed.'

'Cowpats?' said Dr Leighton, astonished. 'Do you mean there are cowpats on the pitch?'

'Oh yes, Rosemary and her husband keep seven or eight cows in the field. An hour before every match, Clarence the cowman moves the cows out and clears up the cowpats which he takes home for his vegetables. Once a month or so he gives the grass a quick once over with the mower,' said Jeffrey. 'But he always misses a few cowpats. I stopped diving for the ball after I landed in a fresh one he'd missed. I had to wash my shirt and shorts that week.'

Dr Leighton looked at him and then at Rosemary who smiled, shrugged and nodded to confirm the accuracy of what Jeffrey had said. Dr Leighton shuddered slightly and took another sip of her coffee. 'So, with the dart, the skittles, the football and so on you're the local entertainment centre?'

'Yes we are,' laughed Rosemary. 'If people want entertainment they come here! To be honest, Stratford Peverell is just too far from cinemas or theatres or restaurants for anyone to make the effort. Who wants to drive 30 miles there and 30 miles back to watch a film or have a meal when you can watch a thrilling darts match in the pub, or have a meal here without all that driving and the hassle of trying to find somewhere to park when you get there?'

Dr Leighton finished her coffee. 'What's Dr Hill like?' she asked.

'He's a sweetheart. He was my Mum and Dad's doctor and he delivered me. I've known him all my life. I'd be devastated if he ever retired. Some people think he's a bit eccentric but he's a real old-fashioned gentleman.' She laughed. 'But that's no real worry. He'll never retire and I hope he'll live forever.' She paused. 'I'm glad you'll be joining him, though. He needs some help. He's been looking tired recently – which isn't surprising really, I don't suppose. He hasn't had a holiday for years. Martha says he's been getting tired too, but he never says anything to her or anyone else. And selfishly it'll be nice to have someone my age to talk to. Not many women my age come to the pub – they're mostly at home looking after their children. Their husbands come in for a pint and a game of darts but the women don't come so often, except on Saturdays, of course. You'll like our Saturday evenings!'

'I haven't got the job yet!' said Dr Leighton. 'I'm just here for an interview.'

'Oh, I'm sure you'll get the job if you want it,' said Rosemary. 'If anyone else comes here for an interview I'll give them the wrong directions and send them off up to the Gibbet. They'll probably never find their way back. The lanes around there are very narrow and there aren't many road signs. Most of the signs were all taken down in the Second World War so that if any Germans landed they wouldn't know where they were, and no one has ever got round to putting them back up.'

Dr Leighton finished her coffee (which was, she told Rosemary, infinitely better tasting than the watery stuff sold in any of London's specialist coffee shop chains) paid for it, got instructions from the barmaid on how to find the surgery (the name of which, she already knew, was still 'The New Vicarage' as it had apparently been for at least three hundred and fifty years), said thank you and goodbye and climbed back into her car. She was quietly pleased that the doctor's premises were still known as the 'surgery' rather than as a 'health centre'. She also suspected (quite accurately as she later discovered) that Dr Hill did not conduct 'clinics', as they were referred to at the London practice, but preferred to define the times when he saw patients as 'surgeries'.

Less than five minutes later, at one minute to one o'clock, she pulled up in front of the village surgery; a large, extremely elegant red brick house in the Queen Anne style. The house, which had a wonderful view over the valley through which Dr Leighton had driven, would, in summer be partly shaded by a huge yew tree on one side of the driveway and a massive oak tree on the other. The house had an in-out driveway with stone griffins perched on all four stone pillars. The griffins and the pillars were covered with multi-coloured moss and lichen growths. Dr Leighton parked her Lotus, a little dustier than it had been when she'd set off, between a very battered and dirty four door Ford truck and an equally battered and dirty Massey Ferguson tractor, neither of which looked quite at home in front of such an elegant building. The truck was higher than other similar versions of the same model and had clearly been fitted with massive tyres, which made it look like a slightly smaller version of one of those Monster trucks which run in circus style events in certain parts of the world. There were no other vehicles in sight. A slightly tarnished brass plate on the front door carried the names of Dr Hill and Dr Croft.

Chapter Ten

The man who answered Dr Leighton's knock on the door was notably more than six feet tall and slim. Dr Leighton, who had never been very good at guessing people's ages thought at first that he was somewhere between 50 and 80 but decided almost immediately that the extremes of her guess were too close together. He had a headful of hair, which is uncommon in men in their 60s or beyond, but does happen, and although it was thinning slightly at the front, the hair that remained, clumped above both ears and at the back of his head, was blond and curly and hadn't been troubled by a hairdresser's scissors for some considerable time. There were a good many wrinkles around his eyes but that can occur in many 30 and 40-year-olds who had spent a good deal of time in the sun as he clearly had. Perched on the top of his nose he wore what Dr Leighton thought at first were a pair of half-moon spectacles but which she noticed were actually a pair of pince-nez. He wore an elderly, rather baggy sports coat that looked as if it had been well-made by a decent tailor but which now had leather patches on the elbows, one leather button missing and a rather notable piece of stitching holding one of the pockets in place. The stitching looked as if it had been done in a blanket stitch with a piece of fine catgut – the sort more normally utilised in sewing up cuts and incisions. Below the waist he wore baggy, plum coloured corduroy trousers and beneath the ancient jacket he wore a checked, woollen shirt and what was instantly recognisable as a Garrick club tie. On his feet he wore an ancient pair of brown, brogue shoes that were scuffed and needed care and attention with brushes and polish.

'Dr Leighton, I presume!' said the man whom Dr Leighton rightly assumed to be Dr Hill.

'What a wonderful house!' she said, looking up and around. 'And the view is magnificent.'

'I bought the house when I was young and daring,' replied Dr Hill.

'Did it look as smart then as it does now? Or did you have to restore it?'

'The place was falling down. The roof had huge holes, there was dry rot in two bedrooms, wet rot in the window frames and woodworm in the floorboards. It took me five years to get everything restored and for years I had a bank loan that kept me awake at nights. It seemed a lot of money at the time but I've never regretted it.'

'It has a wonderful garden!' said Dr Leighton, looking round.

'There was nearly 200 acres of farmland and woodland with the house when I bought it, but I sold off some woodland and a few fields to help pay for the repairs. The house has still got nearly 100 acres which is more than enough. I employ a couple of fellows to do a bit of light farming and that helps bring in some money and we coppice the woodland, of course. The wood we cut doesn't bring in much money but it keeps me in logs and kindling and we supply a chap in the village who makes wonderful furniture. The upkeep of the house takes most of my income now but I don't begrudge a penny of it. As they say, you don't own a house like this – you just look after it for the next tenant. The house is a listed building so everything that needs repairing has to be done very carefully. If a roof tile cracks and needs replacing I bring in a specialist roofer and I've got a good friend who runs a reclamation yard. He can usually find tiles, cast iron downpipes and guttering and bits of window frames.' He sighed, but it was an affectionate sigh. 'There always seems to be something that needs doing.'

'Is this where you live as well as practise?'

'Oh yes,' nodded Dr Hill. 'And Dr Croft lives in a cottage half a mile away, closer to The Jolly Roger – the pub I always think of as 'The Smug Pirate'.'

'The Smug Pirate?'

'Rosemary's parents commissioned a pub sign from a local artist. I think they wanted the usual portrait of a traditional pirate with a patch over one eye and a parrot on one shoulder but the painter produced an extremely jovial pirate looking very smug.'

'Mallory owns the white cottage with dormer windows and a thatched roof. You undoubtedly passed it but probably didn't notice it because just as you pass Mallory's front gate you have to pass a farmyard, and you'll have been distracted by the hens and geese which always wander out onto the lane. They come out when they hear any traffic. I think they're suicidal, though none of them ever seems to get hit.'

'Mallory is Dr Croft?'

'Indeed he is. And I'm Crawford, Crawford Hill. I'm sorry. I should have introduced myself. Mallory did want to be here for our luncheon but I think he's chickened out at the last minute. He's something of a recluse I'm afraid. He rather hates meeting people.'

'Oh dear, does that mean that the interview is cancelled?' asked Dr Leighton, unable to hide her disappointment and thinking to herself that if Dr Croft did not like meeting people it was difficult to see how they could ever meet.

'No, no, not at all,' replied Dr Hill immediately. 'Mallory doesn't play an active part in the clinical side of the practice. The decision is entirely up to the pair of us, Dr Leighton. And, although I would have liked you to have met him, we must look on the bright side and recognise that Mallory's absence means that we have an extra steak and kidney pie to share between us. Rosemary sent us a huge pot of cooked vegetables to go with the pies and I've followed her instructions to the letter though if anything is over-cooked or under-done then I must take all the blame. My aunt was a cook in a pub in the next village but, sadly, I never learnt anything from her.'

'Were you brought up round here?'

'Oh yes, my father was a blacksmith and my mother was the only lady farrier in the county. We had a cottage the other side of The Jolly Roger. You'll notice that everything in the village is referred to according to its geographical relationship to the pub. My mother was exactly five feet tall and weighed seven and a half stone but she could shoe a horse as fast and as well as any man. She was very feminine and always worked in a frock with a leather smock over it.' He paused. 'And that's more than enough about me and my family. It's you we need to talk about. We need to find out what you're looking for out of life so that you can decide whether we're the right fit for you. I have to warn you that this is a terribly old-fashioned practice in some ways. I like to think that we're up-to-date about medicine and treatments but we don't hold with all the computers and so on that many people think so highly of. My own view is that they get in the way rather a good deal.' He stood aside and ushered Dr Leighton into a long, wide hallway which had terracotta tiles on the floor and a series of paintings on both walls. The paintings, all in oil and all looking as if they were in need of a good clean from a professional restorer, were of a mixture of men and women, and judging by their wigs and dress they had been painted in the 18th century.

'Are those all your relatives?' asked Dr Leighton.

'They're someone's relatives, but they're not mine. I bought all the paintings as a job lot at a house auction in the 1970s. I remember they cost me £22 including auctioneer's commission and since I couldn't get them into my car boot, I had a Mini at the time, I gave a fellow with a van £5 to bring them here. I needed some big paintings to cover up damp patches on the walls in the drawing room. Later, after I'd had that room plastered, I brought the paintings into the hall to give the entrance a grander look; I thought they'd add a touch of much needed gravitas. I was a rather young GP at the time. When I came here, my predecessor had already died and a locum was looking after the practice, not very well it has to be said for I gather he was rarely sober after noon.'

'The pictures fit into the house very well. Do you know who any of the people are?'

'I don't have the foggiest,' admitted Dr Hill. 'I keep meaning to get a valuer to look at them – just in case there's anything worth selling.' He looked at the nearest photo, a very severe man in a long wig. 'But I confess I've grown rather used to them all. I gave them all names. This one has always been known as my Great Uncle Joshua.'

Dr Hill moved on, and continued the tour. 'The waiting room is on the left, my surgery, consulting room if you prefer, is just beyond it and yours, if you decide to join us, will be here on the right. It used to be Dr Croft's room but he hasn't seen patients for some considerable time and he prefers to work at his cottage now. He deals with all the paperwork; looks after the accounts and keeps details of investigations. He sends off referral letters and chases up the various consultants if we haven't heard anything from them. You'll meet him soon. He came up earlier this morning and decanted a couple of bottles of wine from his cellar to go with our lunch. He's something of an oenophile and takes it rather seriously, though I'm pleased to say that he doesn't go in for all that stuff about tasting rhubarb, bonfire smoke and autumn mornings; he just knows what he likes. And I generally find that I like what he likes, which is convenient.'

As he spoke, Dr Hill opened the doors of the appropriate rooms.

With one notable exception the waiting room looked very much like the one her own GP had when she was a girl. There was a large mahogany table in the centre of the room with a couple of dozen mismatched chairs arranged around the walls. The one difference was that there was a fire in the hearth with a huge basket full of logs beside it.

'We light a fire in here from the beginning of October to the end of April,' explained Dr Hill. 'The room's warm enough but I always think a fire in winter is emotionally comforting.'

'Doesn't it mean you have to keep rushing out to put on another log?'

'Oh no, I leave the patients to see to that. There's always someone happy to keep the fire going. Usually, at the end of the evening surgery, I find that someone has emptied the ashes out.'

Dr Leighton looked at the fire, now dying down since all the patients had gone, and wondered what the Health and Safety Officer at her old practice would have thought about it. She decided that he would have had forty fits and would have needed to spend an hour in a dark room, with a cold flannel on his forehead. He would have then not just put a stop to the business of having a lit fire in the waiting room (with children around!) but would have insisted on having the fireplace sealed and, just to be really safe, the chimney permanently blocked.

Dr Hill's consulting room was surprisingly small. In addition to the usual desk (with one chair behind it, two in front of it and an old-fashioned sphygmomanometer sitting to one side of a leather cornered blotter pad and an old-fashioned black Bakelite telephone sitting on other side), the rest of the furniture consisted of a large bookcase (crammed full with medical books, some old and some new), a side table, a couch and a stainless steel trolley packed with bits and pieces of medical equipment. The bookcase was over seven feet high but was still a long way below the ceiling. The walls were decorated with numerous paintings, most of which looked like original oils but with a smattering of watercolours.

The former consulting room of Dr Croft (and the one which Dr Hill had indicated would be for the use of Dr Leighton if she joined the practice) was roughly the same size as Dr Hill's consulting room and was quite empty except for a desk, the usual complement of chairs and a bookcase.

'The new doctor will obviously be free to decorate the room to her – or his – taste,' said Dr Hill. 'Mallory removed all his personal stuff when I put the advertisement in the *British Medical Journal.*' He closed the door and led the way further into the house which, to Dr Leighton, seemed vast. It was more like one of the National Trust properties she remembered visiting with her parents, than a house someone might live in. 'You must be starving,' he said. 'And the smell of the pies warming up in the oven is making me pretty hungry too.' He suddenly stopped. 'I say, you're not vegetarian or vegan are you?'

'No, I'm not,' said Dr Leighton. 'I'm looking forward to trying the steak and kidney pie from The Jolly Roger!'

For the first time it occurred to her that Dr Hill's home, which was also his surgery of course, did not smell like a doctor's office. There was no smell of disinfectant. There were none of the smells that she usually associated with doctors' offices and hospitals. She breathed in and realised that the house smelt of furniture polish and flowers.

'Did you call in at the pub and meet Rosemary!' asked Dr Hill.

'I did! We got on very well. She's very easy to talk to.'

'She's a wonderful girl, terrific barmaid and a marvellous cook. I don't know how she manages it all. She and Jack, her husband, run the pub and she does all the cooking. She's the barmaid in the mornings and at lunchtimes, though a girl from the village helps out in the evenings. And she has two adorable children to look after and a whole menagerie of animals. She sent along a wonderful apple pie which you can have with custard or ice cream. The secret of making a good apple pie, she tells me, is putting in enough cloves and just the right amount of cinnamon and sprinkling just the right amount of sugar on the top of the pastry. My contribution was to supply the cooking apples. I have a decent sized orchard.'

Dr Hill led Dr Leighton into the dining room where three places were set at one end of a table that was equipped with chairs to seat twelve. The high ceiling, beautifully proportioned room was so vast that the massive oak dining table seemed almost lost. At the end of the room French windows, which were open, led into a huge

Victorian conservatory filled with masses of flowers, some already in bloom and others in bud and not far away from flowering.

'I'm sorry, I didn't think to offer you an aperitif. I don't drink much at lunchtime. Shall we start straight in on the wine?'

Dr Hill had brought the steak and kidney pies and the vegetables from the kitchen, wheeling everything in on a rickety, old, wooden trolley with the dishes covered in silver plated domes to keep the food warm. The silver domes reminded Dr Leighton of a hotel her parents had once taken to when she'd been small. The waiter had removed two domes with a practised flourish and had, she remembered, repeated the gesture twice when she'd begged him to do it again.

'A little wine would be lovely. But only half a glass, I've got to drive back to London.'

'Do you really have to drive back tonight? It seems a good deal of travelling in one day. I spoke to Rosemary when she brought up the pies and she said they've got a spare room at The Jolly Roger. I reserved it for you and if you decide you can stay, Mallory and I will pay the bill, of course. It seemed slightly inappropriate to offer you a room here.'

'Thank you. That's very kind of you. I was thinking I might stop at a motel on the motorway but I haven't brought any things with me.'

'Oh, don't worry about that. I'm sure Rosemary will be able to fix you up with what you need – towels and a nightdress and so forth. And the village shop sells toothbrushes, toothpaste and all that sort of thing and they don't shut until around nine.' He thought for a moment. 'Actually, they sell most things but I don't think they sell pyjamas and nightdresses. Maybe they do! If Rosemary doesn't have any nightwear you can use I could lend you a pair of clean pyjamas. You'll just have to roll the trouser legs up a little.'

'Thank you! I'd probably need to roll them up a foot or so, but I'm sure I can sort something out. And you really haven't had any other applicants for the job?'

'No, you're the first person to show any interest at all – the only application we've received. I think that perhaps our advertisement wasn't terribly attractive. I suppose I should have put in more about prospects, salary and so on. And the lady who took down our advertisement seemed surprised that we didn't have a website to which we could refer interested applicants.'

'You don't have a website?'

'I'm afraid not. I don't own a computer I'm afraid, though Mallory has a computer and a printer. He does all our letters and keeps on top of the paperwork!' Dr Hill removed the domes from two plates and put the plates on the table. He then put a dish containing vegetables on the table in front of them, opened a bottle of wine and poured some into two glasses.

'And you do the surgeries and the visits?'

'Exactly. Each to his own, as my grandmother used to say. Mallory enjoys paperwork and so on. I hate that sort of thing. If I get stuck with a diagnosis I talk to him about it on the sole condition that the final decisions are always mine. That's his condition, by the way, not mine. Mallory is a fine diagnostician but a little reserved. He'll explain about himself when you meet. Tell me a little about yourself. What is your job at the moment? Are you still working there? If you've left, may I ask why you left, or would that be intrusive? Are you married or expecting to be married? Do you have children? I don't mean to be inquisitive or rude but I suppose these are things I should ask and you would doubtless think me remiss if I did not. And you must ask me anything you like that will help you understand what your life here would be like.'

'I'm divorced and single. I have no children or dependants and have absolutely no plans at all to remarry. The practice where I worked until recently was very modern. In fact it won an award for innovative administration, and the practice was considered something of a pioneer in the use of new software. One of the partners was constantly flying off to conferences to talk about new software applications in general practice. It was, or rather is, one of the biggest health centre practices in the country with over 40 members of staff, doctors, receptionists and so on. Around half of all the consultations were conducted through video-links and another quarter were conducted on the telephone. We even had someone who did nothing else but take blood samples. But I found it all a bit soulless, frustrating and disappointing. It wasn't what I'd hoped medical practice would be about. I resigned suddenly one day because I couldn't see myself spending the rest of my working life there. To be honest, I became rather disillusioned because the

Practice Manager seemed to regard management meetings as being rather more important than seeing patients. I did speak to one of the doctors after I'd left and he assured me that they would give a reference. He tried to persuade me not to leave so I didn't leave because I was fired.'

'You had management meetings?' Dr Hill sounded astonished.

'Three times a week. There was a good deal of talking but no one ever seemed to say anything. There was a lot of discussion about administration and most of the people who spoke seemed to me to be either defensive about the way they thought the practice should be run or overtly antagonistic towards patients – almost as though they regarded them as the enemy.' Dr Leighton pointed to the plate in front of her. 'This pie is delicious.'

'Rosemary's pies are well known in the county!' said Dr Hill. 'Do you think a medical practice should have regular meetings?'

'Do you not have any?'

'None whatsoever, I'm afraid. If you joined us here and felt strongly about it I suppose we could have the occasional meeting.' Dr Hill paused and pulled a face. 'Once every three months or so perhaps…on a daily basis, you and I would meet informally, of course. And I'd always be happy to discuss patients with you. But I'm not terribly keen on formal meetings.'

Dr Leighton laughed. 'Don't worry! I'm not keen on meetings at all. There's a good deal of time wasted and nothing very useful ever seemed to get decided. The practice actually had lots of committees where people discussed some of the topics that came up at the meetings. And then a spokesperson for the committee would come to a meeting and report what they'd decided. I found it all very boring and frustrating.'

'Exactly. My view entirely. But even when they asked you to stay you still wanted to leave? Even in the cold light of day – when you realised that you had no income, but still had bills to pay and so on?'

'Yes. I knew I could never go back there, or to any practice like it. I think I'd rather give up medicine completely than spend my life working in that sort of practice. I was actually beginning to feel ashamed of what I was doing by the time I left.'

They ate, and drank, for a while.

'I'm afraid we don't do any consultations by video or telephone here,' said Dr Hill. 'Of course, I do speak to people on the telephone, but usually when they ring up needing a visit. Occasionally people will ring up to ask something – what to do if they've missed one of their pills, for example – but I don't much like trying to make diagnoses over the telephone. I think it can lead to some terrible mistakes.'

Dr Leighton agreed with him. 'I only used video links or the telephone if patients insisted,' she said.

'And what did you hope that medical practice would be about? In an ideal world what would you look for in a medical practice? You must have thought about this'

'I think I'd want a practice to be simpler, much simpler,' replied Dr Leighton. 'In the practice where I worked the emphasis seemed to be on administration. I suppose I'm a bit old-fashioned but I think the needs of the patients should come first, the needs of the doctors second and the administration a long way third. I know I don't have much experience, I know, but it seemed to me that in the practice where I was working there were too many layers of administration between the doctor and the patients. And because of the way the practice was organised, I never saw the same patient twice. I know there has to be a certain amount of administration, appointment systems and so on, but we had a Practice Manager who seemed to do nothing else but introduce new rules. And everything was about maximising income. I understand that a practice has to make a profit and I had an excellent salary, for which I was very grateful, but if medicine is just about money you might as well go into, oh I don't know, investment banking or something similarly cold-blooded and single-minded.'

The two of them ate for a while, without speaking, each thinking private thoughts. The silence was broken only for them both to agree that the steak and kidney pie was excellent and the claret, which Mallory had chosen for them, was a perfect accompaniment.

'If you want an 'old-fashioned' practice, then you have certainly come to the right place,' said Dr Hill. 'I should warn you that we don't have an appointment system, I'm afraid,' said Dr Hill, as though making a confession. He put down his knife and fork and poured out more claret for them both. 'I've always thought they should be called disappointment systems because no one ever seems to find them satisfactory, though I gather they're very popular.'

Dr Leighton looked at him in astonishment. 'How do you manage without patients making appointments?'

'Very easily. You'd be surprised how well it works. Patients who have something wrong with them, or think they might have something wrong with them, or who need a fresh prescription or want their ears syringed or their blood pressure taken, turn up, sit in the waiting room, take their turn and I see them. A lady from the village, Mrs Onions, comes in for a couple of hours every morning to make sure everyone knows their position in the queue. She hands out raffle tickets with numbers on and collects the tickets when the patients come in to see me. Once a week, when the raffle tickets look a little dog eared she starts a new roll.'

Dr Leighton took a sip of her wine and thought about this for a moment. 'People don't have to telephone beforehand? To say that they're coming to the surgery, to tell you what's wrong with them?'

'Good heavens, no. There wouldn't be any point in not having an appointment system if they had to go through that sort of palaver. And I've always thought it was my job to tell my patient what is wrong with them – rather than their job to tell me why they need an appointment. Besides, if patients rang to say they intended to visit, we'd have the phone ringing all morning for no good reason at all. Of course, people telephone if they need me to visit them at home.'

'I always thought that having an appointment system was compulsory.'

'I think it might be,' admitted Dr Hill. 'Mallory deals with all the paperwork so I'm not entirely sure what the official position is. I do remember a couple of bureaucrats turning up around ten or twelve years ago and telling me that if I didn't have an appointment system they would throw me out of the National Health Service. I told them to go ahead and I'd set up in private practice.'

'They obviously didn't! So, what happened?'

'We're too far away from any other practice to join up and form one of those huge group practices that are so fashionable, and the bureaucrats knew that they'd have a job finding a new doctor to take over a remote, lonely country practice so they went away and I never heard from them again. At least I don't think we did. Anyway, I'm still here, I'm still employed by the National Health Service and I still don't have an appointment system. I think we'd probably be paid more if we did have an appointment system but I'm happy with things the way they are. And the patients seem happy. No one has ever asked why we don't have an appointment system.'

'The appointment system was the backbone of the practice where I used to work,' admitted Dr Leighton. 'Everything was done by appointment. If a patient was too ill to attend the surgery by appointment, they were told to go the local Accident and Emergency Department to be seen. Most other local practices did the same.'

'How long did patients have to wait for an appointment?'

'Usually about three weeks, but there were three appointments kept free each day for what were called 'emergencies'.'

'And if a patient rang with a desperate need to see a doctor but the three emergency appointments had been taken?'

'Then they had to wait three weeks or try the following day for one of the next day's emergency appointments.'

'There must have been a huge queue of patients in the local Accident and Emergency Department!'

'Oh, there was. The average waiting time there was between ten and twelve hours. Some patients waited 24 hours to be seen – or even more.'

'Emergency patients had to wait 24 hours to see a doctor?'

'Oh yes. And even then they often saw a nurse or a care assistant rather than a doctor.'

Dr Hill looked shocked. 'It sounds as if medicine has been taken over by the bureaucrats.'

'Yes, it has. That's why I resigned. Medicine is run by and for the administrators now. They've taken over. They make all the rules, they take all the important decisions, they tell us how to work, they control virtually everything. Our practice employed more administrators than doctors and some of them are incredibly well paid. And they clearly want everything to be controlled by computers. They've made medical practice more remote and they're encouraging practices to stop seeing patients in what they call 'a face to face situation' and to treat them only via a computer or a telephone. Not dealing with patients who have emergency problems makes that easier of course.'

'And that's not the way you want to practise?'

'No!' said Dr Leighton firmly. 'What staff do you have, apart from Mrs Onions?' she asked.

'None. There's just Mrs Onions. If I need to send a letter she can type. Or if she's not around I write a letter in longhand. If I want a copy I'll photocopy it. It means I don't have to wait for her to read her shorthand, type something out, put it in a nice folder, hand it to me, get it signed and then put it out for the postman. Our postman, a really nice fellow called Gerry, usually comes at midday, so if I'm quick I can get letters in the post after I've finished the morning surgery. If I'm out visiting patients I just leave the day's mail in a basket in the porch and he picks it up and takes it away.'

'What about taking blood samples? Who does that?'

'I take the blood and Gerry takes them into town and drops them off at the hospital. He's not supposed to do it but the hospital is on his way back to the sorting office.'

'You don't have a nurse attached to the practice?'

'There is a district nurse who pops in once or twice a week to see if I have any patients who need dressings changed and so on.'

'So, who does things like take blood pressures, remove stitches and syringe ears?'

'Oh, I do all those things myself,' said Dr Hill with a wave of his hand. 'I've always thought that doing little practical things helps me build up a real relationship with my patients and it doesn't take much time. I'm guessing that you had people to do all those things at your previous practice?'

'Yes, the argument was that it saved a lot of doctor time to have nurses or aides do those jobs.'

'And the time which you saved was spent having meetings?'

'Yes, that's right,' said Dr Leighton, who felt a little embarrassed.

'So how did it work, having nurses take blood pressures?'

'Well, if I thought I needed a patient's blood pressure taking, I'd send them off to the reception desk to make an appointment to see the nurse. When the nurse saw them, usually ten or fourteen days later, she'd take their blood pressure and write it in their notes and then they'd make an appointment to see me again.'

'After waiting another three weeks for the new appointment?'

'Yes.'

'Dr Leighton,' said Dr Hill, 'how long does it take to obtain a blood pressure reading?'

'Not very long,' admitted Dr Leighton.

'Three minutes, perhaps, if you do it twice? Once to get the patient used to it and the second time to get a proper reading?'

'I suppose so.'

'And what about if you wanted to know a patient's weight?'

'I'd get them to make an appointment with one of the clinical assistants.'

'And it would take a few weeks to get the result?'

'Maybe a month or, more probably, six weeks.'

Dr Hill smiled. 'If you do it yourself you don't have to wait weeks to get any of these results, the patient avoids two unnecessary visits to the surgery, you don't have to employ receptionists to make all the appointments, and if the patient's blood pressure is worryingly high, or low, you know straight away. All in two minutes. The same is true of giving injections, taking blood samples and all those other little chores. I think it's much quicker and easier – and better for the patient – to do it yourself. Plus, if you take blood pressure readings yourself, the patient's blood pressure is taken every time by the same doctor using the same machine.'

Dr Leighton nodded, instantly understanding. 'Of course,' she agreed. 'Different people taking the same blood pressure will often get different readings, and readings invariably vary when different machines are used.' Dr Leighton picked up the wine glass in front of her, thought about it, took another sip of wine, then another, and decided that she would almost certainly be staying overnight at The Jolly Roger. 'Did I hear you say that you visit people at home?'

'Oh, yes, I certainly do. Would you like half of another one of Rosemary's steak and kidney pies?' asked Dr Hill. 'The third pie is still untouched. Or would you rather move straight onto the apple pie?'

'I hate to say 'no' to the steak and kidney pie but if I eat any more of that I won't be able to manage any apple pie.'

'Don't worry about it. The remaining steak and kidney pie will make a splendid cold dish for supper. Would you like custard or ice cream on the apple pie?'

'Oh, ice cream I think, if that's not any trouble.'

'No trouble at all!' Dr Hill assured her. 'I think I'll have the same. Whenever I try to make custard it turns out horribly lumpy, but I never have any trouble with ice cream.' He thought for a moment and then expanded on his answer to Dr Leighton's previous question. 'I've always felt that it would be absurd not to visit people at home. If patients are feeling really poorly they don't want to drag themselves to the surgery. And some of my patients don't have motor cars. It would be quite cruel to expect them to walk two miles to the surgery and then two miles back home again. I've got a four-wheel drive truck and I know my way round the village very well. As long as you regard the Jolly Roger as the centre of the village, it's difficult to get terribly lost. If you were to join us here I'd take you round and show you where people live – and fix you up with a copy of a local map. One of the estate agents publishes an excellent map which has the names of most of the lanes marked on it.'

Dr Hill put their now empty plates onto the wooden trolley and started to wheel it away towards the kitchen to fetch the apple pie which was warming in the oven. The wheels squeaked comically and one of them wasn't happy about the way the other three were travelling.

'Let me help you,' said Dr Leighton, standing and following Dr Hill.

'There's really no need,' Dr Hill assured her. 'But do come into the kitchen and take a look around.'

The kitchen was a huge room with a ceiling at least fifteen feet high. There was a huge Welsh dresser on the left side of the room, the largest kitchen table Dr Leighton had ever seen in the centre of the room and another long, free-standing table along the right hand side. There were no fitted cupboards at all. There was a massive, cream coloured AGA, an equally enormous fridge freezer which looked as if it probably belonged in a museum, two Belfast sinks, side by side, a half glazed door out into the garden and, apart from a kettle and a magnificent, shiny toaster which Dr Leighton remembered had been a Christmas present from the couple at The Jolly Roger public house, few other signs of the 20th or 21st century. There was no dishwasher, no microwave oven, no mixers, no coffee machine and no other electrical equipment. One door, wide open, led into a scullery where Dr Leighton could see an elderly, green enamelled washing machine and a wooden clothes dryer suspended from the ceiling. Another door led into an enormous and surprisingly well-stocked pantry.

Dr Hill opened one of the AGA's doors and pulled out a massive apple pie that looked big enough for a party of a dozen hungry guests. He put the pie onto the trolley and carefully placed a silver, domed dish cover over it to keep it warm. 'There are plates in the dresser and cutlery in the top left hand drawer. And there's an ice cream scoop there too.'

Dr Leighton went to the dresser to find these essentials.

'I suspect that being a country GP is rather different to being a GP in a big city,' said Dr Hill, as Dr Leighton found one large, yellow plate and one light blue one and put them onto the squeaky wheeled trolley. It didn't look to her as though any two pieces of crockery in the cupboard were matching. She then opened the drawer Dr Hill had indicated and found two spoons and two forks. They were surprisingly heavy, and turning over the forks Dr Leighton noticed that they were solid, hall marked silver. She found an old-fashioned ice cream scoop that looked as if it had probably started life when Queen Victoria was on the throne.

'I would imagine so,' said Dr Leighton, who was beginning to think it would be more difficult to find similarities than differences.

'I bought a job lot of cutlery at a house auction forty years ago,' explained Dr Hill. 'Either the auctioneer hadn't noticed that they were all silver or he didn't care. No one wanted silver cutlery at the time – it was considered too heavy and ugly. I found that it was often possible to get bargains at the end of a country house auction. The auctioneer is usually tired and slightly hoarse by the time he gets round to stuff from the kitchen, the garage and the garden. The big dealers will have all gone to pay for and collect the furniture they've bought, ready to cram their purchases into their vans and onto the roof-racks on their Volvo estate cars, and the nosy parkers who've just turned up for a poke around, with no intention of ever bidding for anything, will have gone off to find somewhere to have a cup of coffee. I actually bought a lot of what they call 'brown furniture' at auctions: cupboards, tables, wardrobes, chairs and so on. British buyers turn up their noses at Victorian furniture but it's usually very well made. Most of it is bought by dealers and sent to America.'

Dr Leighton made a mental note that if she ever bought a house in the country she would visit local auctions in order to furnish it with good, solid, old-fashioned furniture.

'Have you ever worked in a small practice?' Dr Hill asked.

'No, I did my two house jobs, a house physician and then a house surgeon, and worked as a junior registrar in anaesthetics for a year before deciding I didn't want to spend my life working in hospitals. They were very bureaucratic and getting worse by the month. I decided I wanted to be a GP so I took a job as a trainee in a practice with 8 doctors – all partners. It was very efficient. When I qualified as a GP I took a job at a practice in London – the one where I've been working up until recently.'

'And then you resigned. Good for you!' said Dr Hill. 'That must have taken courage. If you decide to take the plunge and join us here, you really will find it quite different to anything you're used to. Working in an old-fashioned country practice looks very relaxing on a nice day but when there's a storm raging and the roof tiles are flying about and trees are crashing down and you get a call to a farm, that's just twenty minutes away on a sunny day, it can seem a trifle daunting. And it's not much fun having to walk to a cottage to deliver a baby when there's two feet of snow in the lanes and not even a tractor can get through the drifts. How many patients did you each look after in your London practice?'

'We had just over 2,000 patients per doctor. That was slightly higher than the local average. How many patients do you have here?'

'I can tell you exactly – it's 1,472,' replied Dr Hill. 'And it's no coincidence that the population of Stratford Peverell is also 1,472. We look after the entire village and we don't have any patients outside the village. The total was 1,471 two weeks ago and then XL had a baby. It'll probably go back to 1,471 in the next few days because we're about to lose Mr T. He's 93, a grand fellow, and his heart is giving out.'

'When you say 'we look after' you mean yourself and Dr Croft?'

'That's right. But as I explained, Mallory doesn't deal with patients any more. If he wants to tell you why then he'll tell you. But that's up to him. He does all the administration for the practice. He deals with the bureaucrats who come round occasionally and tell us how to do our jobs. He keeps them off my back.'

'So why do you want another doctor?' asked Dr Leighton. 'Your list isn't all that large and I doubt if you're planning to retire.'

Dr Hill laughed. 'No, I'm not planning to retire. I'll work until I drop but I'm not a young man anymore, and I run out of energy rather more speedily than used to be the case. I do sometimes feel rather tired – more than used to be the case. I've never understood why healthy people who enjoy what they do want to retire when they reach a certain age. If you hate what you do then I suppose it makes sense to reward yourself with a few years playing bowls, making matchstick models of the Eiffel Tower, helping out in the local Oxfam shop and visiting National Trust properties. All wonderful activities for some people I don't doubt, but not for me. But I love what I do. It's my life.'

'So why did you advertise for another doctor?'

'I'm not getting any younger,' said Dr Hill. 'I'm 70 next month and Mallory is 72 and no one knows better than a country doctor that sickness and death are never far away from any of us. I try to keep fairly fit but if I'm ill there is no one to look after the village. Mallory and I talked things over and decided we could afford to split the practice income into thirds instead of halves. If I had a heart attack or a stroke we'd have to hire a locum we didn't know – if we could find one. He or she wouldn't know us, our patients or the village. It wouldn't be fair to anyone – especially the patients. So we decided that we'd try to find a young doctor so that we didn't have to spend too much time thinking about the unthinkable.'

'Are you looking for an assistant or a junior partner?' asked Dr Leighton.

'Not an assistant, certainly. That would imply some sort of hierarchy and I don't think that works well in a medical practice. Mallory and I talked it over and decided that we needed a third partner and that the best way would be to bring someone in and appoint them as a full partner on a sort of probationary contract for a few months. We'll pay the new doctor a third of the practice income for that period. If you join us then I suspect that you will be earning less than you were earning in London, I'm afraid. But your personal expenses will doubtless be substantially lower. We don't do a lot of the things that bring in money. We don't charge to sign passport forms or sick notes, for example. On the other hand our practice expenses are considerably lower than they would have been at your practice in London, with that big purpose built health centre and all those members of staff. If at the end of the trial period we all get on then we'll sign a full partnership agreement. If things don't work out then we can all shake hands and call it a day. How does that sound to you?'

'It's unusual but it sounds sensible,' agreed Dr Leighton.

'The thing is,' said Dr Hill, 'that being a country doctor in an old-fashioned practice is so very different. We do much of our healing in people's houses. We practise in a rather old-fashioned way. You'll find out that being available 24 hours a day for 365 days a year is quite different to turning up for a few surgeries a week and then going home at the end of each surgery.'

'When did you last have a holiday?'

'I haven't had a holiday since Mallory stopped practising. Not even a weekend off. I'm married to the job and married to Stratford Peverell.'

'But you enjoy it?'

'I enjoy it more than I could have ever imagined I would enjoy being a doctor. For me, being an old-fashioned country GP is the best job in medicine.'

'I can understand that,' said Dr Leighton softly.

'But at times it can be exhausting, heart breaking, frustrating and terrifying,' warned Dr Hill. 'And I know I wouldn't be able to do it if I didn't have Mallory to look after the paperwork and to keep the regulators and the bureaucrats off my back. If you come to work here never make the mistake of thinking he's not an essential part of the practice.'

Dr Hill tapped the silver dome over the apple pie. 'And we ought to start on the pie before it goes cold.' He opened the freezer door. 'I'm afraid I've only got vanilla, chocolate or strawberry ice cream. The village shop doesn't stock any of those fancy flavours and it's such a long drive from the nearest supermarket that anything I bought there would have melted long before I got home.'

'Oh, vanilla, I think don't you?'

'Excellent choice,' agreed Dr Hill, taking out a large, plastic tub of vanilla ice cream.

And then, with the exquisitely painful timing that all old-fashioned GPs know, understand and come to expect as entirely normal, the telephone in Dr Hill's surgery started to ring.

'I'm sorry about this,' apologised Dr Hill, handing the ice cream tub to Dr Leighton. 'The telephone always knows if you're having a meal, running a bath or doing something intricate and tricky.'

He hurried off to answer the telephone. 'Just help yourself to ice cream,' he called over his shoulder. 'Put two scoops on mine and then pop the ice cream back in the freezer. Start without me and I'll be as quick as I can.'

Chapter Eleven

Dr Leighton was still scooping ice cream out of the plastic container when Dr Hill returned.

'I'm so sorry about this. There's an emergency on the other side of the village. I've got to go. A farmer I know well. From what his wife says it sounds as if he's having a heart attack. She's not a woman to panic. You can either stay here and wait or, if you like, you can come with me.'

Dr Leighton didn't hesitate. 'I'll come with you.'

'Pop the apple pie and the ice cream into the freezer,' said Dr Hill, heading for his consulting room. 'I'll just get my bag.'

Moments later the two of them were seated in Dr Hill's rather battered old Ford truck, with Dr Hill's equally battered black bag sitting on the back seat. Before setting off, Dr Hill had paused only to put the truck into four-wheel drive.

'Should I take my car and follow you?' Dr Leighton had asked.

'Probably better if you come with me. You might have a job keeping up. And we have to go down a farm track to get to the Taylors'. I'm not sure that fancy sports car of yours would make it in one piece.'

Dr Leighton was prepared to accept that her low slung sports car might not make it down a farm truck but she was a little aggrieved by Dr Hill's comment about her ability to keep up. She didn't think Dr Hill's truck was likely to have the power or speed of her Lotus.

Five minutes later, after Dr Hill had overtaken a tractor by bumping along a grass verge and had screamed along country lanes at a speed she would have never dared to try, she had revised her opinion.

'You don't hang around, do you?' said Dr Leighton, tightening her seat belt and hanging onto the grab handle that she assumed had been added as an optional extra.

'I find it's always best to get there as quickly as is safely possible,' said Dr Hill, quite calmly. 'The Taylors are lovely people but they're both big worriers. He'll calm down a lot when we get there and, as you know, panic can make a bad situation worse. I know the Taylors very well and they don't cry wolf.' He slid round a bend with the side of the truck brushing against a hawthorn hedge. It wasn't difficult to see why the vehicle was battered and scratched. 'One of the advantages of a truck is that we're a little bit higher up than the hedges so I can see if there is anything round the corner. I had the suspension lifted and big winter tyres put on to give me even better visibility.'

'Does it ever snow round here?' asked Dr Leighton, as they drove up a steep, narrow lane, only just wide enough for the truck.

'We're quite high up here and we usually get a couple of weeks of snow at some time during the winter. But autumn is often just as tricky. Snow isn't all that bad unless it drifts across the road; it's wet leaves which are a real nightmare for driving. Our local postman's little red van has two wheel drive, of course, and he can't get up this hill very well, for a couple of months of autumn at least. There are only two farms up this way so one of the farms leaves an old milk churn by the side of the road and the farmers come along and pick up their own mail.' Dr Hill slowed for a sharp bend and then accelerated again. 'The village shop likes to get stocked up in October, ready for the winter. They have three huge freezers in their barn and they also keep a good supply of tins and dried goods in case their delivery lorries can't get to them. They're the only place in Stratford Peverell where we can buy petrol and diesel and they've run out a few times. If I get low on diesel, one of the farmers will bring me a few cans of their red diesel but I don't think that's entirely legal so don't tell anyone. And the pub always keeps a few extra barrels of beer in their cellar. They ran out three years ago and I don't think they want that to happen again!'

'So this is a good time of the year to be visiting,' said Dr Leighton.

'Spring is my favourite season. It's the end of the harsh weather and the beginning of the countryside's New Year. All the promise of the summer lies ahead.'

Dr Leighton couldn't help thinking how appropriate it was that she should be contemplating a big change in her own life, just as Nature was preparing for her annual change. If she were offered the job (and if she took it, for she was still feeling very nervous about the change) just how well would she be able to cope through what would doubtless be a dark, cold winter? She remembered what Peter had said about being cut off from the world. He hadn't meant that he thought that she would be cut off literally but it sounded as if that could happen. How would she cope if she had to treat really sick patients without benefit of knowing that an ambulance could come to collect patients she couldn't treat?

'Do you ever use a helicopter service to take patients to hospital?' she asked. A huge bird, sitting on a gate post, disturbed by the noise of Dr Hill's truck, lazily took off and flew across a field and up into the sky. 'What was that?' she asked. 'It looked like an eagle!'

'It was a buzzard. Yes, we do sometimes use the local helicopter service. But if the weather is bad they can't get here and they always have trouble finding anywhere to land. The only really flat patch of land is the football field behind the pub. A brave pilot once tried to land on Mr Whitehall's croquet lawn but he's got a row of poplar trees which made it too dangerous.'

'You were right about my not being able to keep up with you!' admitted Dr Leighton, who knew that she and the Lotus would have been left far behind. She was suddenly thrown up into the air as the truck jumped over a bump in the road. 'Do you always drive this fast?'

'Oh, good heavens no!' laughed Dr Hill, who seemed surprisingly calm. 'Only in genuine emergencies. I usually drive like the proverbial old lady – pootling along in the middle of the road.'

Dr Leighton suspected that this was probably something of an exaggeration. And the road was, in any case, so narrow that there was no middle.

The last half a mile of the journey took them along a deeply rutted farm track, with grass growing in the middle. The track, which was clearly home built, was made up of stones and broken rocks, which would, without doubt, have ripped the bottom off Dr Leighton's Lotus.

A woman in an old-fashioned pinafore was standing on the step of the farmhouse when Dr Hill braked and halted the truck just yards away from her. A cloud of hens and geese made a good deal of noise. Some flew away and some ran off, protesting noisily, and a sheep dog, asleep in the back of a truck even more battered than Dr Hill's, poked his head above the side and looked to investigate what was causing so much noise. Apparently unconcerned, perhaps recognising the doctor's truck, he didn't bark, but lowered his head and went back to sleep.

'He's in his favourite chair in the kitchen,' said the woman, whom Dr Leighton assumed to be Mrs Taylor. She was wearing a full length pinafore over a blue skirt and a red jumper. Her hair was tied back and she wore no make-up, not even a smear of lipstick.

'This is Dr Leighton,' said Dr Hill. 'She's a doctor from London and she's working with me today.' He somehow made it sound as though Dr Leighton, coming from the nation's capital, were an important specialist of some kind. Dr Leighton somehow knew that he'd done this not just to make her feel more important (which it did) but to add a little extra comfort to that which his own arrival would have brought to Mr Taylor and Mrs Taylor.

Mrs Taylor, who looked terrified and was clearly trying hard not to cry, nodded to Dr Leighton, thanked her for coming, and led them both through the front door and into the house. She then led them along a narrow passageway that would have been wider had it not been artificially narrowed by sacks of animal feed stored along one side, and then into a large, traditional farm-house kitchen.

Two cats, slept on a mat in front of a huge old AGA (was ownership of one of these old ovens a pre-requisite for living in Stratford Peverell, wondered Dr Leighton) and a huge, white-faced man, sat in a huge, battered old leather armchair. He was wearing brown corduroy trousers which had probably enjoyed their heyday in the 1970s, solid looking leather boots and an elderly dress shirt that needed, but did not have, a detachable collar. The leather of the chair had been used as a scratching post by the cats and there was a large tear in one side which had been repaired with half a dozen pieces of grey duct tape. You didn't have to be a detective to identify the man in the chair as Mr Taylor, the reason for their visit. The house smelt strongly of wood smoke and the room smelt of cheap tobacco.

Dr Hill introduced Dr Leighton, as he had introduced her to Mrs Taylor, put his black bag down on the kitchen table, a huge piece of pine furniture, took a wooden chair across to the old man in the armchair and sat down. Dr Leighton thought about picking up a second chair but didn't. She hung back.

'Have you got any pain?' asked Dr Hill. He took gentle hold of Mr Taylor's wrist and, without fuss, started to take his pulse.

'Not at the moment,' said Mr Taylor, he reached out a hand and touched Dr Hill's arm, as though the doctor's presence alone was giving him some comfort. There was sweat on the big man's forehead and the little hair he had was plastered to the top of his head. He'd obviously been sweating a good deal.

'Tell me what happened?'

'I was moving some sacks around – bringing them in from the truck – and I came into the house because my dinner was ready. I ate, sat down to have a beer and do a bit of paperwork, and I suddenly got this massive pain in my chest. I thought I was going to die.'

'Describe the pain,' said Dr Hill, who had taken his hand off Mr Taylor' s wrist.

'We have to keep the feed in the hallway,' said Mrs Taylor. 'We've got rats in the barn and the two cats we keep are too darned lazy to get rid of them.'

Dr Hill turned very slightly on the chair. 'You two need to earn your keep!' he said to the two cats. Then he addressed Mrs Taylor. 'Would you put the kettle on, Ada?'

'Of course, doctor,' said Mrs Taylor. 'If you need lots of hot water I could put a couple of saucepans full of water on the stove.'

'I just want you to make us all a cup of tea,' said Dr Hill, with a smile. Dr Leighton looked at him with new respect. She realised he was trying to keep Mrs Taylor occupied so that he could talk to Mr Taylor and get the answers he needed first hand.

'It was like someone sitting on my chest,' said Mr Taylor.

'But it's eased now?'

'It's gone now,' agreed Mr Taylor.

'How long did the pain last?'

'From about five minutes before Ada rang you until just before you arrived. Oddly, when I heard your truck coming up the track the pain started to fade.'

'And when the pain came you were sitting where you are?'

'I'd just moved into this chair to have my beer. I always like a beer after I've eaten.'

'Were you short of breath?'

Mr Taylor nodded.

'Have you ever had anything like this before?'

'Nothing. I had a tooth abscess three years ago and that was terrible. And I broke my leg when I was 19. But this was the worst pain. I thought I was going to die, doctor.' Dr Leighton could see tears in his eyes.

'And the pain was just in your chest?'

'It started in my arm. And I had pain up here, too,' said Mr Taylor, touching his neck and jaw.

'Which arm?'

'The left one.'

'You've never had anything like it before? No pains in your chest at all?'

'Oh just the usual indigestion,' confessed Mr Taylor. He nodded towards the mantelpiece. Both doctors looked there too. A large bottle of antacid sat on the shelf, alongside a large brown clock, a mug containing half a dozen pens and a comb and three or four postcards. There was also an opened packet of cigarettes and a disposable lighter.

'Just unbutton your shirt, I want to listen to your heart.'

While Mr Taylor unbuttoned his shirt, Dr Hill stood, took out his keys and unlocked and then opened his black bag and took out his stethoscope. It was, Dr Leighton noted with surprise, an old-fashioned one of a style she'd never seen before. Dr Hill listened carefully for a couple of minutes before standing up again and handing the stethoscope to Dr Hill.

'Tea or coffee?' asked Mrs Taylor.

'Oh, nice cups of tea all round, I think, Ada,' said Dr Hill. 'Just a splash of milk and two sugars in mine.'

'Oh I know how you like yours,' said Mrs Taylor. She reached into a dresser and took down four cups. 'How about the young lady doctor?'

'Just a little milk but no sugar,' said Dr Leighton, turning away from Mr Taylor's chest.

'Sounded fine to me,' said Dr Hill to Dr Leighton. 'What did you hear?'

'Nothing abnormal,' agreed Dr Leighton. She handed the stethoscope back to Dr Hill who, after rummaging in his black bag, pulled out a rather elderly sphygmomanometer. This too was like nothing Dr Leighton had ever seen. The blood pressure measuring machines she was used to were electronic. You read the blood pressure reading from a small screen. Dr Hill's machine, like the freezer in his kitchen, and his stethoscope, looked like something that would not have looked out of place in a museum.

'What were you doing when the pain started?'

'I'd been moving sacks around.'

'After you'd eaten – what were you doing after you'd eaten? You said that you'd been doing some paperwork.'

'He was sorting through some paperwork for the taxman,' said Mrs Taylor, who had made the tea. 'He hates doing paperwork.'

'The damned tax people have been onto me again,' said Mr Taylor, unable to hide his anger. His voice rose and started to shake a little. 'You answer one question and they come back with six more. I've done nothing wrong but they opened an inquiry into my accounts six month ago.'

'Don't you have an accountant?'

'Yes,' nodded Mr Taylor. 'But he charges a fortune. I thought I'd save money by doing some of it myself.'

'I told him he's crazy,' said Mrs Taylor. 'We can afford the accountant.'

'Where's the paperwork you were looking at when the pain started?'

'On the table.' Mr Taylor pointed to a thick pile of papers.

'Have you got a big envelope?' Dr Hill asked Mrs Taylor. 'Big enough for all those papers? And a piece of notepaper?'

Mrs Taylor didn't say anything but disappeared from the kitchen for a few moments. She returned carrying a large, padded bag and a plain piece of notepaper.

'Write a short note to your accountant asking him to reply to the taxman on your behalf,' said Dr Hill handing the plain piece of paper to Mr Taylor. He turned to Mrs Taylor. 'Do you have the accountant's address?'

'It's on some of those papers,' replied Mrs Taylor.

Five minutes later the taxman's letter, a wodge of paperwork and the note from Mr Taylor were tucked neatly inside the padded envelope.

'I'm going to take this away with me,' Dr Hill told Mr Taylor, picking up the envelope and putting it beside his black bag. 'I'll put it into the post for you.'

'Yes, doctor,' said Mr Taylor, obediently.

'You'll have a piece of cake,' said Mrs Taylor, taking a huge old tin out of a cupboard. It was a statement not a question. 'I only made it two days ago. It's a fruit cake. The sort you like, doctor. It'll have settled in nicely by now.'

'I'd love a piece,' said Dr Hill, who was now struggling to roll up Mr Taylor's sleeve.

'Thank you,' said Dr Leighton, who didn't really want any cake but didn't want to upset Mrs Taylor more than she didn't want a piece of cake. Mrs Taylor took four plates and four forks from a large Welsh dresser, and put four large slices of cake and four forks on the four plates.

Having wrapped the cuff of the sphygmomanometer around Mr Taylor's upper arm, Dr Hill was now taking his blood pressure. Moments later he sat back and again offered the stethoscope to Dr Leighton.

'Just a little high, I thought,' said Dr Hill when Dr Leighton handed him back the stethoscope and removed the cuff from around Mr Taylor's arm.

'Just a little,' agreed Dr Leighton, politely, after struggling to master the sphygmomanometer, though it had seemed to her that Mr Taylor's blood pressure was considerably higher than it should have been.

'Leave the cuff where it is. We'll check it again in a few minutes,' said Dr Hill. 'Now let's all have a piece of that cake while we decide what to do.' He turned back to the patient. 'But before you have any cake I want you to put this under your tongue and let it dissolve.' He opened his black bag, reached inside and took out a small bottle of tablets.

'Hold out your hand!'

Mr Taylor held out his hand while Dr Hill shook a single white tablet into the large man's palm. Mr Taylor obediently then popped the tablet into his mouth.

Dr Leighton was flabbergasted. She had no doubt that Mr Taylor had just had a heart attack. It wasn't just an attack of angina. It was a full-blooded heart attack. And she was certain that Dr Hill could also have no doubt about the diagnosis. She also suspected that the indigestion pains of which Mr Taylor had complained were angina, early warning signs of heart trouble, rather than anything to do with his stomach. She was flabbergasted because there had been

absolutely no mention of calling an ambulance and sending Mr
Taylor into hospital. Instead, they were all about to enjoy a slice of
Mrs Taylor's fruit cake. She wondered whether she should say
something and maybe ask if Dr Hill wanted her to call an
ambulance.

Dr Hill was now washing his hands in a huge Belfast sink under
the kitchen window. Before he'd finished, Mrs Taylor had opened a
drawer in the table, taken out two clean hand towels and put them on
the back of a chair ready for him and Dr Leighton.

'When you get to know Mrs Taylor a little better she will possibly
tell you the secret of her fruit cake,' said Dr Hill, picking up one of
the plates. For the first time he noticed the forks. 'What on earth is
the cutlery for?' he asked.

Dr Leighton washed her hands and picked up the second towel.

'Well, since we have a visitor,' said Mrs Taylor, blushing a little.

'Oh, I think Dr Leighton can manage to eat a slice of fruit cake
without a fork!' said Dr Hill. 'Put the forks back in the drawer!'

'Are you going to work with Dr Hill?' asked Mrs Taylor,
collecting up the four forks and putting them away.

'I'm just visiting at the moment.'

'I have hopes,' said Dr Hill. 'Much to my surprise and
disappointment I'm not getting any younger. The practice needs
some new blood.'

This was the first real indication Dr Leighton had had that the job
might be hers if she wanted it. And she realised that she really didn't
know whether she did want the job or not. Dr Hill's way of
practising seemed utterly alien to everything she'd learned or
experienced. Why hadn't he called an ambulance? She'd been taught
that it is vital to get a heart attack patient into hospital as quickly as
possible. Mr Taylor needed to be in a Coronary Care Unit, connected
to a heart monitor. He needed a drip and constant attention from
specialist nurses. He needed to be put on drugs to bring down his
blood pressure and he needed an anti-coagulant to make sure that he
didn't have any more blood clots in his cardiac arteries. All Dr Hill
had done had been to give him what looked like an aspirin tablet and
feed him a cup of tea and a piece of fruit cake. None of what he was
doing made any sort of sense. Indeed, it all seemed so crazy she
began to wonder if both she and Dr Hill might find themselves in

trouble with a coroner if Mr Taylor were to die. She felt she really ought to say something. But she didn't.

'Let's check that blood pressure again,' said Dr Hill, finishing the last of his cake and washing it down with a third of a cupful of tea. He stood up, bent over the patient, pumped up the cuff and put the business end of his stethoscope back into position.

'The systolic is down by 20,' he said to Dr Leighton after a moment or two. He turned to Mr Taylor. 'It's improved.'

'So what was it?' asked Mrs Taylor. 'Was it a heart attack?'

'I'm pretty sure it was,' replied Dr Hill.

'Does he have to go into hospital?'

'I'd rather he stayed here.' He turned to Mr Taylor. 'If you stay at home will you rest? And will you do what I tell you to do?'

'Do I have a choice?'

'Oh yes. You have a choice. You can bounce around in an ambulance for an hour or an hour and a half and travel to the hospital. When you get there they'll put you in a Coronary Care Unit and fit you with a lot of tubes and leads and shine bright lights on you for 24 hours a day. They'll give you a pile of powerful drugs. Or you can stay at home and rest and I'll monitor your heart and your blood pressure and give you some simple medicine to take.'

'I don't want to go into hospital,' said Mr Taylor. 'I really don't.'

'I know that,' replied Dr Hill. 'But if you stay at home then you have to make some serious attempts to change the way you live.'

'You mean I should lose weight?'

'You don't just need to lose weight – a lot of weight – but you also need to change your diet. And you have to change it quite considerably. You also have to start learning to relax, and when you're feeling better than you do at the moment you have to start taking the right sort of exercise – aerobic exercise that doesn't just involve you in lifting heavy sacks of animal feed and moving them about.'

'Oh I'm too old for leaping about,' said Mr Taylor.

'I'm not talking about leaping about. Just a brisk walk once or twice a day will do it. And that was the last piece of cake you have for a while. I'm going to leave you with some pills to take every three hours and also some very small pills which you can take if you get any pain again. You just put one under your tongue and let it dissolve. I'm going to come back tomorrow with a diet plan.

Meanwhile, you're going to rest. You're not to move any sacks.
You're not to do anything around the farm. And you're not to look at
any paperwork that doesn't make you smile or feel good inside.'

'Geoff can deal with the farm,' said Mrs Taylor.

'Geoff is your cowman?'

'He is. He's reliable. I'll tell him not to bother Alfie with
anything. If he needs instructions he can ask me.'

'You'll ring Tony? He'll help won't he?'

'I rang Tony after I rang you. He'll be here in ten minutes at
most. For as long as I can remember he and his Dad have been more
like best chums than father and son.'

'How are you feeling now?' Dr Hill asked Mr Taylor. 'Any
pain?'

'The pain has gone completely. And I hope it stays away.'

'And how is your breathing?'

'I'm feeling fine. I can breathe normally now.' He took a deep,
deep breath to prove this point. His colour was a good deal healthier.
He looked more like a human being and less like a corpse or an
overweight version of Paul the white-faced clown in a three ringed
circus.

'Can you get up to bed by yourself?'

'Oh yes, I think so.'

'Then, let's see you do it.'

Mrs Taylor and the two doctors watched and helped a little as Mr
Taylor made his way to the staircase and then up to his bedroom.
Mrs Taylor helped him to undress, got him into his pyjamas and into
bed.'

'How's your chest?' asked Dr Hill when Mr Taylor was
comfortably settled.

'It's fine. No pains.'

'You can get out of bed to go along the corridor to the bathroom,'
said Dr Hill. 'Otherwise you stay in bed. I'll be back to see you
tomorrow.'

When they got back downstairs, Dr Hill handed Mrs Taylor two
small bottles of pills. 'He's to take two of these every three hours,'
he told her. 'And these tiny pills are for him to take if he gets any
chest pain again. I'll bring another supply tomorrow. You ring me if
anything worries you. I'll be back tomorrow morning. Tell Alfie that

if he's not in bed when I get here I'll ring an ambulance and send him into the hospital. Are there any cigarettes upstairs?'

'No. Just the ones downstairs. There are a couple of fresh packs in the larder.'

'He doesn't have any cigarettes tonight or tomorrow morning,' said Dr Hill. 'Unless he gets agitated. He can have one cigarette only if he becomes very restless.'

'It's Sunday tomorrow, doctor,' said Mrs Taylor. 'Can he not go to church? He likes going to church?'

'You'll both have to miss this week. Do you want me to ask the vicar to call in after his morning service?'

'Would you? Do you think he'd come?'

'I will do that,' promised Dr Hill. 'And I'm sure the vicar will pop round.'

Dr Hill took out his keys, locked his bag and picked up the bag and the large envelope full of Mr Taylor's tax papers and he and Dr Leighton left the house. They'd been there, noticed Dr Leighton, over an hour and a half.

'You think I should have sent him into hospital, don't you?' said Dr Hill, as they drove away from the Taylors' farm. 'That's what would have happened in London, isn't it?'

'He'd almost certainly had a heart attack,' said Dr Leighton. 'We both know that.' She paused 'How old is he?'

'Late forties.'

'He looks older, much older.'

'He's a farmer. Most of them look older than they are. They work hard and they're out in all weathers.'

'In London, he'd have gone straight into hospital,' agreed Dr Leighton. It came out rather bossily, rather coldly. 'There would have been no question and no hesitation.' She thought hard for a moment before saying what she said next. 'To be honest I was surprised when you didn't send him into hospital.' And she stopped herself. She had been about to add: 'I think you could lose your medical licence for what you've just done – or rather, not done. And so could I.' But she didn't and was, for ever after, grateful that she had stopped herself.

'Then thank you for not saying anything back there,' said Dr Hill. 'It would have confused the Taylors if you had. And I'd have had to send him into hospital.' He turned slightly and looked at Dr

Leighton. 'I think that sending him into hospital would have killed him. Medicine here is quite different to medicine in a big city, and although I know we can appear rather backward I sometimes suspect that big city doctors might have something to learn from the way we practice.'

'But hospitals are especially equipped to deal with heart attack patients. We couldn't even do an electro cardiogram.'

'What difference would an ECG make?' asked Dr Hill. 'We both know he had a heart attack. We know he's probably been getting angina. And we know that when we left him he was feeling much easier than he had been. An ECG reading wouldn't change how we treated him.' He paused, thinking for a moment. 'How long does it take to move a patient from home to hospital in London?'

'Ideally, no more than 30 minutes from the first phone call. Usually rather less than that.'

'It would take at least two and a half hours to get Mr Taylor into hospital,' Dr Hill told her. 'At least. Probably more. It would take over an hour to get the ambulance to their farm – even if they could drive the ambulance along that track. And to get him to hospital he'd be bounced and jolted about for ninety minutes. Once he arrived at the hospital he'd be put into the CCU, assuming they had a bed, and there he'd be frightened out of his wits by all the excitement. His wife would have to wait somewhere and he wouldn't have her by his side. I know for a fact that they've been married for 20 years and they haven't been parted for more than an hour or so in all that time.' He slowed the truck as a pheasant walked across the road. 'I think that knowing your patients well, as people as well as patients, makes a huge difference. If Mr Taylor had been a close relative or my dearest friend I would have treated him in exactly the same way. And that's the secret of good medicine isn't it? You have to ask yourself if you have treated your patient in the way that you'd like to be treated, or that you'd like your nearest and dearest to be treated if someone else was looking after them?'

Dr Leighton didn't say anything but just nodded slightly. 'You told his wife he could have a cigarette,' she said, accusingly. 'You must know as well as I do that his heart attack was probably partly a result of his smoking.'

'I agree. But now is not the time to push him to give up cigarettes completely. I agree that he needs to stop them. But at the moment I think it is more important to stop him feeling stressed. One more cigarette isn't going to kill him.'

'You could have given him a tranquilliser to stop him worrying?'

'Something like a benzodiazepine?'

'Exactly.'

'But the incidence of serious dependence among those who take benzodiazepines suggests that they're probably the most addictive drugs in the world. Mr Taylor is going to be vulnerable for the next few weeks. There's plenty of evidence to show that patients who take benzodiazepines for more than a week or two can become very dependent on them. In fact I think the Government's advice is that they shouldn't be prescribed for more than two weeks at the most. The side effects associated with these drugs are horrendous. I think I'll find it easier to wean Mr Taylor off his cigarettes than to wean him off both cigarettes and benzodiazepine tranquillisers.'

Dr Leighton who had known about the benzodiazepines but had forgotten just how dangerous they could be, began (not without justification she realised) to feel as though she were losing the debate.

'There was a report published in the *British Medical Journal* nearly half a century ago,' said Dr Hill. 'It was a large study of patients who had suffered heart attacks. Around half the patients were sent to hospital and half were kept at home. Do you know what the result was?'

Dr Leighton had to admit that she hadn't heard of the study and didn't know the result.

'They concluded that the mortality rates of the two groups were similar whether they were treated in hospital or at home. But the medical profession has never taken much notice of the results because they're rather inconvenient. Hospital doctors don't like to have to accept that patients are just as well off staying at home, rather than being treated in a very expensive, specialist hospital unit. And, of course, another doctor in America has published extensive work showing that patients with serious heart disease can be treated as well with diet, exercise and relaxation as with surgery and an extensive diet of expensive drugs which carry a host of unpleasant and dangerous side effects.'

'But what about treatment? I assume those were aspirin tablets that you gave him?'

'Aspirin is good at helping to stop clotting, and in my experience much safer than warfarin. And, of course, there is evidence that keeping heart attack patients in bed for too long can do more harm than good.'

Dr Leighton was beginning to feel like a medical student struggling to keep up in a particular strenuous seminar. In just a few hours her world had turned upside down. When sitting in the kitchen at the Taylors' farm, she had pretty well decided that she didn't want to work with Dr Hill. She had decided that everything her former husband had warned about was proving true. She'd decided that Dr Hill was dangerously out of date in just about every conceivable way, and she had begun to wonder if it was possible that if she rang the senior partner at her previous practice she might be able to get her old job back. She could, she thought, claim that the death of her mother had left her upset, depressed and slightly off balance. Now her mind was in turmoil.

'By the way,' said Dr Hill. 'Apropos of absolutely nothing we have discussed recently, I would always recommend that if you're in a patient's house and you get a chance, you have a look in the bathroom cabinet.'

Dr Leighton looked at him. 'Isn't that rather rude?'

'Not at all,' replied Dr Hill. 'As a GP I am entitled to know everything about my patients. I will always keep their secrets but they cannot have secrets from me or I can't offer them the best advice. The whole relationship between doctor and patient must be one of trust. If I tell them to undress there must be a reason for it. If I stick a finger into a very personal orifice there must be a reason for it. Medical care, especially in general practice, is built upon trust and mutual respect. That's why rural practice is the most perfect form of medicine. I live among my patients. If medicine becomes too bureaucratic then individuality gets crushed, as does any individual sense of responsibility. You'll find all sorts of clues in someone's bathroom cabinet. You learn a lot about what symptoms they have and what illnesses they fear they have. Just knowing what medications they're buying for themselves will tell you a great deal. Mr Taylor had his medicines sitting on the mantelpiece in plain sight but most patients hide them away in the bathroom – the worst place in the house to keep medicines, of course. And patients don't always tell you the whole truth, you know. Sometimes they're too nervous or embarrassed to tell you something. And when they talk about the alcohol they drink or the cigarettes they smoke you can always double what they tell you!'

Dr Hill looked at his watch. 'Since our ice cream has almost certainly melted by now, do you mind if I make one more stop before we get back to the house?'

'No, of course not.'

'It won't take a minute. But we're passing the home of a patient I try to see once a fortnight or so at least.'

'Why once a fortnight?'

'Well, mainly because she's rather frail and nervous and for some indiscernible reason, a doctor's visit helps to reassure her,' said Dr Hill with a smile. 'She's 96-years-old and she's been chronically ill for the last 40 years. Besides, she's got a younger sister who would be terribly upset if there needed to be a post mortem. If a GP has seen a patient within 14 days he can sign a death certificate without a post-mortem or an inquest.'

'We usually send our patients into hospital or a nursing home if they are seriously ill,' said Dr Leighton. 'Since I've been a GP I don't think I've signed any death certificates. Most of our really elderly patients were in hospital or in nursing homes or care homes and they were looked after by doctors employed by the homes.'

'There aren't any care homes round here,' said Dr Hill. 'The nearest one is…'

'…thirty miles away!' interrupted Dr Leighton.

'Exactly! Most things are at least thirty miles away. The nearest care home is probably a bit more than that to be accurate. That's a hell of a long way for anyone to travel to deliver a hug, good wishes, a home baked Victoria sponge or a bunch of wild flowers. Neighbours might go once a week but no one could expect them to visit daily. Around here, if they're ill, most of the villagers like to stay in their own homes if they can. They have their furniture around them, their books and their records and since everyone around here has a garden, they have a view they know and can enjoy. Nearly everyone has a pet or two and most feed and know the wild birds, the squirrels and even the badgers. There are three badger setts that I know of in the village, I've got one no more than 300 yards from my back door, and badgers are inquisitive and surprisingly friendly. When folk who are ill stay in their home their friends can visit them, bring them treats and bits of gossip, and they're looked after by a doctor they know rather than some stranger.'

'But what if they fall ill at night?'

'Well, they can ring me if they are ill. If they're living at home they're happy to take the risks that are involved with living alone. No one is under any illusions. They prefer those risks to the knowledge that in a care home they'll probably be filled up with tranquillisers and sleeping tablets. And at home they can make whatever meals they want. The village shop will deliver and is just a phone call away and the pub will deliver hot meals at a reasonable price. The vicar is a good fellow, he's very sensible, he belongs to a very broad church, he visits everyone – Anglicans, Catholics, Jews – anyone who wants spiritual comfort. Occasionally, very occasionally, a social worker has managed to get out here, visit someone and tried to persuade them that they'd be better off living in a residential home somewhere. These days they don't bother. It's too far for them to come and there's no mobile phone signal so they get terribly frightened and upset. The younger social workers, in particular, hate being out of touch with their Facebook page, their Instagram Page and their Twitter account. They can't wait to get back to town to update what they've been doing and to check out what everyone else has been doing.'

Dr Hill swung his truck off the lane down which they driving and moved onto a narrow track. This one was comprised of grass and earth and although it was bumpy there were no stones or rocks. 'Mrs Parton doesn't have a car,' he says. 'And everyone who visits has a four-wheel drive something. Most people round here drive trucks like this one. In the winter it gets rather muddy so you have to drive carefully. I slid into the ditch once and had to get my tree guy to pull me out with the tractor.'

Dr Leighton looked out of the side window of the truck and noticed a three foot deep ditch on her side of the track. It was three foot wide too. Through the windscreen she could see that there was a similarly sized ditch on the other side of the track. She swore quietly to herself that nothing would persuade her to part with her Lotus. If the time ever came when she contemplated selling her sports car and buying a truck, she'd pack her bags and get back to London as quickly as she could. She was not the sort of person who would ever drive a truck let alone buy one.

Two hundred yards down the lane Dr Hill stopped outside a small, quintessential English cottage. Made of stone, it had a thatched roof with two dormer windows, downstairs windows with leaded lights and a climbing plant around the front door. There was a white picket fence at the front of the tiny front garden, and a path down the centre, between two rose beds.

'Clichés have to start somewhere,' said Dr Hill, noticing Dr Leighton staring at the cottage.

'I'm sure I've seen this cottage before somewhere,' said Dr Leighton. 'Or are there thousands of country cottages looking just like this one?'

'No, I'm sure you have seen this one,' said Dr Hill. 'A few years ago the cottage appeared on a TV advertisement for something or other. I can't remember what it was. The advertising people gave Mrs Parton a big chunk of money to let them film the outside of her cottage. The white picket fence wasn't there when they arrived but they added that and let Mrs Parton keep it. And they even put in the dormer windows in the roof. The director thought they made the cottage look friendlier. Just why the director didn't find a cottage which already had dormer windows and a picket fence – there were already two in Stratford Peverell – was a mystery to be explained only by those operating with someone else's money. The fee they paid her kept her out of poverty. A chap in the village advised her on how to invest it, and the money has helped her survive on an old aged pension that wouldn't pay her heating and food bills. Then after the advert appeared on the television, a photographer took photographs which were used on a greeting card and a calendar. He didn't have to give her any money but he turned out to be a decent fellow who was utterly charmed by her – she invited him for a cup of tea and gave him scones with jam and cream – and he gives her a small royalty which pays around half of her electricity bill. So her little cottage has earned its keep.'

Dr Hill picked up his black bag and, before leading the way up the garden path, stopped, turned back and spoke to Dr Leighton.

'Mrs Parton, the lady we're going to see is well into her nineties – she admits to 97 or 98 but she's always played around with her age and I suspect she could have received her congratulatory telegram a year or two ago – and there really isn't anything wrong with her that cannot be explained by old age. Her Christian name is Ephemia but everyone calls her Effie, by the way. They don't like doctors putting 'old age' on death certificates but it's what she'll die of when she finally reaches the end of a quite extraordinary life. She's a fascinating woman. During World War II she was one of the few women to fight in the French Foreign Legion. She was rejected for the British armed forces because of her heart but she had a French mother so she somehow got herself to France and joined the Legion. She stayed in it for over 20 years then came back to England. She worked in the theatre for a while, designing sets and costumes in the West End, and then married an Egyptian. They travelled in the Far East for several years. He wrote books about China and she illustrated them with photographs. When he died she came back to England and opened a second-hand book shop in Cambridge. She also taught piano – though she doesn't play now, not since she developed rheumatoid arthritis. She ran the bookshop for a long time and when she retired, she saw an advertisement for her cottage and came here on the spur of the moment. That's her life in a nutshell. She's frail and leaves her door open so that visitors can just walk in. She has her bedroom downstairs and there's an extra bathroom downstairs too so I don't think she's been upstairs for years. The chap who looks after her garden goes upstairs once a week to check that everything is OK – no leaks and so on.'

As he spoke, Dr Leighton realised that she knew very little about the patients she looked after in London. She had been trained to think of them as patients ('the woman with a dodgy heart', 'the man with a faulty liver', 'the child with asthma') rather than as people. She suddenly realised just how much she'd missed by not enquiring more about her patients.

'Do you know this much about all your patients?' asked Dr Leighton, who was quietly impressed.

'I would find it a very dull job if I didn't know a little about my patients. Don't they teach you to ask people about their lives, their jobs, their achievements, their successes, their failures and so on?'

'Good heavens, no!'

'When you take a medical history you don't ask about work, hobbies, family and so on?'

'No,' said Dr Leighton. 'I was never taught to do that.'

'If you don't understand the person then you cannot possibly hope to treat the patient,' said Dr Hill, rather sadly. 'I've never yet met anyone who hadn't had a life that wasn't fascinating. And I've never yet met someone from whom I didn't learn something.' He started to say something else and then stopped and led the way up the rest of the path. Even though she had been warned, it was still a surprise to Dr Leighton that Dr Hill didn't knock on the door as might have been expected, but opened it and walked straight in, shouting his name and a greeting as he did so.

Mrs Parton was sitting in an easy chair in a room at the back of the cottage. Her hair was beautifully done and was clearly cared for professionally. She wore a velvet skirt and a colourful blouse and had a shawl around her neck. The French windows were wide open and there was, almost inevitably, a log fire burning in the hearth. There were two large basketsful of logs – one on each side of the hearth. Mrs Parton was listening to music.

'Bach?' said Dr Hill.

'Congratulations, Crawford!' said Mrs Parton, with a big smile. 'You're getting better. Concerto in A minor.'

'That's what I thought it was,' said Dr Hill.

Mrs Parton laughed. She had a light, girlish laugh. 'Of course you did!'

Dr Hill introduced Dr Leighton. 'She's working with me for a day or so, just to see what old-fashioned GPs do with their time!'

'Watch, listen and learn, my dear,' said Mrs Parton. She held out a hand to Dr Leighton. The two women touched fingers lightly. 'Your hand is cold, my dear. Sit by the fire. Would you like a sherry? Of course you would. Would you do the honours, doctor?' She looked at Dr Hill as she said this. He looked at Dr Leighton and raised an eyebrow a quarter of an inch or so. She smiled and nodded. She didn't really want a sherry, she didn't much like sherry, but it seemed rude to decline. Dr Hill went to a drinks trolley on the other side of the room and poured sherry into three glasses. He took the glasses back, gave one to Mrs Parton, who insisted that Dr Leighton call her Effie, and one to Dr Leighton and kept one himself.

The two doctors sat side by side on a sofa on the other side of the fire. They talked with Mrs Parton for what seemed five minutes or so about what had recently happened in America, about a new book that had been published that week, about a play that was getting rave reviews in London and about a scandal in Australia.

'I've brought you a bottle of your medicine,' said Dr Hill. He stood up, unlocked and unopened his black bag and took out a brown bottle of medicine which he placed on a small table next to Mrs Parton. To Dr Leighton the bag seemed to have conquered the usual rules of space. And the five minutes of conversation had, she noticed, lasted over half an hour.

'Ah my magic medicine!' said Mrs Parton to Dr Hill. 'Thank you.' She then turned to Dr Leighton. 'Before you go you must ask Dr Hill for the secret of this medicine,' she said. 'Whatever it is, I swear by it. It keeps me alive. I call it 'Dr Hill's Mysterious Tonic'. He makes it himself you know. I think he's a secret alchemist.'

The two doctors said goodbye to Mrs Parton and Dr Hill promised to call in again in a fortnight or before if she needed him.

Dr Hill reversed down the track which led to Mrs Parton's cottage. There was no room to turn round. And then he headed back to his house. 'We can try some of that apple pie if you've still got an appetite for it.'

'Do you mind very much if I just go back to the pub,' said Dr Leighton as Dr Hill drove back into his own driveway and parked beside Dr Leighton's sports car. 'I'm mentally exhausted. There's so much I need to think about. And I really need a bath or a shower. I got up very early this morning for the drive down here.'

'No problem at all,' said Dr Hill. 'You can pick up your car and drive yourself down to the pub. Call me in the morning if you want to discuss the job – but call me please even if you decide you aren't interested.' He paused. 'I'm rather afraid you were thrown in at the deep end today.'

'Not at all,' said Dr Leighton. 'And of course I will call,' said Dr Leighton. 'Thank you.' She paused. 'What was in that bottle you gave Mrs Parton? She said I should ask you.'

'It's a Gentian Alkaline Mixture. Rather old-fashioned, I'm afraid. I make it up myself.'

'I've never heard of it,' confessed Dr Leighton. 'What does it do? What's it for?'

'In harsh pharmacological terms it doesn't do anything very much,' said Dr Hill. 'But in human terms it does a great deal. Mrs Parton believes in it. I've got a dozen patients who take it regularly twice a day.'

'It's just a placebo?'

'Yes, it is.'

Dr Leighton didn't say anything.

'You don't approve of placebos?'

'We were taught that it is unethical to prescribe a placebo,' said Dr Leighton. She paused and then apologised. 'I apologise,' she said. 'That sounds rude.'

'It's not rude at all. It's what you were taught,' said Dr Hill. 'But the reality is that in practice everything you do or prescribe has a value and a quality as a placebo. If you don't take advantage of that then you're ignoring one of the most powerful healing forces there is.'

'I don't understand,' said Dr Leighton. 'How can there be a placebo response when you give a patient an antibiotic or a painkiller? Surely they either work or they don't. As I understand it a placebo is a dummy pill that contains nothing of value – just lactose or starch – and one that doesn't do the patient any good. It only works if you can trick the patient into believing it's of value. It's a confidence trick – the sort of thing used by witch doctors to convince primitive people that chicken feathers and bits of bone gave them special powers.' She looked rather uncomfortable. 'I was taught that's why it is unethical to use a placebo.'

'And yet you'll have heard of apparently healthy individuals dying within days or hours after being cursed by a witch doctor?'

'Yes, of course.'

'Well the power of a doctor in a white coat, or not in a white coat but someone just called 'doctor', is just as great as the power of the witch doctor. So, to start with we have to acknowledge that the doctor has a placebo power. If we don't use that power then we deprive our patients of a massive healing force.'

Dr Leighton suddenly realised that while they'd been sitting in the truck the sky had darkened and rain had started. The raindrops made a steady, gentle tattoo on the truck roof.

'I don't understand.'

'If a doctor gives a bottle of pills to a patient and says: 'Try these, they might help you' then the pills, however powerful they might be in scientific terms, will be far less likely to work than if the doctor says: 'Take these, they will make you better'. That's not theory – it's fact as you can easily check out for yourself. Tons of scientific papers have been written about placebos. In fact the placebo power is even easier to invoke than that. The doctor who smiles and builds a relationship with his or her patients will be far more likely to be able to make them better than the doctor who scowls, is brusque and has no sort of relationship.'

'Yes, I can see that,' admitted Dr Leighton.

'OK, now take it one step further,' said Dr Hill. 'If I have a patient who thinks she's poorly, but who doesn't actually have anything wrong with her that I can treat, and who needs something to pep her up a bit, what do I do? Do I refuse to give her anything, and disappoint her, do I give her a powerful drug that she doesn't need, and which may have unpleasant or dangerous side effects that might make her ill, or do I give her something that doesn't actually do anything at all, and definitely doesn't have any side effects, but which, if I can convince her it will help, will make a tremendous difference to her?'

The rain was getting heavier and the raindrops were bouncing off the bonnet. The sky had gone very dark.

'You're talking about Mrs Parton?'

'I'm talking about her and a great many other patients – most of whom, it must be said, are often given benzodiazepine tranquillisers to which they become dangerously addicted.'

'A lot of the patients in our practice were hooked on benzodiazepines,' admitted Dr Leighton. 'I agree there was a tendency among some of the doctors in the practice to hand them out as a cure-all for all sort of vague illnesses. And I agree quite a lot of patients got hooked, suffered a great many side effects.'

'Doctors first started using placebos during the Second World War,' said Dr Hill. 'An American army medical officer had run out of morphine while treating injured soldiers. Rather than admit to the soldiers (many of whom were in terrible pain) that he had nothing to give them, the doctor found some vials of plain water and gave those by injection. But he didn't tell the soldiers that they were being given water. In fact he implied that they were being given morphine. To his amazement, the water proved to be just as powerful a painkiller as morphine. The soldiers' pains were eased though they'd been injected with nothing more powerful than water.'

'Is that really true?' asked Dr Leighton, incredulously. The rain was now heavier and they both had to speak a little louder to make themselves heard. Through the waterfall on the windscreen they could just see raindrops bouncing several inches off the bonnet of the truck.

'Absolutely. You can check it out sometime. I remember reading about a researcher called Jellinek who found that out of 199 patients who complained of having a headache, 120 lost their headache when given nothing more powerful than a sugar tablet. It's been found that 30 per cent of patients with severe, steady, post-operative pain get relief from placebos. And according to a report in the *British Medical Journal*, no less than 60 per cent of patients suffering from angina had fewer attacks when given placebo tablets and told that their attacks would be less frequent.'

Dr Hill, who had clearly spent some time researching the subject, pointed out that research work involving many patients, and a good deal of study, had shown that a third of patients with a variety of serious pains including angina and post-operative pain received relief from placebos. Moreover, he added that placebos had proved equally effective in treating other problems including anxiety and nausea.

'What this means,' he said, 'is that any new drug which is tested must have a positive effect of greater than 30% to be worth prescribing.

'It is, of course,' he went on, 'a prerequisite of the placebo prescriber that the patient should believe in him and the treatment he prescribes. If the prescriber does not seem to have faith in the drug he prescribes, then the patient will be unlikely to respond favourably. Even more important perhaps is the image of the whole medical profession, for the placebo effect depends upon public trust in doctors. Anything which destroys that trust will immediately reduce the effect of all drugs in practice'.

Outside, the rain was still pouring and the sky was still getting steadily darker.

'No one ever taught me any of this,' said Dr Leighton.

'Don't take my word for it. When you get back to London, pop into your medical library and take a look at some research.' He paused and smiled. 'You've got your internet, of course. I expect you can do all the research you need with a laptop or your telephone. What do they call them now?'

'Smartphones.'

'That's it. Do a search on your smartphone. You'll be surprised. You'll even find research which has shown that patients with heart disease, who had been considered suitable subjects for open heart surgery, recovered after going through an operation in which all that happened was that their chests were cut open and then stitched up again. The surgeon didn't touch the heart at all but the patients improved massively, and because they hadn't been through the actual trauma of open heart surgery, they recovered far more speedily. That's how powerful the placebo response can be!'

'Now you're pulling my leg!'

'No, I'm not. I promise. There's some research work showing that patients who merely had cuts in their chests were just as well after their non-existent surgery as the patients who had had potentially dangerous and debilitating surgery. Another experiment showed that patients who thought they'd had knee surgery – and who had bandages to convince them – did just as well afterwards as patients who had real surgery. There's tons of other research which shows the same thing. The placebo power is incredibly powerful. A good deal of surgery is clearly unnecessary.'

'How on earth do you know all this stuff?' asked Dr Leighton, who was by now feeling extremely sceptical. She rather liked Dr Hill and thought he was probably well-meaning, and good to his patients in an old-fashioned sort of way, but she also suspected that either he'd misunderstood something he had read or else he'd been reading some very dodgy research published in alternative health magazines.

'I read a lot,' said Dr Hill. 'I don't waste any of my time on running an appointment system or dealing with administration.'

'Dr Croft does all the practice administration?'

'Absolutely!' laughed Dr Hill. 'But he reads as much as I do. We're both fascinated by the unrecognised truths in medicine.'

'But if placebos are so effective, and you clearly believe that they are, why aren't they more widely recognised and written about?'

'Ah, I'm afraid it's the usual thing: money!' said Dr Hill. 'Placebos tend be generic or very cheap and nowhere near as profitable as many of the drugs they can be used to replace. The fact that placebos are often far more effective than infinitely more expensive and dangerous products is of no interest to the medical establishment which was long ago bought, lock stock and syringe barrel, by the pharmaceutical industry. That's why it is often considered improper and even unethical to use a placebo. And can you really imagine surgeons who make fortunes out of their private practices telling their patients that the complex and potentially dangerous operation they're contemplating is probably unnecessary?'

Dr Leighton didn't say anything. She was slightly confused and more than a little shocked by what she had learned. She still didn't really believe what she had heard. If it were true why hadn't anyone else ever told her these things?

'None of this is new,' said Dr Hill. 'Have you heard of Sir James Mackenzie?'

'I'm afraid I haven't.'

'Read about him,' suggested Dr Hill. 'There's an excellent biography of him available. I can't remember the name of the author but Mackenzie was one of the most celebrated 19th century physicians. He was a general practitioner and he was well aware of the power of the placebo. When Mackenzie started practice in Durham, he discovered the value of a special mixture which consisted of burnt sugar and water with a pinch of ginger. This stuff had a high reputation among miners in the area who believed in its powers as a tonic. Mackenzie learned that the medicines a doctor prescribes contain more than drugs and work by means which are not entirely physical. He also understood, by the way, that if a placebo is to do its job properly it needs to look and taste powerful.'

'I've never heard of him,' confessed Dr Leighton softly but it would, she thought, be easy enough to check up that he existed. 'Not many GPs were given knighthoods in those days.'

'No, they weren't. Mackenzie was a special sort of doctor. So too was a Yorkshire doctor called Dr Pickles who practised in the 1930s. He was one of the earliest epidemiologists in general practice. And, of course, Dr John Snow, the greatest epidemiologist of them all, was a general practitioner.'

'Dr John Snow?'

'You haven't heard of him?'

Dr Leighton shook her head.

'Snow was the doctor who guessed that cholera in London was being transmitted in the water supply. He took the handle off a water pump in Broad Street in London and stopped a cholera epidemic.'

Dr Leighton looked embarrassed.

'You really haven't heard of him?'

'No, I haven't.'

'Look him up. He was one of the most brilliant and courageous of all medical men. He was the first English doctor to use chloroform as an anaesthetic for a woman in labour. The patient he experimented upon was Queen Victoria.'

Dr Leighton laughed. 'Now you really are kidding me!'

'No, I'm not. Check it out.' Dr Hill peered out through the windscreen. 'And now the storm seems to have passed. If you're going back to the pub then now is a good time to go without getting soaked.' Oh, and one last thing – do read A.J.Cronin's novel *The Citadel*. It's rather old-fashioned but it'll tell you more about general practice than most textbooks.'

And so Dr Leighton, her head so full, crammed from side to side and top to bottom with new ideas, that she was no longer quite sure who she was or what she was doing, climbed into her Lotus and drove back to The Jolly Roger, while Dr Hill went indoors, looking forward to a large slice of apple pie decorated with two spoonsful of vanilla ice cream.

As he went into the front door, he looked back at his truck. The sudden heavy storm had washed off most of the dust and mud, and if he looked at it through half closed eyes it almost looked as though the paintwork were gleaming in the weak and watery early evening sunshine.

And high in the sky, stretching as far as he could see, was the most beautiful and perfect rainbow he had seen for a very long time.

Chapter Twelve

We all have days in our lives which are 'special', which stand out as in some way different to, and more significant than, the days which preceded and the days which followed. The day on which we are born and the day on which we die are the two most important days but none of us remember much about those particular 'special' days.

For most of us the special days, the essential days in our lives, are the days when we find our true love, when we marry, when a beloved parent dies, when we leave school or graduate from college, when we start an important, life-changing job and so on.

The day that was now just approaching its final hours was, it was already clear to Dr Leighton, going to be one of those 'special' days. Indeed, she was already well aware that it was going to turn out to be a life-changing day.

It was special simply because it had opened her eyes. She still wasn't entirely sure that she was going to accept the job; a job which, privately, she felt sure would be hers if she really wanted it. Dr Hill had already told her that there were no other candidates and had implied that the job was hers for the taking.

But whether or not she took the job wasn't the reason the day was special. The day was special because her eyes had been opened to a whole new way of looking at medicine and at patient care. At least, that is, if she could really believe what Dr Hill had told her.

She was sitting thinking, in her bedroom at The Jolly Roger. It was a comfortable room with a bed, an elderly easy chair, a small table with a chair and a view of the village green. Through a door lay a small bathroom (there was no shower but the bath, an old-fashioned cast iron one with huge feet and massive brass taps looked deep enough and long enough for her to swim in – well just about). And there was a fireplace with, almost inevitably, a log fire. The fire wasn't exactly blazing but a couple of logs were burning and the room smelt pleasantly of wood smoke. A nightdress was laid out on the bed (Dr Hill had clearly found time to telephone) and a toothbrush and a tube of toothpaste were on the shelf in the bathroom. There was a plate of sandwiches on the table, together with a pot of coffee and a cup. There were also a couple of magazines and a paperback book that Dr Leighton had borrowed from a shelf downstairs in the snug.

For the umpteenth time in the last hour, Dr Leighton tried her smart phone. There had been no reception the first time and there was no reception now. Suddenly, on the spur of the moment, she got up, walked over to the bed and picked up the telephone on the bedside table. There was a small printed notice taped to the side of the instrument (an old-fashioned one in green) which said: 'Dial 9 for an outside line and then dial the number you want'.

Dr Leighton sat down on the bed, dialled 9 and then dialled the phone number of Jasmine, a doctor with whom she had studied medicine, who now worked as a medical researcher in a London hospital. After they'd exchanged greetings and the usual 'where are you?' and 'what are you doing?' conversational gambits, Dr Leighton asked the woman (not quite a friend but more than an acquaintance) if she'd do her a favour.

'If I can, I will. What do you want?'

'Look up something for me on the internet,' said Dr Leighton. 'I've got absolutely no reception where I am. See if you find anything about heart operations in which the surgeon just cut open the patient's chest and then sewed it up again – with the patient being healthier afterwards although the surgeon hadn't actually done anything.'

'I remember hearing about something like that,' said Jasmine. 'I don't think I believed it then and I don't think I believe it now.' As she spoke, she keyed a few words into a search engine.

'Got it,' she said. There was silence for a moment as she read. 'This is amazing,' she said. 'You were right. There are papers in tons of major journals. They did do that. And some patients did well – as if they'd had surgery.'

'See what you can find about a Dr John Snow.'

Again, there was a delay of no more than half a minute.

'He was a 19th century doctor. He reckoned that people in London were getting cholera through their drinking water so he took the handle off a water pump that he thought was the source of a localised epidemic. He apparently saved a lot of lives. And, amazingly, he caused a bit of a stir by giving chloroform to Queen Victoria.'

'Just one more,' said Dr Leighton, who now thought she knew the answer to this question before she received it. 'Can you see anything about injured soldiers being given injections of saline because the doctor looking after them had run out of morphine?

This time the delay was a little longer. And then came a whoop of surprise. 'Hey, that's actually true. There are some papers written by a Dr Beecher who reported it. Actually, there's a ton of stuff about it.' There was a pause again. 'I wouldn't have believed any of this, but it's all real. What set you off down this not very well trodden road?'

'I was speaking to an elderly GP I met. He told me something about how placebos work. I wasn't sure whether to believe him.'

'Well, it looks real enough to me. Is there anything else?'

'No, that's great thanks,' said Dr Leighton. And then she changed her mind. 'No, yes, there is one other thing. Just check to see if you can find anything about patients with heart attacks doing better if they were looked after at home instead of going into a Coronary Care Unit.'

Once again there was a pause for a few moments. While she was waiting, Dr Leighton opened one of the sandwiches, and looked inside. As Rosemary had promised, it was cheddar cheese with pickle. She took a bite. The bread was fresh and the cheese tangy.

'Got it!' said her friend. 'Did this come from the same GP?'

'Yes.'

'Well, he's scored 100% so far. There have been several papers proving that patients often do just as well if they stay at home after having heart attacks. This is astonishing. Why didn't I know any of this stuff? Do you want me to email the links to some of the papers?'

'Thank you,' said Dr Leighton. 'Yes, please. I'll look at them when I get back to civilisation.'

'What are you doing down there?'

'Just a job interview,' replied Dr Leighton.

'You're not going to take a job in the middle of nowhere, are you? It's all leeches and take your own bloods out in the sticks you know! A friend of mine took a job with a GP practice in Oxfordshire and six months later she bought a horse and had joined the local hunt. She started wearing tweeds all the time and had her hair cut very short so that she didn't have to bother doing anything with it.'

Dr Leighton laughed. 'I'm thinking about it. Taking the job that is. I'm not so sure about the tweeds and definitely not up for joining the local hunt.'

'Think about it all you like but then say 'no thank you' and scurry back to London as quickly as you can. If you take a job in the country they'll have you milking horses and mucking out cows within a month.'

'I think it's the other way round,' said Dr Leighton.

'There you are – they've already got you hooked. Don't speak to anyone. Don't listen to anyone. Make a loud humming noise if anyone says anything to you. Get in your car and drive straight back to London. If you stay down there any longer you'll die. Your lungs won't be able to cope with all that clean air. You need good, solid London air – rich with lovely, corrosive chemicals. I'm serious…jump into that lovely, sexy little car of yours and hurtle back to civilisation just as fast as you can make it.'

Dr Leighton laughed, thanked her friend, promised not to breathe in too much clean air or to eat too much good, healthy food, said goodnight and put the phone down. She then stood up, poured herself a cup of coffee, picked up a sandwich and settled herself down in the easy chair. She felt as though, like Alice, she had blundered through a rabbit hole and was wandering around in an entirely different universe. Whatever she decided to do, her world would never be the same again. She'd learned things she would never be able to unlearn. She had, she would have admitted to anyone, been slightly shocked to discover that everything that Dr Hill had told her had been the truth. It wasn't that she had, for a moment, suspected of him of lying. He didn't seem the sort of person to tell lies of any kind, let alone such elaborate ones, and what would have been the point?

The problem was that in now knowing that he had been telling her the truth ('the whole truth and nothing but the truth') she had to recognise that the people who had taught her everything she knew about medicine had hidden from her some very important pieces of evidence. Why had all these things been hidden away? Were the lecturers at medical school afraid of sharing these facts? Were they in thrall to the drug companies, as Dr Hill had pretty well suggested?

Or did they just not think that these things mattered? And what other truths had been hidden away from her.

This had, she decided, definitely been one of those very, very special days. She had, she realised, learned more about the essence of medical care in one day than she had learned in six, long, hard years at medical school and several years as a practising doctor.

She ate two more sandwiches ('I didn't know a cheese sandwich could taste so good', she thought) drank two cups of coffee ('better than coffee they sell in London's expensive cafes'), undressed, ran a bath and climbed into the water. She stayed in the bath, lost in thought, until the water grew cold. And then, wrinkled and slightly shivery, she climbed out of the bath, dried herself vigorously to warm herself up, put on the nightdress she'd been lent and got into bed where she lay thinking the same slightly confusing thoughts that had filled her mind when she'd been in the bath. At one point she picked up the paperback she'd borrowed from downstairs. It had promised amusement and some distraction when she'd picked it up. But although she held the book in front of her, as though she were about to start reading it, she didn't open it. And when she eventually fell asleep, the book slid from her fingers, down the bedspread and onto the floor.

Chapter Thirteen

Dr Leighton was woken the next morning by what sounded like a flock of birds talking to one another in the way that flocks of birds are wont to do. Gradually, she realised that what she was hearing was not a flock of birds but a flock of people. She got out of bed, picked up the book that had fallen to the floor and placed it on the bedside table, tiptoed to the window, pulled back a corner of the curtain and looked out.

The forecourt of the public house was full of cars, motorbikes and people. The cars and motorbikes weren't doing anything except sit where they'd been parked and the people, who were whispering to one another, were all festooned with binoculars and cameras, most of which were equipped with the sort of very long lenses popularly used by paparazzi. The people weren't moving about much either but they were clearly all involved in many whispered conversations. Nearly all of them seemed to be men and most of them wore anoraks, though a few wore those multi-pocketed waistcoats that are usually favoured by fishermen. Nearly all of them had books and notebooks stuffed into their pockets. Most were holding platefuls of food or mugs of steaming fluid. Some were eating what looked suspiciously like bacon rolls. The Jolly Roger appeared to be doing a roaring business in providing breakfasts.

Slightly bewildered by this strange sight, and by now thoroughly awake, Dr Leighton went into the bathroom, performed her usual morning ablutions, put on a little make-up and then dressed in yesterday's clothes. She realised, with some disgust, that she didn't even have any clean underwear to put on. She'd meant to go to the village shop to see what they'd got for sale but had forgotten.

When she had dressed, she moved as if to leave her bedroom and go downstairs and then stopped. Instead, she picked up the telephone and rang the reception desk. The phone rang for quite a while before Rosemary answered.

'I'm so sorry to keep you waiting,' said Rosemary. 'It's madness down here. Would you like a cup of tea? Some breakfast? I'll bring it up to your room.'

'I'd love a cup of tea and some toast and marmalade. But I can come down to eat.'

'No, no, you stay where you are. It really is utter chaos down here. I'll be up in five minutes and I'll explain what's happened.'

Dr Leighton carefully drew the curtains and looked out. The crowd of men was still there. And they were all men, she noticed. Most were still eating or drinking. One or two had opened their car doors and were sitting inside them as they ate. Two leather suited motorcyclists were sitting on their machines eating their sandwiches. Half a dozen of them were studying their smart phones and iPads and trying to make them work. They all seemed to be waiting for something, though Dr Leighton had absolutely no idea what it might be. The cluster of men reminded her of something but she couldn't quite remember what it was.

'They're twitchers,' explained Rosemary, when she appeared a couple of minutes later. She put a tray down on the table. 'Are you sure you don't want a cooked breakfast? I can do you a lovely plate of bacon, eggs, sausage, tomatoes, hash browns and mushrooms. The marmalade is home-made by the way. I'll bring it up for you so you can eat here.' Through the open door, Dr Leighton could smell the food being cooked downstairs. She thought she could even hear the sizzle.

'No, I never eat a cooked breakfast, thank you. Toast is fine.'

'Well, I've brought you plenty of toast, some butter and a bowl of the homemade marmalade. Are you really sure that's all you want?'

'Thank you. Perfect. Twitchers? You mean bird watchers?'

'Yes. We've been invaded by them.' Rosemary sighed. 'It's my husband's fault, I'm afraid.'

'Is your husband a bird watcher?'

'Good heavens, no!' laughed Rosemary. 'If you knew him you wouldn't even ask that. He wouldn't be able to tell a seagull from a sparrow if you gave him a pair of binoculars and a bird watching guide. But business has been a bit slack recently, to say the least, and he decided to chivvy things along a little.'

'How?'

'He telephoned a friend who has a laptop and asked him to go onto one of the bird watching sites. Apparently the internet is full of them. The bird watchers all tell one another if anyone has spotted a Lesser Plumed Plover or a South American Sparrow. They type in the name of the bird and where it was seen.'

'I'm beginning to understand,' said Dr Leighton.

'You've got it,' said Rosemary. 'Jack got his mate to go on the site and tell the world that a red flanked blue tail had been seen in the field behind our pub. And now all these bird watchers have turned up in the hope that they'll spot it and can tick it off in their little books. Apparently bird watchers keep little books in which they write down every rare bird they've seen and a red flanked blue tail is something of a rarity. I suppose it's like those I-Spy books children have where they have to tick off things they've spotted on their holidays.'

'I'm guessing that no one has actually seen a red flanked blue tail in your field.'

'You get ten out of ten for that guess.'

'And now all the birdwatchers are having breakfast?'

'Well, of course they are! There's nowhere else for miles. If they want a drink and a bite to eat then we're it. And we don't have room inside for a quarter of them.'

'But if there isn't a red flanked blue tail in your field why don't they all just give up and go home?'

'Oh, apparently they don't do that. They're used to birds just disappearing and then coming back. They're waiting. A couple of them are standing in the field so that they can spot it if it appears. And the minute they see it everyone in the car park will rush round to the field – very quietly I assume – so that they can peer at it and photograph it. They're in the car park so that they can have their breakfast. Most of them seem to know one another. They're a sort of wandering circus.'

'Are more coming?'

'I think so. One of them told Jack that there will be hundreds of them here by lunchtime. The ones here are the real enthusiasts from our region. Some more are supposed to be coming from London and Scotland. I overheard two of them talking and one said that he'd heard that some very keen French twitchers were coming over by plane. He said that when an eagle escaped from a zoo in London, a bunch of French bird spotters chartered a private plane and flew over to look at it.'

'Crumbs! They must be very dedicated.'

'Oh, they are.'

'And there isn't going to be anything for them to see?'

'Not unless they're very lucky and a lesser spotted whatever it is turns up by accident.'

'How long will they stay here?'

'Jack says some of them will stay for two or three days though most will give up and go home tonight or tomorrow. All our rooms are already booked for tonight and tomorrow night. We haven't done this much business for ages.'

'I'll be leaving this morning so you can rent my room to one or two of them,' said Dr Leighton.

'Oh, are you sure? That's disappointing. But you'll be coming back, won't you? Has Dr Hill offered you the job? He'd be a fool not to.'

'I need to talk to him about it,' said Dr Leighton. 'I'll go and see him as soon as I've had my breakfast.'

'Is that toast cold? Do you want me to bring you some fresh?'

'It'll be fine,' Dr Leighton assured her. 'You'd better go and feed your twitchers.'

'Yes, I suppose had. We've got a couple of people in to help out but they're rushed off their feet. And Jack has gone down to the village store to buy up more supplies of everything.'

'At least you should be making some money!'

'I hope so, though I'm terrified they'll find out there is no lesser spotted whatever in our field and want to lynch us!' said Rosemary. She pulled a face, waved and hurried back downstairs, leaving Dr Leighton to enjoy her breakfast in peace.

Chapter Fourteen

Once she'd paid her bill, and thanked Rosemary again for the loan of a nightdress, Dr Leighton had to ask a couple of the putative bird watchers to move their cars before she could get into her Lotus, let alone drive it out of the car park.

One of the bird watchers, a huge fellow, wore a knee length anorak which had a furry collar. The other wore a bulky blue sweater with a picture of a robin on the front. He did not seem at all embarrassed by this. The robin appeared to have only one leg, and the knitter who had produced the sweater had given him a raised eyebrow and a rather quizzical look. Dr Leighton suddenly remembered that the collection of bird watchers who had gathered reminded her of the small groups of train spotters who used to gather on the platforms of provincial and city railway platforms. Their sole aim in life was to write down the names or numbers of the railway engines they spotted.

'What are you all looking for?' she asked them.

'There's a report someone saw a red flanked blue tail in the field behind the pub,' said the big man in the anorak. He was well over six feet tall and more than half as much as that wide.

'You don't sound very confident of spotting it,' said Dr Leighton.

'We're not,' came the reply. 'If birds are nesting then they'll stay in the same place for ages. But if this one was just passing through we could be here all day without seeing a feather.'

'Most of us spent two days in Lincolnshire last month,' said his companion in the blue sweater. 'There'd been word that someone had seen a ring ouzel. In the end, we just all gave up and went home. No problem. We all stayed in a motel a mile away and while we were there we spotted a pair of red kites. That was quite a surprise and a bit of a thrill to be honest with you.'

'It was more successful than the trip we made to Birmingham!'

'Oh yes, Birmingham was a real disaster. A proper embarrassment.'

'Made worse by the fact that *The Sun* sent along a reporter and a photographer to produce a feature about bird watching.'

'I still cringe when I think of that one.'

'Why? What happened?' asked Dr Leighton.

'Someone claimed they'd seen a capercaillie in a bit of scrappy woodland,' said the man in the blue sweater. 'So we all hurtled along the motorway to Birmingham. We come from Manchester and as usual we got stuck in that complicated motorway junction they've got just outside Birmingham…what do they call it?'

'Do you mean Spaghetti Junction?'

'That's the one. We went round and round for an hour.'

'Birds can fly thousands of miles in terrible weather and hit the exact spot they're aiming for,' said the big man in the anorak with the furry collar. 'But we got lost in Birmingham'

'The house and the garden were in a tiny cul de sac,' said the man in the blue sweater. 'The bloke who'd reported the sighting said he'd seen the capercaillie while out walking his dog and then seen it again at the bottom of his neighbour's garden. He was an experienced twitcher. He'd been following birds for ten or eleven years.'

'The neighbours couldn't believe what was happening. Within two hours there were 150 twitchers crammed in this quiet cul de sac, all trying to squeeze down the side entrance of this guy's house so that they could peer at this unfortunate bird.'

'The bird didn't move. It just sat there. We all sat and watched it for eight hours and it didn't move a feather.'

'When you're watching a bird you have to keep very quiet,' said the big man in the long anorak. 'We had a whip round and gave the owner of the house £110 to take his wife and family out for the day and to let us into his garden.'

'Then a bloke who always travels in a motor cycle and sidecar suddenly developed hay-fever and sneezed. It was the loudest damned sneeze I've ever heard. But the bird didn't move an inch.'

'By this time we were getting a bit suspicious,' said the man. 'The bird hadn't budged.'

'So a guy who'd arrived in a beautiful old maroon Jaguar, the same sort as that Inspector Morse drove in that television series, decided to take a closer look. He has a telephoto lens that must be at least two feet long and he crawled down the garden on his belly. One or two people were beginning to think that the bird might have had a heart attack and died with all the excitement. All you could see was this little patch of feathers almost hidden in this hawthorn bush. So the bloke with the long lens crawled to within about ten feet of the bush. Then he lifted up his massive lens and looked through the camera.'

'I'll never forget what happened next,' grinned the man in the blue sweater.

'Nor me,' said his chum. 'This bloke, covered in dirt and grass stains, leaps up into the air, cursing and screaming and throws his camera, complete with telephoto lens down onto the grass.'

'And then,' said the man in the blue sweater, 'he tells us that the bird has the words 'Government Health Warning' printed on its bum.'

'Turns out that what we thought was a bird was actually a screwed up cigarette packet that had blown into the hedge or been tossed there from a path that runs along the other side. Honest, it looked just like a bird.'

'We get a lot of disappointments,' sighed the man in the blue sweater.

'How long have you been here today?' Dr Leighton asked the two birdwatchers.

'We saw an alert on the internet late last night and I was up at 5.30 this morning.' He looked at his watch. 'I've been here an hour or so.'

'But don't you get disappointed if you travel a long way and then don't see anything?'

'No, no,' replied the first birdwatcher.

'Never,' confirmed the second.

'We have a good day out,' said the first.

'Thrill of the chase!'

'And we always find a pub and have a good cooked breakfast. I hear they do a great steak and kidney pie here so we'll be staying for lunch.'

'And I see they have apple pie and blackberry pie on the menu.'

'My wife won't let me have a fried breakfast. She says it's bad for my arteries. Bugger my arteries, what about me?'

'If I'd stayed at home my missus would have me putting up a new cupboard in the bathroom.'

'I was supposed to wash the car, cut the grass and have tea round at her mother's place.'

'So bird watching is just a good excuse for a nice day out?'

'Absolutely!' said the first bird watcher. 'It's my hobby. No one can interfere with a man's hobby, can they? Be grounds for divorce.'

The two men moved their cars and then, after asking her not to rev the engine too much, helped direct Dr Leighton out of the car park and into the lane.

It then took her twenty five minutes to reach Dr Hill's home and surgery because of the traffic coming in the opposite direction. She counted fifteen cars, two motor cycles, a minibus and a small coach with 'Twitcher Tours' printed in white chalk on a large piece of brown cardboard sitting on the dashboard. Every vehicle was full to the brim with men with cameras and binoculars around their necks. It wasn't difficult to see where they were all heading.

Chapter Fifteen

'I hear The Jolly Roger has been doing good business this morning,' said Dr Hill, when he opened the front door and saw Dr Leighton standing there.

'You heard it on the local grapevine?'

'This is a small village,' grinned Dr Hill. 'If someone blows their nose or breaks a shoelace on the other side of the village, I'll know about it within five minutes at most. Come in and have a cup of something. Tea or coffee?'

'I think I'll stick with tea, thank you. I had tea for breakfast at the pub.'

'Not wise to mix your drinks, eh? Did you have one of Rosemary's famous fry ups?'

'No, I just had toast. But I think she was doing good business among the bird watchers.'

'I bet she was. Rosemary's fry ups are legendary. People come from miles around to have one of her breakfasts. Those bird watchers will be there for days if they've got any sense. Rosemary and Jack should make enough money to keep them going for a month. I take it Jack claimed to have seen a Greater Crested Titwarbler on his bird table?'

'Something like that!'

'A harmless enough scam,' said Dr Hill. 'I bet most of the bird watchers don't really care whether they see a new bird or not. They just want a nice day out away from work and chores.'

'That's definitely the impression I got,' agreed Dr Leighton. 'It's Sunday and I only spoke to a couple of them but if they were anything to go by then I guess that most of them were expecting to be washing cars, mowing lawns or putting up cupboards.'

'I've never understood the wild enthusiasm for putting up cupboards everywhere,' said Dr Hill. 'And why do people buy these nasty bits of furniture that need putting together when for half the price they could buy a lovely piece of solid Victorian furniture?'

They went into the kitchen and Dr Hill filled the old-fashioned kettle and put it onto the AGA. He then got a couple of cups and saucers out of the Welsh dresser. Dr Leighton was not surprised. Dr Hill had not seemed to her to be a man who favoured drinking tea or coffee from a mug.

'Rosemary's husband is a bit of a confidence trickster,' said Dr Hill. He paused, thinking and wondering. Then he decided to go ahead. 'I was, I'm afraid, rather sad when Rosemary married him. The pub had belonged to her parents. When they died she took it over, though it was too much for a girl in her twenties to manage. He appeared from nowhere one summer and they were married inside a month. I think that marrying a girl who owned a pub must have been a dream come true for him. I was reminded a little of Martin Chuzzlewit's pal in the book by Charles Dickens – the one in which a young man travels with Mr Chuzzlewit to America and endures all sorts of miseries to prove to himself that he can stay happy when everything is going wrong – and then comes home and marries the comely landlady. The difference between them being, I strongly suspect, that Rosemary's husband never felt the need to stretch himself or to expose himself to trial or tribulation. This bird watching thing is probably harmless enough but he tries some rather tricky scams and one of these days I'm afraid he's going to go too far. Rosemary is a lovely lady but Jack, her husband, is what used to be called a bit of a lad, a bit of a handful.' He paused and shrugged. 'Still, they seem to get on well and in the end that's all that matters, isn't it?'

Dr Hill made the tea. 'Shall we sit in the conservatory?' he asked. 'It's a beautiful morning and the garden is looking well.'

They carried their tea into the conservatory and sat down in beautiful old wicker chairs.

'If you want the job it's yours,' said Dr Hill, when they were settled. 'I spoke to Mallory last night and he's very happy with the idea. May I ask how much you were getting paid at your last job?'

'Dr Leighton told him.

'Were you really?' said Dr Hill, clearly impressed. He whistled lightly and filled the kettle and put it onto the stove. 'I'm afraid we can't get anywhere near to that. But we can offer you less money for more work and that's surely got to be quite an incentive,' he said wryly.

Dr Leighton smiled, pursed her lips as though in deep thought. 'Well, that does make it tempting.'

'Would you like me to lay out the offer we'd like to make you?'

'Yes, please.'

'Mallory and I agreed that if you decide to join us we would like you to consider working with us for three months. It would be a sort of trial period for us all. This is effectively a single-handed practice at the moment and it will, as I think you've seen, be very different to the work you're accustomed to. It would be fairer for us all if we try each other out before committing to a lifetime partnership. If, after that three month period, we all agree that the trial has been successful then we would make you a full partner. If you decide that our practice isn't what you're looking for then you would leave. Actually, of course, Mallory and I will commit to the three month period but if, after a month, a week or a day you really feel that you've had enough then you can just shake hands and be on your way.'

'That's very fair. Actually it's more than fair. It's generous.'

Suddenly, and quite mysteriously, and without having consciously made any decision at all, Dr Leighton realised that she wanted this job more than anything else in the world.

The previous evening she had started making a list of the reasons to take the job and a list of reasons not to take it. The list of reasons to take it included: 'It will enable me to provide better medical care and will be professionally satisfying'; 'I will be more independent and free to practise the way I think is best'; 'I'll have a chance to get to know my patients'; 'I'll be living in a lovely village in a quiet part of the country'; 'I think I can trust Dr Hill and I can certainly learn a lot from him'.

The list of reasons not to take the job were: 'I'll have to work harder than I did in London and I'll have less time to myself', 'I'll be a long way from the city and the people I know', and 'I'll almost certainly earn less money'.

In the end she had also asked herself: 'What would my mum have wanted me to do?' She had been pretty sure she'd known the answer to that.

'You'll be on call for alternate nights and alternate weekends,' said Dr Hill. So in each fortnight you'll work one weekend and you'll be on call for seven nights out of fourteen. We'll deal with bank holidays as we come to them but basically we'll share the work. Neither Mallory nor I believe in paying someone less for doing the same work as someone else so we'll split the practice income three ways instead of two ways. You'll get the same as I get and the same that Mallory gets. That's the deal. If you work here then you and I will share the clinical work and Mallory will continue to deal with all the administration. He'll carry on doing what he's been doing for years. He'll keep the bureaucrats off our backs.'

'But you and Dr Croft will have to take a big cut in income,' pointed out Dr Leighton.

'We will. To start with I wanted to suggest that we should split the income in half, give one half to Mallory and split the other half between the two of us. After all, you'll be cutting my workload but not Mallory's. But Mallory wouldn't hear of it so the total is divided into thirds. And, of course, we'll pay you a third of the practice income during the three months while we are all trying one another out.'

'I think you're being very generous,' said Dr Leighton. 'And I would like to accept the job. You've been very honest with me and I want to be honest with you. I don't know whether I'll be any good at this job. I don't know if I can do it. I feel very much like an old-fashioned apprentice. But I want to try and I desperately want to succeed and the only thing I can promise you is that I'll do the very best I can.'

'We can't ask any more than that,' said Dr Hill.

'When would you like me to start?' asked Dr Leighton.

'As soon as you can. Do you have a good deal to sort out in London?'

'I don't have anything to sell and the lease on my flat runs out very shortly. But I do need to find somewhere to live down here.'

'Just go to London, collect your stuff and your black medical bag and by the time you get back I'll have found one or two cottages for you to look at. There's always something available to rent down here in the country. I assume you'd rather just rent something for the time being?'

'I think renting would make sense to start with,' agreed Dr Leighton. 'But there is one other thing I need help with: advice on finding a suitable black bag!'

Dr Hill looked puzzled for a moment.

'At my practice in London we never did home visits and we didn't do calls at night or at the weekend – so none of us had any need for a medical bag. Not only do I not have a black bag – I have no idea what to put in it!'

'That hadn't occurred to me!' said Dr Hill. 'I believe that one or two companies do still make medical bags. You can get little boxy things with drawers. And I believe there are doctors who use nylon rucksacks to carry their instruments and drugs. But I'd recommend that you have something black, because that's traditional and it's what patients expect, and you want something that is sturdy and stands up by itself when you put it down on the floor. And you must have something about twice as big as you think you'll need. It used to be possible to find old Gladstone Bags – but they're usually far too small for the stuff we need to carry and besides they aren't usually lockable. And if they are lockable then the key usually disappeared decades ago.'

'I noticed that you always keep your bag locked.'

'That's to comply with the Dangerous Drugs Act,' explained Dr Hill. 'I carry ampoules of morphine and other dangerous drugs. The law is that the bag must be kept locked, and when you aren't using it then it should be locked away out of sight – in the car boot or behind a locked door if it's at home. If you go to a decent luggage shop they'll probably have quite a few possible bags for you to choose from. Large, black briefcases work quite well. Or you could use a pilot's bag – one of those large, week-end bags which airline pilots carry with them. You can get an amazing amount of stuff in one of those. Alternatively, if you want something that doesn't look too new and shiny, you might be able to find one for sale in a house auction.'

'And what should I keep in it?'

'Stethoscope, sphygmomanometer, ophthalmoscope, auriscope, patella hammer, small torch for looking down throats, large torch for finding house names in the dark, prescription pad, a few sheets of notepaper and some envelopes, syringes, needles, plasters, bandages, cotton wool, a decent thermometer, a pair of tweezers, you'll be surprised how often you need a pair of tweezers, a scalpel and a packet of blades, a couple of pairs of Spencer Wells forceps and two pairs of scissors, one large and one small – all that sort of stuff. And you need some drugs that you know inside out and back to front.

You need surprisingly little to be honest. A decent all-purpose antibiotic for adults and one for children who have ear infections; some aspirin tablets and ampoules of morphine and something in between the two; some gylceryl trinitrate tablets for anyone with angina; adrenaline and a steroid in ampoule form to give patients with severe allergy reactions or who are in status asthmaticus; something good for allergies and a bottle of a decent tonic.'

'Mist Gent Alk?'

'Exactly – though that's optional, of course,' smiled Dr Hill.

'How can I possibly find a bag big enough for all that stuff?'

'Oh, you'll be fine. Most of that stuff is quite small. I carry an old sphygmomanometer around with me because I'm used to it and so are my patients but you can get ones that are much smaller. Oh, and you need a dressmaker's tape measure.'

'A tape measure?'

'Oh yes. More useful than you'd think and essential if you think someone has a deep vein thrombosis and you want to see if their calf is swollen. And a map to start with, of course, though you'd keep that in the car. And a notebook and pen. And a list of useful phone numbers.'

Dr Leighton, who was by now thoroughly bewildered and perhaps even a little frightened, had been scribbling down all these ideas in a small notebook which she'd found in her handbag and which, being a child of a technological age, she had hardly ever used and had, many times, been close to throwing out.

'Shall we confirm the arrangement then?' asked Dr Hill, holding out his hand.

'I'd be delighted to,' agreed Dr Leighton. She took his hand and they shook. 'What do we do now? Do you have to send me contracts? Paperwork?'

'We just did everything we need to do,' said Dr Hill. 'Unless you want me to put something in writing?'

Dr Leighton looked at her new partner (albeit on three months trial) and frowned. 'Is that really all we have to do?'

'I don't see why we need anything else,' said Dr Hill. 'Bits of paper just complicate things. We both know what we've agreed to. No contract drawn up by a lawyer is going to make things any clearer is it? But if you have a lawyer and you want him to draw up an agreement then you must do that.'

Dr Leighton shook her head. 'I'm very happy with the handshake.'

'I'm guessing that your last job involved quite a bit of paperwork?'

'It did. There was a 24-page contract and I had to provide my passport, my driving licence, three recent utility bills, six months' worth of bank statements, a certified copy of my General Medical Council registration certificate and a copy of my licence to practice. Someone at the practice photocopied everything and filed it all away in a personnel file. The contract was written in the sort of English that no one can understand, and I had to have a lawyer look it through to see what I was agreeing to do. I remember it cost me nearly £1,000 just to join the practice.'

'Ah, we're a little more old-fashioned here,' said Dr Hill. 'And now if you have time there's someone I'd like you to meet – and he's desperately keen to meet you.'

'Who's that?' asked Dr Leighton, bewildered.

'Mallory. He's invited us to lunch. Can you manage that before you have to drive back to London?'

Chapter Sixteen

Mallory wasn't anything like the person Dr Leighton had expected to meet.

She had, for absolutely no good reason, assumed that Mallory was probably rather frail. She'd imagined that he would probably be sitting in a wheelchair and almost certainly suffering from some chronic disorder that had left him wasted and unable to do anything other than sit at a desk working on a computer screen.

Everything she had imagined was wrong.

Mallory turned out to be apparently perfectly strong and healthy. But, as she had expected, he appeared to be enormously shy and seemed nervous about meeting her. That seemed odd, since he was one of her two employers.

About five foot ten or eleven inches tall and weighing, she guessed, slightly less than average for his height, Mallory wore tailored jeans, a plain white dress shirt without a tie and a blue short sleeved sweater. His full head of hair, worn rather long, made it difficult to guess his age and, Dr Leighton thought, probably made him look younger than he was.

There was a Mrs Croft too. And again Dr Leighton's imagination had been wrong. She'd assumed that Dr Croft was, like Dr Hill, a bachelor. He wasn't. His wife, who was perhaps an inch or so taller than her husband, and also slim almost boyish in appearance, smiled and welcomed Dr Leighton with what seemed like genuine enthusiasm. She had blonde, shoulder length hair and wore a sleeveless cotton dress in light blue. Dr Leighton noticed that she constantly touched her husband, as though comforting or reassuring him.

The Crofts lived in what had once been two small thatched cottages connected to a bakery. The three buildings had been knocked together to make one long home. Visible in an open fronted garage, there was a Land Rover. It was one of the basic but tough models used by farmers to ferry animals and bales of hay and straw around in mud and snow, rather than one of the smart Range Rover models favoured by celebrities and royals and used almost exclusively in Chelsea and Kensington. Also visible in the garage were a couple of powerful looking motorcycles; one a classic Brough Norton, which Dr Leighton recognised as being similar to the sort of machine T.E.Lawrence had been riding when he'd crashed and died, and the other a modern Honda. There were also a couple of ordinary bicycles.

'We didn't know whether you'd be able to come or not,' said Mrs Croft, after insisting that Dr Leighton call her Poppy, 'or how long you'd be able to stay, so I just made a buffet salad. I hope that's OK?'

'That'll be lovely,' said Dr Leighton.

'Would you like any wine or do you prefer a soft drink? Or water from our spring? It's been checked by the water people and apparently it's as pure as water can be.'

Dr Leighton explained that she had to drive back to London that afternoon and said she'd love a glass of their water.

Poppy Croft's idea of just a simple buffet seemed to Dr Leighton to be more akin to the sort of buffet you'd be likely to find at a wedding. There were plates of cold meats; small, individual pork pies and several different types of cheese (brie, Emmental, cottage cheese, red Leicester, stilton and something that looked like Cheshire cheese but which had a pinkish tinge to it). There was a bowl full of salad greens, radishes and cherry tomatoes and one dish containing olives and another with sun dried tomatoes. And there were three different types of bread. For pudding there were several dishes of fresh fruit.

'In the summer we have a huge harvest of raspberries, gooseberries and strawberries,' Poppy told Dr Leighton. 'You'll have to come and take some off our hands.'

'Poppy makes amazing pies and jams,' said Mallory Croft. It was almost the first thing he'd said. He spoke very quietly and rather slowly. Dr Leighton got the feeling he wasn't a man who chattered a great deal.

They talked of the village, of Dr Leighton's work and life in London (Poppy said that she and her husband hadn't been to London for over a decade and said that although she'd like to go, she didn't think she had the courage and that if she did go she'd probably stick out as a country yokel and either be mugged or run over within the first hour) and they talked about where Dr Leighton was going to live when she moved to the village.

'We have a spare room here,' said Poppy. 'But when you're on call at night and at the weekend you'd need a phone. We don't have one in the spare room and it'll take months to get British Telecom to put one in.'

'No, I couldn't impose on you,' insisted Dr Leighton who was relieved that there was a good, solid reason for her to decline. She realised that Dr Croft, having retired from active medical practice would not want to be disrupted again by night calls. 'I thought I'd stay at The Jolly Roger until I've found somewhere to live.'

'That wouldn't be a problem. In the hope that you would say 'yes' to our offer I had a word with Rosemary,' said Dr Hill. 'It's apparently possible to switch phones from one number to another number and she says she's happy for me to put my phone through to theirs. This has the advantage that Rosemary can take any messages for you if you're out on a call.'

'I hadn't thought about that!' admitted Dr Leighton.

'It's a bit of a problem for unmarried GPs who do night calls,' admitted Crawford Hill. 'Martha has a small cottage attached to the back of my house and answers the phone for me if I'm out but when she's away, my receptionist comes in and stays in Martha's rooms.'

'I've got a couple of two-way radios,' said Crawford Hill. 'The sort of radio phones the military use. When you start doing calls on your own I'll give you one of the radios so that you can call me if you get completely lost or stuck.'

'Mallory and I are convinced that Mrs Onions has a thing for Crawford,' said Poppy. She turned to Dr Hill. 'You'll come back from a night call, climb into bed and find Mrs O lying there waiting for you.'

'Complete with floor length flannelette nightie and hair curlers,' said Crawford Hill. 'Did you know that she insists on bringing her budgie with her when she stands in for Martha?' He turned to Dr Leighton. 'You haven't met my housekeepers or the receptionist, have you?'

Dr Leighton admitted that she hadn't.

'You've got quite a treat in store,' promised Dr Hill. 'And you'll understand Poppy's jest at my expense when you meet Mrs Onions.'

After they'd eaten, the four of them sat in a large conservatory and drank excellent coffee made with freshly ground beans.

'Come and help me fill the dishwasher,' said Poppy to Dr Hill, when they'd all finished their coffee.

'I'll help,' said Dr Leighton immediately, starting to get up.

'No, no, you stay here and talk to Mallory,' insisted Poppy. She and Crawford Hill stood up and started to clear away the cups. In a moment they were gone.

'You have a beautiful house,' said Dr Leighton.

'Thank you,' said Mallory Croft. He cleared his throat, rather nervously. 'My wife thought I should talk to you,' he said. 'She said I ought to tell you why I no longer see patients. She said it would be better than letting you wonder about it. And much better than you having to hear second-hand gossip.' Each sentence was separated from the others by long pauses. 'She and Crawford understand that I find it difficult to explain why I don't practise medicine anymore, and they decided I'd find it easier if they were out of the room.' He smiled. It was a very watery sort of smile.

'Dr Hill tells me that you do all the paperwork,' said Dr Leighton, thinking that she ought to say something.

There was a long pause. Dr Leighton could see that Mallory was struggling to speak.

'I do,' he said at last. 'And Crawford and I talk about patients quite often. But I don't see patients myself and I don't make diagnoses. Crawford has been so kind.' There was another pause. 'He's been very kind and understanding.'

Dr Leighton sat quietly, nodded and waited. There was another long silence during which they both sat and watched birds on a feeder outside the conservatory window.

'Do you know anything about veterinary surgeons?'

'Nothing at all. Well, nothing other than what everyone knows.'

'Most of them specialise. There are vets who deal almost exclusively with pets – dogs, cats, budgies and so on. There are vets who deal with farm animals. And there are vets who look after race horses.'

'I hadn't thought about it but I can see the sense of that,' said Dr Leighton.

'Vets in towns obviously don't see many cows or pigs.'

Dr Leighton didn't think she was expected to comment and so she just nodded.

'There aren't any racing stables round here. There are some horses, of course. But just horses that people use for hack riding. There are a few point to point meetings.'

'Hack riding?' said Dr Leighton, who hadn't heard the term.

'Just riding for fun. Riding along the lanes or the bridle paths. There are no riding schools around here but quite a few people have one or two horses.'

Dr Leighton nodded her understanding.

'We had a patient who was a vet with a practice in the village. He looked after the animals on several local farms. He was married to a lovely lady called Imogen and he had two sons.'

Dr Leighton had no idea what was coming next but she could feel the tension mounting. Mallory was having difficulty in talking. 'If it's too painful to talk about you don't have to continue,' she said softly.

'You should know what happened,' said Mallory Croft. 'You're joining the practice. If I don't tell you then you'll always wonder.'

Dr Leighton nodded.

'One day, some years ago, the vet had a phone call from a well-known horse trainer who has a racing stable about twenty miles away. Their usual vet was away at a dinner in London. They'd tried all the other local racing stable vets and they were all away at the same dinner. It was some annual thing where they hand out awards and one or two well-known vets make speeches. The vets were all staying in London and wouldn't be back for another day.'

Mallory picked an apple from a bowl on the table in front of him. He held the apple in both hands but didn't make any move to start to eat it.

'One of their race horses, a valuable mare, had developed a limp and because she was worth a few million pounds, they wanted her seen straight away. They wanted the vet from our village to go and take a look at her.'

Mallory put the apple back into the bowl.

'The vet told them firmly he dealt with cows and pigs and sheep and didn't know anything about race horses. They're a very special breed, you know. They tend to suffer from problems that don't much affect your ordinary pony. But the trainer was very insistent and offered to pay the vet a pretty huge fee if he'd turn out. It was £500 just to go and take a look at the horse, make a diagnosis and prescribe some treatment.'

'So he went,' said Dr Leighton, after another silence.

'So he went,' said Mallory. 'He got out his old Volvo Estate Car, put his bag of tricks in the back and drove off to the racing stables. And he made a mistake. He made the wrong diagnosis and prescribed the wrong treatment. He'd never treated a race horse before. He should never have gone to the stables.'

A tear appeared in the corner of Mallory's right eye.

'The end result was that the horse had to be put down and the trainer and the horse's owners sued the vet for several million pounds.' The tear ran down Mallory's cheek. He wiped it away hastily, obviously hoping that Dr Leighton hadn't seen it.

'Didn't he have insurance?' asked Dr Leighton. I thought that vets, like doctors, had to be insured in case they got sued.'

'Oh, he had insurance. But his insurance policy didn't cover expensive race horses and like most of us, the vet had never studied the fine print. The policy was good for cows and sheep and pet Labradors. But there was a limit on the cover for each animal and anyway the vet's policy, his name was Wilf by the way, didn't cover race horses.'

Dr Leighton still had no idea how Mallory had become involved in what was obviously a tragic story.

'So the trainer and the horse's owners, who turned out to be a syndicate in the Middle East, set the lawyers on Wilf and before he knew it the writs were coming in thick and fast. They didn't just want the money for the horse, they also claimed that the horse would have had valuable foals. And they wanted the money they'd lost on those. It came to ten million pounds or so. There was no way that Wilf would ever be able to pay. The lawyers knew that but it didn't stop them. They took Wilf's house, they took his car, they took everything he owned. Everything. They left him with nothing. And the bad publicity meant that his reputation was ruined. They even made a formal complaint about him to the vets' equivalent of the General Medical Council. Wilf knew that he'd be lucky to get a job as a farm hand.'

The tears were now flowing down Mallory's cheeks and he had given up his attempt to wipe them away.

'I was still practising medicine then. Crawford and I ran the practice together. Wilf came to see me. He was in a terrible state. He was in despair. I talked to him for a long time. And I gave him a prescription for an anti-depressant called Prozac. And I told him to see me twice a week.'

Dr Leighton nodded.

'I don't know what good I thought Prozac could do. But I didn't know what else to do. His life, and his family's life, had been destroyed. They all moved into a small rented cottage. We helped them out by paying the rent and paying their bills at the village shop. It was a damp and really rather squalid cottage. The lawyers had even taken all the furniture. All Wilf had left was his veterinary equipment. He'd gone bankrupt and the bankruptcy people aren't allowed to take a man's tools. Wilf sold them because they weren't any use to him. Wilf's wife had helped run his practice so she was out of work too. They didn't have a car and so she couldn't get a job. They had a two mile walk every day – there and back – to take the children to the village school.'

Dr Leighton now thought she knew what must have happened next.

'He kept back his captive bolt pistol. It was one with a penetrating bolt, designed to kill the animal it was used on.'

Mallory's voice broke and he paused for a moment.

'He shot his two boys while they were asleep. Then he shot his wife. And finally he killed himself.'

Dr Leighton stared aghast. This was worse than she'd feared.

'He was due to come and see me the following day. When he didn't turn up I called in to see him. I found the bodies.'

'Oh no!' whispered Dr Leighton.

'At the inquest the coroner concluded that Wilf had murdered his wife and two sons and then committed suicide. He blamed the Prozac I'd prescribed.'

Dr Leighton now felt tears coursing down her own cheeks.

'I gave up medical practice that day,' said Mallory. 'Crawford tried to talk me out of it. He suggested I take a month off. But I knew I could never practise medicine again. So we worked out a scheme where he looked after the patients and I dealt with all the paperwork. The bureaucracy takes up more time than seeing patients so it wasn't entirely a one-sided arrangement. And I talk to Crawford quite often about patients.'

He then stopped talking and lowered his head into his hands.

Poppy Croft and Crawford Hill came into the room a few moments later. Poppy went straight to her husband, sat beside him and put her hand on his arm.

Dr Leighton, stunned and her face stained with tears, stood up. 'I'm so sorry,' she murmured.

Poppy stood up and took a few steps to where Dr Leighton was standing. 'I thought it best that you heard what had happened,' she said softly.

Dr Leighton nodded.

Five minutes later, Dr Leighton and Crawford said goodbye to the Crofts.

'I'll take you back to your car,' said Crawford.

They drove in silence back to Dr Hill's home.

'What an absolutely awful story,' said Dr Leighton. 'But it wasn't Mallory's fault! The coroner didn't blame him did he?'

'Of course it wasn't,' agreed Crawford. 'And no one blamed him.'

'Was there ever a complaint?'

'Good heavens, no! There was no reason for a complaint.

'Do you think he'll ever practise again?'

'No.' said Crawford firmly. 'He describes himself as being a cracked plate.'

'I don't understand...'

'Scott Fitzgerald noted, after his own breakdown, that someone who has had a breakdown, or has in his words 'cracked up', must be kept in service as a household necessity but can never again be shuffled with other plates, or warmed on the stove or brought out for guests, and is only good enough to hold crackers and cheese late at night or to be used in the fridge to hold leftovers'. That, I'm afraid, describes my dear friend Mallory.'

Crawford Hill drew up in the driveway and turned off the car's ignition. 'Of course, it was all made even worse by the fact that Wilf was Mallory's twin brother. He may not have mentioned that.'

'No,' said Dr Leighton. 'He didn't mention that.'

'They were very close,' said Crawford softly.

On the long drive back to London, Dr Leighton had to slow down several times to wipe the tears from her face.

Chapter Seventeen

It took Dr Leighton longer than she thought it would to sort out her affairs in London.

The solicitor and estate agent handling the sale of her mother's former home had finally managed to arrange for the completion of a process which seemed to have taken forever. Her mother had spent the last part of her life in a specialist care home for patients with dementia and the house had remained empty, gathering dust.

After her death, the contents had been split between two local charity shops and a man who had described himself in his advertisement as a 'house clearance specialist'. The charity shops had expected her mother's ornaments, books, pictures and clothes to be delivered to them and that had taken Dr Leighton three trips in her small car. The 'house clearance specialist' had turned up in a large removal van and had, after leering at her a good deal, shaking his head at the quality and condition of the furniture and sucking in much air through his brown and broken front teeth, said that he would take away the furniture as a favour but that Dr Leighton would have to pay him £500 in cash for the petrol for his van and the fees at the local authority recycling centre. He said that he would have to charge an additional £50 to take away the accumulation of wine bottles which had filled three kitchen cupboards and the cupboard under the stairs. Dr Leighton, too exhausted by the trips to the charity shop to cart the bottles to the nearest bottle bank, had paid him the £50 and left the sad and empty house in tears. She had kept no mementoes for herself. Her mother's only jewellery, including her wedding and engagement rings and a gold crucifix on a chain, had mysteriously disappeared after her mother's death. The care home staff insisted that the undertaker had taken everything, and the undertaker was quite certain that there had been no jewellery on her mother's body when they'd collected it.

Dr Leighton told the solicitor to pay the money straight into her bank account while she decided where to invest it. The solicitor had received a legally binding letter from her former husband confirming that the payment of £50,000 which she had made was 'in full and final settlement' of their agreement. Naturally, she found that she was expected to pay both legal bills for this outrageous piece of extortion, and that meant that her inheritance was reduced by another £2,375 (including fees, photocopying, postage and VAT). And, of course, she had to pay back the £50,000 bridging loan she had taken out to prise her ex-husband off her back, together with the usurious interest payments which the bank had demanded.

'We could fight this for you,' said her solicitor, full of that special variety of righteous indignation enjoyed by those who fight battles with other people's money. 'It is outrageous that you should be making this payment. I could arrange for us to see a barrister specialising in this very type of litigation.'

'No thank you,' said Dr Leighton, remembering that it had been her solicitor who had encouraged her to settle and astonished that there should actually be someone specialising in combatting such a specific type of financial chicanery. She wanted nothing more than to remove her former husband from her life forever. 'I've given my word and although my ex-husband is a contemptible rat, I'm going to stick by what I promised.'

'I read in *The Times* that he's going to stand for the Conservative Party at the next election,' said her solicitor. 'There was a big feature on him. He was photographed with his fiancé in their apartment in Jermyn Street.'

'How nice,' said Dr Leighton, who, although she had now been told of the article by three separate people, still hadn't seen it.

'I can arrange for you to see our associated investment partner,' said the solicitor. 'I'm sure she can help you invest the sum profitably. Even after all your costs the estate is worth considerably north of a quarter of a million pounds. There are some very tax-advantageous schemes available. A good many of our clients are investing in a scheme which is building an office block in Malta. Or we could put you into a small software company being set up by one of our other clients – very hard working young people, all still in their teens. They're organising a web-based business with an associated bricks and mortar subsidiary. The company is called 'Sock it To Me'. They're going to specialise in selling socks. They're opening a shop just off Oxford Street but the company will have its own website and these days most investors are only interested in retail ventures which are primarily internet based.' The solicitor leant forward and lowered his voice. 'I myself have put some of my pennies into the business,' he whispered. And he then touched the side of his nose with a forefinger, though he didn't wink.

'Maybe later,' said Dr Leighton. 'I don't have enough brain left to make any sensible decisions about investments. Besides, I might need the money.'

At the back of her mind, right at the back, in a secret, very private corner, she was already thinking that if all went well with her new job she might want to buy a cottage in Stratford Peverell. 'That's a crazy idea', said the sensible bit of her mind. 'It's far too soon to be thinking like that.'

She realised that there probably wouldn't be enough money to buy a cottage outright, not if London prices were anything to go by, but with a bank loan she could surely buy something. She'd never owned a property of her own and she rather fancied the idea of owning a small (very small) piece of England, something with a small garden; a garden she could manage herself, big enough for a bird table, a few flowers and some herbs which she could go out and pick whenever she wanted: some mint, some sage and a patch of rosemary. She'd have to learn to identify trees, bushes, flowers and weeds. Maybe she'd allow the weeds to co-exist, she thought with innocence. After all, didn't someone once define a weed as a plant growing where you didn't plant it? And there had to be a hearth where she could sit and watch dancing flames and smell wood-smoke. And maybe a few trees of her own so that when it had been windy she could go out and pick up her own kindling. Maybe a badger would come and visit; he would snuffle through her flower bed but that would be OK.

She would, she thought to herself, much rather own a small cottage that she could call her own, than own part of an office building in Malta or have shares in a web based business (with an associated bricks and mortar subsidiary) selling socks.

The most exciting day of her sojourn back in the capital was spent touring luggage stores in central London. Eventually, she found what she was looking for: a black, leather pilot's case (as Dr Hill had recommended) which contained three suitably sized compartments and a firm brass lock. It cost her a small fortune (actually, about as much as one Jimmy Choo shoe, she thought to herself) and made her feel very professional. She couldn't remember buying anything apart from her Lotus motor car that had given her quite as much pleasure.

She visited a medical equipment supply store in Wigmore Street, just round the corner from Harley Street, the traditional home of doctors in London, and spent an even larger fortune on the medical equipment she needed to put inside the bag.

The small amount of furniture that her ex-husband had left behind in the flat they'd shared was of little or no financial value. It had absolutely no sentimental value and it certainly wasn't worth putting into storage. She contacted a firm of removers who charged her £300 to take it away and insisted that it would cost them nearly that much to dispose of it at the local authority's recycling centre. She didn't believe them and was silently convinced that most if not all of the furniture would end up in a junk shop or for sale in auction rooms.

The remainder of her personal belongings she managed to cram into two suitcases, an overnight bag and a black bin liner. That was it. She looked at the small collection of stuff before she packed it into the Lotus and felt rather sorry for herself. In a materialistic age it wasn't much for a life time of accumulating – albeit, so far, a fairly short one.

She then telephoned Dr Hill and told him that she was coming back ready to start work. He promised to have acquired details of one or two cottages available to rent by the time she returned.

And, after that, she phoned Rosemary at The Jolly Roger and booked herself a room.

'Your old room is available,' said Rosemary. 'Would you like that one? Or would you prefer another? Actually, to be honest, you can always pick a room when you get here. The bird watchers have all gone and we're very quiet.'

'The room I had before will be perfect!'

'Are you coming back here for good?'

Dr Leighton said she was, that she was going to work with Dr Hill for a three months' trial and that he'd promised to look out for a cottage available to rent.

'That's fantastic!' said Rosemary, who sounded genuinely excited. 'I'll keep my ears open and if I hear of anything I'll let Dr Hill know about it. If he and I can't find anything you can always try the local shop.'

'Don't tell me they sell cottages as well as everything else?

'No, no!' laughed Rosemary. 'They have one of those boards with little adverts pinned to it. You can put an advert there. They charge £1 a week for a postcard sized advert.

Chapter Eighteen

Dr Leighton started her life as a country doctor the morning after she'd arrived in the Stratford Peverell.

'I assumed you'd prefer to get your feet in the water straight away,' Dr Hill had said, when he'd telephoned her at The Jolly Roger on the evening of her return. But if you'd rather wait a couple of days that's fine.'

Dr Leighton said she was happy to start work the following morning. 'But will there be any patients booked in to see me?' she'd asked.

'We don't have an appointments system,' Dr Hill reminded her. 'We have an old-fashioned first come first served system. I thought we'd tell Mrs Onions to send patients in alternately – one for you and one for me. Is that OK with you?'

'That's fine!'

'And when morning surgery is finished we'll share out the calls,' Dr Hill had said. 'I've got you a map, by the way. And unless we've very busy with calls there should be time to go and look at a couple of cottages Rosemary and I have found for you. As far as night calls and weekend calls are concerned, Mallory and I talked about it and thought it would be sensible for you to wait a couple of weeks before you start doing those. You need to get to know your way around the village a bit first. I know you'll manage perfectly well with the medical side of things but finding your way around some of the lanes can take a little time – especially in the dark. But if you do ever get lost, just try to find your way back here – to the surgery. I'll always be available. Or use your half of the two-way radio I mentioned. '

Dr Leighton who had very little experience of visiting patients in their own homes, and none whatsoever of finding their homes and then treating them in the middle of the night (when, she knew from her experience in hospitals, every problem seems magnified a hundred times and everything becomes an emergency) was grateful for this and grateful too for what she realised was Dr Hill's generosity in extending to her the professional courtesy of assuming that she would be able to cope with whatever illnesses with which she was faced. She wished she had his confidence in herself.

The first three patients Dr Leighton saw in her first surgery had nothing much wrong with them, and she quickly surmised that those patients had merely called in so that they could say that they'd been the first to have seen the new doctor. In a small village there would be some kudos in that. The first needed a repeat prescription for Dr Hill's special tonic. The second needed her ears syringing. And the third wanted to know what Dr Leighton thought about a new remedy for arthritis which she'd read about in a popular magazine.

Dr Leighton had dispensed the requested medicine herself (she was accustomed to writing out a prescription and sending the patient off to the nearest pharmacy, and it was the first time she'd ever prescribed and dispensed a medicine without the aid of a pharmacist), syringed the blocked ears (the first time she'd done that and although the end result was very satisfactory from the patient's point of view, both she and the patient ended up soaked with warm water and convulsed with giggles) and explained to the patient with the magazine cutting that she quite agreed with the treatment Dr Hill had initiated and could see no reason to change it. She'd been a GP long enough to know that some patients will, for whatever reason, try to play a new doctor off against the patient's original doctor. The patient had folded the cutting, put it back into her handbag and smiled happily. Dr Leighton congratulated herself on passing that particular test with flying colours.

Dr Leighton noticed one unexpected difference with her new practice.

In London the patients had been aware that their time was limited. They had their stories well prepared; some even seemed to have rehearsed what they needed to say in their allotted five minutes. In Dr Hill's practice, the patients were more at ease and felt able to take their time in telling their stories and explaining why they were there.

None of the patients she saw had been seriously ill, though several were definitely individuals who could properly be described as 'characters', and at least two of them would, in London, have been considered prime candidates for residential care.

Several of the patients led lives which would, if described on a television programme, have merited exclamations of delight and exhortations. If there had been a live audience they would have burst into genuinely spontaneous applause. (Dr Leighton knew, though she wasn't entirely sure how she knew it, that when a television audience bursts into spontaneous applause it is usually in response to the assistant studio manager holding up a sign saying 'CLAP'. And she knew that the assistant studio manager would have another sign which carried the word 'BOO' and he would occasionally hold this one up as an alternative.)

'Do you manage to get around satisfactorily?' she asked one old lady, who was clearly suffering from severe arthritis and who came into the surgery leaning on two walking sticks. She wore a shawl and a poke bonnet. This was the second time Dr Leighton had someone wearing a shawl but she'd never before seen anyone not in a film wearing a poke bonnet.

'Oh yes,' replied the old lady, leaning her sticks against Dr Leighton's desk and settling in the chair on the other side of the desk. 'I try to exercise as much as I can. I do line dancing.'

Dr Leighton was startled. 'Line dancing? Is there a group in Stratford Peverell? Where do you do that? How do you manage?'

'Oh, I do it alone,' replied the patient, replying to all the questions with one answer.

'But how…'

'I sit down and just wave my legs about in the air. I have one of those DVDs with line dancing music on it. My grandson gave me his DVD player when he bought something else. I don't think they use DVDs now, do they? It's all just on computers these days.'

'Splendid!' said Dr Leighton who meant it.

'Did you know that I'm 101?' asked the woman.

'I didn't,' said Dr Leighton. She looked at the woman's medical notes which did indeed confirm her age.

'I put my longevity down to eating lots of fat, suet and dripping,' said the old woman. 'They keep out the cold.'

'I shall endeavour to eat more of all three!' said Dr Leighton, crossing her fingers under the desk as she spoke.

Another elderly woman, Mrs Udall, explained that she thought she'd caught a bit of a cold and might need a tonic to help fight it off. She explained that Dr Hill always gave her a tonic if she felt she had a cold coming on. 'It stops a cold developing,' she explained. 'Thanks to Dr Hill I haven't had a cold or the flu for nine years.'

'How did you catch a cold?'

'I was carol singing.'

'When was this?' asked Dr Leighton, puzzled for she had always associated carol singing with the pre-Christmas period.

'Last week. Friday and Saturday.'

'But it's Spring.'

'Oh yes.'

'So why were you carol singing in Spring?'

'It was too cold to go carol singing in December. Last week was the warmest week we've had for a while. Dr Hill said I wasn't to go out in the cold weather.'

'No,' agreed Dr Leighton. 'That was very sensible of him.'

'Besides, I was the only one carol singing last week so people were surprised and pleased to see me. I collected £7.55, half for the Church roof fund and half for the Salvation Army Christmas Appeal.'

Dr Leighton, not sure what to do, looked at Mrs Udall's medical notes and found that Dr Hill had at least once a year prescribed a vitamin tonic. She did likewise and then went into the small dispensary and poured 150 mls of the tonic into a bottle and handed it to Mrs Udall with as much ceremony as she could manage.

'Dr Hill always puts on a label with my name and the instructions,' whispered Mrs Udall, very softly. 'One teaspoonful to be taken three times a day before meals.'

'Of course,' said Dr Leighton, apologetically. She took the bottle back to the small dispensary, found the sheet of labels, wrote on the patient's name and the instructions and stuck the label on the bottle.

'That's perfect, thank you doctor,' said Mrs Udall. 'I think you're going to do very well here.'

By the end of the morning Dr Leighton had seen nine patients (half as many as Dr Hill) but she'd managed without needing to call on Dr Hill for help and congratulated herself on successfully avoiding a couple of potential pitfalls.

'You passed your first test this morning,' Dr Hill told her, as they met at the end of the surgery. 'Mrs Carpenter slipped in between patients to congratulate me. She's decided you're an excellent doctor.'

'Mrs Carpenter...?' said Dr Leighton, thinking hard.

'The woman in the coat with the fox draped round the collar,' explained Dr Hill. 'She showed you a magazine article about something or other. She brings in a magazine article at least once a fortnight. She liked your answer. And since she is the village gossip you'll have an enviable reputation by five o'clock tonight.'

'You make it sound like a review on Trustpilot!' laughed Dr Leighton.

'What on earth is Trustpilot?'

'Haven't you heard of it? No, I suppose you wouldn't have. You'd need the internet and a smart phone. It's a website that enables people to review businesses, hotels, restaurants, garages…doctors…everything!'

'Ah well, Trustpilot is just a modern version of village life then,' said Dr Hill. 'Villagers like Mrs Carpenter have been reviewing doctors, publicans, vicars and village shop keepers since people started living in communities. Their reviews are prejudiced, sometimes unduly critical, very one-sided and, generally speaking, best ignored'

'That does sound like Trustpilot!' agreed Dr Leighton.

'But village reviews do have the advantage of having a fairly short lifespan. Today's gossip is quickly superseded and once it has been replaced it is usually forgotten quite quickly.'

'That's a distinct advantage. A review on Trustpilot stays there forever and becomes a permanent burden.'

'Well, let's hope the internet never finds us,' said Dr Hill.

'One of your patients told me that the secret of reaching 100 years of age is eating lots of suet, fat and something else which I've forgotten.'

'Ah, yes,' said Dr Hill, with a nod. 'I know who that would be. And they're our patients now, by the way. That would be Mrs Instow. We have more than our fair share of centenarians and nonagenarians in Stratford Peverell and they all have differing explanations for their longevity. Mr Quirke insists that he's got to 100 because he started smoking early, at 14 I think it was, and although he never smoked to excess, he always made sure that he smoked every day. He claims that smoking settles the nerves. We have two who claim that the secret of a long life is plenty of alcohol. Mr Yarnold claims he's lived a long healthy life through drinking whisky every day. He claims it kills all germs and all the bad cells in the body (by which I think he meant cancer and who knows he may be right). Whisky may be more medicinal than we imagine. I remember reading that the actors and crew making the film 'African Queen' all contracted terrible intestinal infections after drinking the water. The only two who remained immune were Humphrey Bogart and John Huston, the director, who drank only whisky throughout the making of the picture. And we have a woman in her 90s called Miss Barnes who claims she has never touched fruit or vegetables. She says they're full of poison and bad for you. And we have a 90-something-year-old patient, whose name escapes me at the moment, who has never done any exercise at all. He says that exercise wears out the body and I could easily be persuaded that he's right about that.'

'Oh, I like that one,' said Dr Leighton. 'So if we drink lots of whisky and take no exercise we should do well?'

'Absolutely!' agreed Dr Hill. 'There are only three visits,' he said, holding up a piece of paper that his receptionist had given him, and looked at his watch. 'Shall we do them together? We can have some lunch at The Jolly Roger and then afterwards drive past the cottages which Rosemary and I have found. I don't have the keys to any of them but we can take a look from the outside and see what you think. We'd better go in my truck if you don't mind. I'm afraid that lovely little car of yours wouldn't get where we need to go – not in one piece at any rate.'

Dr Leighton, who was very attached to her Lotus (and as proud of it as she was of her new medical bag) no longer felt hurt by this, on behalf of her car. The Lotus was wonderful for cruising on motorways, excellent for nipping around city streets and best of all when parked in a driveway as a sign that the owner had 'arrived' (in more than one sense) but it was not going to be quite at home on narrow lanes where grass growing in the centre of the road was more usual than surprising, or on rutted farm tracks which offered a challenge even to Dr Hill's heavy duty, four-wheel drive truck.

'I suppose I'd better get myself something a bit higher off the ground,' she said, rather sadly.

'Get something with four-wheel drive,' suggested Dr Hill. 'I'd suggest a truck. They're excellent value, well built, good in snow and wet weather, great on farm tracks and inside they're just like posh cars. Mine even has lights that come on when it goes dark and windscreen wipers that automatically wipe the windscreen if it starts to rain!'

Dr Leighton, who remembered thinking that she definitely didn't want to drive around in a truck, said nothing.

'Meanwhile, you can borrow the tractor for your calls,' said Dr Hill. 'You don't need a key. Just climb up, press the starter button and drive away.'

Dr Leighton, aghast, looked at him. 'Am I allowed to drive a tractor with an ordinary car licence?'

'I don't have the foggiest idea,' confessed Dr Hill. 'But I would have thought so. They're not exactly speedy. I doubt if anyone has ever been arrested for speeding in a tractor. And I haven't seen a policeman around here for seven or eight years. That, I seem to remember, was when Mrs Reynolds claimed that her garage had been broken into. She reported that her ladder had been stolen but the policeman they sent out found it in her greenhouse.'

'Aren't you worried that someone might steal your tractor?'

'Who would steal it?' asked Dr Hill, who appeared genuinely puzzled. 'Everyone who wants a tractor has already got one. And if someone stole it, to whom would they sell it?'

The three visits were quite straightforward but Dr Leighton was grateful that she hadn't tried to do them in her Lotus. The first patient, Mrs Waters, needed her regular prescription for blood pressure medicine. She lived in a cottage on the only lane in the village which actually had a B road identity. The second patient, who lived no more than 100 yards away from the first, was a seven-year-old with earache which had started during the night. Her mum reported that her little girl had been crying a good deal. A bottle of antibiotic medicine and an instruction to collect another supply from the surgery sorted out that problem. And the third patient was a farmer who thought he had pains in his neck, shoulder, arm and back. To reach his farm they had to bounce down a long ill-kept track and across a field which didn't seem to have a track at all. Even the truck complained noisily about the journey. When they finally got to the farm, the two doctors examined the patient and agreed that he had merely strained some muscles lifting too many sacks of cattle feed. The treatment, they agreed, was warmth, mild analgesia and a few days' rest.

'Shouldn't we ring the surgery to see if there are any more calls?' asked Dr Leighton, as they headed for The Jolly Roger for their lunch.

'No need. Martha knows where we'll be,' said Dr Hill. 'I eat lunch here most days. She'll ring if she needs us.'

Chapter Nineteen

After an excellent, rather late lunch at The Jolly Roger (thick, homemade vegetable soup with crusty bread, chicken pie with an inch thick pastry crust as light and full of air as a soufflé, thick cut moreish chips and carrots and a huge bowlful of 'I cannot possibly eat all that' treacle sponge with custard for pudding) the two doctors set off around the village to look at the cottages which were available to rent, Dr Leighton having decided that if she carried on eating the sort of meals they served at The Jolly Roger she'd soon need a whole new wardrobe – several sizes larger.

'What sort of cottage did you have in mind?' asked Dr Hill, as they moved away from the otherwise empty pub car park.

'Oh, I don't know. The usual sort of corny country cottage, I suppose. A thatched roof, roses growing round the front door and ivy or clematis round all the windows, a fireplace so big I can sit almost inside it on cold winter days, a tiny, twisting staircase and thick beams across the ceiling. And a little stream outside the back door – preferably one that bubbles and has trout in it.'

Dr Hill turned to her and smiled. 'We can find you one like that and maybe it would be good for you to live in it for three months so that when you come to buy a permanent home, you are careful not to choose anything with a thatched roof, a huge hearth so big you can sit in it, roses around the doors and ivy or clematis round all the windows, a tiny staircase, thick beams in every room and a bubbling stream at the bottom of the garden.'

'I don't want something like that?'

'Well, you may want something like that. But I'm not sure I'd recommend it.'

'Why not?'

'Thatched roofs look lovely from outside, when they're on someone else's cottage, but they have to be replaced more often than you'd imagine and there are so few thatchers around that when you suddenly notice that you are walking on a wet carpet, look up and spot the leak in the ceiling, you'll find that there is a two year waiting list to have a proper repair done. It'll also cost you a fortune because decent thatchers can charge pretty well what they like. And what money you have left over will be spent on insurance because of the risk of a fire. And it's no good saying that you don't smoke so there won't be any risk of a fire, because fires in thatched roofs are caused by other people's fireworks, Chinese lanterns and a spark from either your chimney or a neighbour's – and you'd be surprised how far a spark can travel on a breezy night. In fact the risk of a house fire with a thatched roof is so great that most people who have them never light a fire. The roses around the door and the ivy around all the windows will need pruning back every year or else you won't be able to get into the cottage or see out through the windows. A huge hearth will use up so many logs that you'll need a delivery of cut logs at least once a week. A tiny, twisting staircase will be amusing the first time you use it and a damned nuisance every other time you use it and a nightmare if you ever want to have a bed or a wardrobe upstairs. And low beams will mean that every visitor to your house will crack their head at least six times in the first hour. And what was the other thing?'

'A bubbling stream right outside the back door?'

'No, you definitely don't want one of those. In the winter it will flood and after a storm you'll come downstairs and find a foot of water in every downstairs room. Your insurance company won't pay up because they'll have asked you if there is a stream anywhere near to your house, and they have maps which will tell them the answer anyway. It's better to have a stream nearby that you can visit. A small stream at the bottom of the garden would be nice.'

'Oh,' said Dr Leighton. 'I hadn't thought of all that. But I don't want something new and made of concrete and cardboard.'

'No, of course you don't. You won't find one of those around here. And you don't want something on a hill top or at the bottom of a valley either.'

'I don't?' said Dr Leighton who was beginning to think that choosing a home was going to be infinitely more difficult than she had imagined.

'No, you don't. If you live on the top of a hill you will be buffetted by every bit of wind. During a gale or a storm, you will lose most of your roof and if there are trees nearby you'll worry constantly that one of them is going to crash down on your bedroom and kill you while you're sleeping. And if you have a house in a valley, there will be a risk that the house will flood. In a valley there will always be a river or a stream, even if it's difficult to see, and the land and the air will always be damp. And valleys usually have a micro climate all of their own so while your neighbours who are half a mile away are enjoying wonderful sunshine you'll be shivering or shovelling snow off your front step.'

'Phew!' said Dr Leighton, exhausted by this litany of terror. 'Have you found anything that is habitable?'

'I think so! Most of the cottages around here are at least 100-years-old, and 100 years ago builders were much more sensible than they are these days. And most of the houses that were built were commissioned by their owners, who knew what sort of house they wanted and where they wanted it built – even if they intended it to be lived in by one of their farm labourers or estate workers.'

Dr Hill slowed and pulled onto a narrow verge, bumping his truck over small hillocks and thick tufts of grass. 'This one is called Sunset View and it's a bit hidden,' he said, unfastening his seat belt. 'Unless the original owners had a wicked sense of humour they were slightly confused because it faces due east.'

Dr Leighton looked around and thought that since she couldn't see anything that looked like a building, Dr Hill's remark about the cottage being a bit hidden was probably something of an understatement.

'The main snag with it is that it's completely on its own. If you want privacy that's fine – you can play music as loud as you like and do the gardening in a swimming costume if you're brave enough to take on the insect life. But it's a bit lonely and you might find it a trifle scary if you get called out at night and have to come home at 4 o'clock in the morning.'

They got out of the car and Dr Leighton followed Dr Hill through a five barred gate and across a field full of sheep.

'The other problems are that access is a bit tricky and there really isn't anywhere to park a vehicle. You can only reach it by going through this field which belongs to the landlord.'

After tramping through the grass for 100 yards or so, they eventually found themselves standing looking at what was obviously an empty cottage. It was brick built, solid looking and had that unoccupied look that houses always acquire when there is no one living in them. Not even the presence of curtains could change that.

'It looks nice, but I do think I'd find it a bit scary at night,' admitted Dr Leighton.

She was, she realised, beginning to feel slightly scared about this move to the country. Ever since she'd left home she'd lived in a series of flats. When she'd been at medical school she'd lived in a hall of residence, on the 14th floor of a 16 storey building that offered as much privacy as the concourse of a mainline railway station. And every lane they went down looked the same as every other lane. There was a hedge on the left and a hedge on the right and every so often there would be a tree on the left or the right. 'Can I really do this?' she asked herself silently. She felt that a day's complement of visits would take her hours and hours. And how would she find cottages in the dark when there was an emergency? She realised that she was, in short, well out of her comfort zone. And the prospect of living in such an isolated place terrified her.

'I agree,' said Dr Hill. 'But I thought I'd show it to you. The owner has been letting it to holidaymakers for a few years. They don't seem to mind the isolation. But then I doubt if many of them were returning back here in the middle of the night. I think coming back to it at 4 am would be a bit unnerving. I'd bump into a sheep and break the world high jump record.'

There were also significant drawbacks with the second cottage, Daffodil Cottage, which was available to rent. It was in the middle of a terrace and not only was there absolutely no parking and no garden but the lane in which the row of cottages was situated was very narrow.

'You'd have to park on a patch of land about 150 yards away,' said Dr Hill, rather apologetically. 'And I should tell you that the man who has the house next door keeps chickens and has a very noisy cockerel. And he is something of a hypochondriac. I'd worry that he would be knocking on your door six times a day to tell his latest worries.'

'I don't think it would be much fun on a wet night!' said Dr Leighton, looking around. 'I'd feel much happier if I could find somewhere with a parking space quite close to the front door.'

'I agree,' said Dr Hill. 'But don't be upset. I've kept what I think is the best cottage until last and I rather think you'll like this one.'

They went back to the truck and drove to the third cottage on Dr Hill's short list.

Called Squirrel Cottage this one was far less lonely. Indeed, far from being lonely, it was situated centrally and conveniently overlooking what the locals referred to as the village green (but which was in reality little more than a small patch of grass just about big enough for a kick about game of football). A dozen detached cottages, most of them painted white but two painted that shade of pink which seems popular among the owners of cottages and modestly sized homes in the country, were well-spaced around the village green. All of the cottages were different but most had a white picket fence in front of them. All had small front gardens but, according to Dr Hill, much bigger gardens at the rear. To the left, about a hundred yards away, there was the village pub, The Jolly Roger, and about the same distance to the right lay the village shop. The village church was within walking distance, too.

The cottage, which had a slate roof rather than the thatch which Dr Hill had warned her against, even had a small garage, big enough for Dr Leighton's Lotus, and a driveway big enough to park her new truck. Two dozen birds, nesting in a tree in the front garden, were making a good deal of noise.

'You've got your own rookery,' said Dr Hill, looking up a trifle warily. 'Bit noisy, of course. Rooks are very social birds. There's also a large yew tree in the garden at the back. According to country lore both are signs of good fortune.'

'It's wonderful!' said Dr Leighton immediately. They both climbed out of Dr Hill's truck. 'Can I afford it?'

'I would think so,' said Dr Hill. They both stood in front of the cottage. 'The rent is £550.'

'A week?' asked Dr Leighton, who was used to London prices.

'It's £550 a month out of season and since you'd be taking a three month let you could rent it for that – and that includes local taxes and insurance for the cottage – everything except what you spend on electricity and oil. There isn't any gas, of course but there is an oil central heating system. The nearest gas supply is 20 miles away and never likely to get any closer. And it's fully furnished so you could move in straight away. I don't think the furniture is anything special but I gather it's perfectly serviceable. There's even a small greenhouse and a few fruit trees in the garden. The owner of the cottage has a gardener who pops in once a week for a couple of hours. If you want him to carry on that would be fine, and included in the price. And best of all from the practice's point of view I know there is a telephone. And, of course, we can switch phone calls from my number to yours!' said Dr Hill. 'I don't know how they do it, but it's possible. We just ring the telephone people and they'll arrange it. When you are no longer on call, you just do something with your phone and then all the calls come through to my phone. When I'm no longer on call I do something with my phone and all the calls go back to your phone. Everyone who rings the practice always dials the same number and they don't know where the phone rings. Isn't that marvellously clever? What will they think of next?'

'Oh, I think they've been able to do it for some time!' said Dr Leighton, with a smile. She rather liked her employer's rather charming otherworldliness. 'The practice where I was a trainee had it fixed up for their phones, though it was never used because by the time I worked there they had stopped doing visits or night calls. They used it once when both their receptionists were off work at the same time. They switched the phones through to someone else who was available to answer the phones and take calls but not able to come into the surgery.'

'Golly,' said Dr Hill, clearly still impressed.

'I'd definitely like to take this cottage!' said Dr Leighton, without any more thought.

'Don't you want me to get the key so that you can have a look around inside?'

'Oh yes. But I know I'll take it. How soon can I move in?'

'It's empty so you can move in as soon as you like.'

And so, two days later, having signed a lease for three months, and with surprisingly little fuss, Dr Leighton moved herself and her belongings (two suitcases, an overnight bag and a bin liner – plus, and definitely not forgetting her new black medical bag) into Squirrel Cottage. As Dr Hill had warned her, the furniture was elderly but solid and serviceable. As a very welcome bonus, the owner had even filled the woodshed with logs. A trip to the nearest town enabled her to purchase sheets and towels and the other bits and pieces which any house needs before it can be thought of as a home.

The first phone call Dr Leighton made was to Jasmine, her friend in London. 'Would you check something on the internet for me?'

'What do you want to know?'

'Can I drive a tractor with an ordinary car driver's licence?'

It took her friend several minutes to stop laughing long enough to check the Government website.

'It says that you can,' she assured Dr Leighton. 'You can drive an agricultural tractor, a mowing machine and a pedestrian controlled vehicle – I assume that is one of those that you have to walk behind.' There was then more laughter. 'Have you got a part time job? Or are you just helping out on the farm? It isn't harvest time down there is it? Don't they usually do all that stuff in autumn? Is it possible to retain your dignity and climb up into a tractor? You'd have to wear trousers or there'd be a crowd watching you go up and down into the cab. Have you got those trousers with the straps that go over your shoulders? What are they called? Dungarees, isn't it? You can probably get them made out of canvas. Or you could wear a boiler suit or one of those siren suits that Winston Churchill wore.' Her friend, now giggling uncontrollably, knew that Dr Leighton hated wearing trousers, and always wore skirts or dresses.

'I'm not going to start wearing trousers and don't you dare tell anyone I asked about driving a tractor!' said Dr Leighton.

'No, no, of course not!' said her friend. 'Well, can I just tell one or two people?'

'No! And the tractor is only temporary – just for a few days until I can get myself a truck.'

Unfortunately for Dr Leighton that confession did nothing to stop the merriment at the other end of the telephone line.

Chapter Twenty

In the event, Dr Leighton never needed to drive the tractor.

The day after she had moved into Squirrel Cottage, Dr Leighton spent some of her inheritance on a more suitable vehicle for driving around Stratford Peverell.

She became the proud owner (well, fairly proud owner) of a bright blue Mitsubishi truck with 45,000 miles on the clock and a sizeable ding in the tail gate. 'It'll save you the bother of doing it yourself,' said the man who owned it, a rather over jovial fellow who was retiring from his gardening business and, at his wife's instigation, wanted to trade in his truck for something small and powered by electricity. He was unhappy about selling the truck and he spent half an hour extolling its various virtues. 'All trucks have a ding in the tail gate,' he said with a shrug. 'I'm surprised they don't put the ding in when they make them. It would save a lot of heartache.'

'Don't people have the dents repaired?' asked Dr Leighton, and to the man's simple, straight forward reply of: 'Why would they?' she could not think of an answer. He had seemed genuinely puzzled by her query.

Dr Leighton had originally visited a garage in the nearest town, some thirty miles away from Stratford Peverell, but the salesman there, who wore a cheap electric green suit that would have probably fitted a much larger man, and sported an ambitious comb over which appeared to have been glued into place, reeked of Old Spice aftershave and had a sneery look which Dr Leighton found disconcerting. He had two trucks for sale and assumed that she was buying one on behalf of a husband or boyfriend. He managed to keep a straight face while claiming that one of them, which was 11-years-old, had done only 14,000 miles, and when Dr Leighton asked him if it was possible that the odometer had gone round back to the beginning at least once, he laughed and assured her that it had not. She was surprised he had not tried to convince her that the truck had been driven by a careful old lady who had used it only to attend church on Sundays. He had offered a derisory trade-in price for Dr Leighton's smart sports car, the only real connection to her previous life, and with the money from the sale of her mother's house now safely in her bank account, she found the offer easy to reject.

Eventually, she had remembered one of the few things her father had told her – that when buying a second-hand car from a dealer one could be sure of only one thing: that the dealer was guaranteed to behave on a scale moving from mild deceit to outright crookedness. The corollary, he assured her, was that private owners selling their vehicles would be dishonest only 50% of the time and would not be as ruthless or as efficient at being dishonest as the professionals. So she bought a local newspaper, looked through the cars for sale and found a Mitsubishi truck which sounded promising and which was being sold privately.

In order to push through the sale and accommodate his customer, the retired builder agreed to deliver the truck to Dr Hill's new home – Squirrel Cottage, The Village Green, Stratford Peverell. He said he had a friend who would follow him there and then, afterwards, take him back home afterwards. When Dr Leighton offered to reimburse him for the cost of the petrol for both vehicles, he was delighted and she felt strangely pleased that he hadn't even asked her to pay for the fuel.

Chapter Twenty One

The days went by quietly and determinedly and Dr Leighton settled into her new life as a country doctor with an ease which surprised and comforted her. She was aware that her life had changed dramatically. In London, life had been a constant bustle and even though she worked far fewer hours than she did now, the days had gone by with a sort of relentless fury.

Here, in her new job, she did a surgery in the morning and one in the afternoon. At first she just shared the patients with Dr Hill so that the patients saw whichever doctor was free. After ten days or so the receptionist reported that some patients were actually asking to see her, usually because they'd seen her a few days earlier and were happy with the treatment programme she'd initiated.

One thing she had noticed was that the patients in the waiting room at her new surgery seemed alert and very much alive. They talked to one another while they waited. Occasionally, laughter could be heard. In London, in the clinic where she had previously worked, the patients in the waiting room looked as if they were already dead. No one spoke to anyone else and there was an air of determined pessimism bordering on relentless doom and gloomy expectations. The receptionist, Mrs Onions, who sat in a corner of the waiting room among the patients, was indestructibly cheerful, welcoming and friendly. At the clinic in London the receptionists had been tough, stony faced and ruthless and most of them appeared to Dr Leighton to have been trained by the same people who trained Post Office counter staff.

After the morning surgery had finished, Dr Leighton would routinely share the visits with Dr Hill and then, after lunch at the pub, or a salad or a sandwich at home, she would go back to the surgery in the late afternoon for the evening surgery. If she fancied company and chatter, she ate her dinner at The Jolly Roger, often sitting at the bar and talking to Rosemary when she wasn't busy serving drinks. If she wanted a quiet evening she made a meal for herself and sat and read or listened to music. There was a television in her cottage but she felt absolutely no urge to watch it. The world portrayed on the television (even the programmes about or based in the countryside) seemed somehow distant from the new world in which she had immersed herself. She had no interest in the news and hadn't looked at a newspaper since she'd been living in the village. She was far more interested in local issues such as, for example, the problems which were caused when flooding closed one of the village lanes (caused by half a dead tree falling into a stream and blocking it so very effectively that not even Land Rovers or trucks could pass through the resultant flood). In the town such a mishap would have merited calls to the council and the emergency services. The police would have put up cones and 'Road Blocked' signs. Many men (and possibly women) wearing high visibility jackets or vests, and Wellington boots of course, would have visited and inspected the site, taking photographs and measurements. Risk assessment specialists would have been called in. The local newspaper would have sent a reporter with a smart phone as a camera and, on a quiet day, the local television company might have sent a two person crew with a presenter with a can of hairspray and entirely unsuitable shoes. The fire brigade would have been called and would have hurried to the scene with bells ringing. Naturally, however, nothing would have been done to solve the problem for days or possibly weeks.

Here, in Stratford Peverell, a group of farmers dealt with the problem themselves, with three tractors being involved in moving the tree. The first tractor had got stuck in mud and the other two tractors had been needed to extricate it. There had been much laughter at the expense of the tractor driver whose machine had needed dragging out of the mud but it had not been cruel laughter, and the hapless driver had been laughing too.

The biggest change was in the way she worked.

In London she had been working as a GP but it had been like working in a factory. The patients had been numbers and diseases, not real people. She rarely saw the same patient twice. If they needed anything more than a prescription for an antibiotic or a painkiller she was encouraged to send her patients to hospital. Simple procedures such as taking blood, syringing ears or removing stitches were all done by a practice nurse. If a patient had a small cut she sent them to the hospital to be stitched up, regardless of the inconvenience for the patient. And, of course, she never saw her patients in their homes. She knew nothing, absolutely nothing, about how or where they lived. She knew nothing about their work life or their home life. In Stratford Peverell, the people were real and she was, for the first time that she could remember, a member of a community. Oh, of course there were people who didn't get on with one another. And she knew, from things that Dr Hill had said, that there were feuds between families that had gone on for generations. At her London practice the ulcers, the diseased joints and the gall stones had existed almost in isolation, their owners being incidental. Here, in her new world, she thought not of diseases with people attached but of people with diseases troubling them.

Soon it was Dr Leighton's first night on call.

She checked the contents of her black bag at least three times and made sure that the tank of her truck was filled to the brim with diesel. She studied a map of the village at great length and she checked that the telephone was working by ringing the speaking clock four times. She and Dr Hill had decided that if the telephone rang while she was out on a call, an answering machine would be an adequate substitute for a human receptionist. She had checked the answering machine that she'd bought and fitted to the telephone. She had recorded a short message, explaining that she was out on a call and asking callers to leave a message with their name, address and telephone number.

She was both excited and terrified and could not remember being so tense since the day when a boy called William Gladminster had invited her to go the pictures with him. He had been sixteen, three inches shorter than her and sorely afflicted with acne and a stammer. She had been fifteen and her parents had lectured her for twenty minutes on the things to watch out for during what they had clearly both feared was going to be an evening of unremitting debauchery. She had left home absolutely full of fear and apprehension and she had been instructed to be home at 10.30 pm according to the clock in their kitchen which she knew, was always at least five minutes fast. In order to meet this requirement, the two teenagers had had to leave the cinema a good ten minutes before the end of the main picture. They had, she remembered, held hands in the cinema because it was dark. Neither of them had wanted to hold hands on the bus home, lest someone spot them and reports them to their respective parents, and although she had been relieved that he had not tried to do so, she had also been quietly disappointed. The young Gladminster had taken her to her door, as a gentleman should, and before walking home he had kissed her on the cheek. She somehow knew that this overt exhibition of romantic interest had taken all his courage. She had watched as he had sprinted down the road in order to meet the deadline of his own curfew. The following week their exams had started and he had not invited her out again. But she remembered, and would never forget, the way she had felt before that first date. She wondered, quietly, whatever had happened to him and to the other pupils with whom she had been at school. She had never been a person eager to maintain old friendships. Her parents had made friends easily. When she was small, her mother had sent Christmas cards to (and received from) at least a dozen people they'd met on their summer holidays. Now, she could hardly remember the names of any of the students she'd shared life with when she'd been a medical student. Even the names of the people she'd worked with in London were beginning to fade. All these thoughts flitted through her mind as she waited for the telephone to ring.

At nine o'clock the telephone rang. She had the telephone on a small table beside her chair. She'd been reading and, although it wasn't cold, had a fire lit in the hearth. She picked up the receiver on the second ring and could feel her heart beat faster as she did so.

'How are things?' asked a voice she knew well – that of Dr Hill.

'Yours is the only call so far,' she replied.

'I always find the calls go in clumps,' replied Dr Hill. 'Sometimes there will be three or four calls in a night. Then we'll go a week without getting a single call. It's the same at the weekends and on bank holidays.'

They'd talked for another few minutes about a patient Dr Hill was dealing with: a man in his 40s who had nerve pains. They both thought he was suffering from vitamin B12 deficiency and were waiting for a blood test result to come back.

'I'd better get off the phone,' said Dr Hill. 'In case a patient is trying to get through. I'll be glad of a night off to be honest. I've been feeling rather tired recently – though it's probably just my age!'

'Maybe you need one of your own tonics!' suggested Dr Leighton.

'Well, if you prescribe one for me make sure you do so with confidence and conviction!' said Dr Hill.

At 11 pm the telephone went again. This time it wasn't Dr Hill, but a patient who lived on the other side of the village green.

'I'm sorry to ring so late but could I speak to Dr Hill, please?' said the caller. 'It's Daphne Pettigrew.'

'Dr Hill isn't on call this evening, this is Dr Leighton.'

The caller seemed surprised. 'Oh, hello Dr Leighton. I didn't expect to hear your voice. I thought you lived across the green. Have you moved in with Dr Hill?'

'I live in a house on the edge of the village green,' said Dr Leighton quickly. It occurred to her that it would be very easy for a rumour to start that she and Dr Hill were cohabiting and although she liked him, and enjoyed his company, she really wanted to bang that theory on the head as quickly and as firmly as possible.

'But I telephoned Dr Hill at the surgery.'

'The phone was switched through to my home. I live in Squirrel Cottage by the green. I go to Dr Hill's home to do surgeries but I live here.'

'I didn't know they could do that – with the telephones, I mean.'

'I don't understand how it works, but it seems to work which is all that matters. What can I do for you?'

'It's my Richard,' said the caller. 'He has earache. It started this afternoon and I thought it would settle but it hasn't. Keith came in from the pub a few minutes ago and insisted I call you. He plays for the darts team. He said I shouldn't have waited.'

'Which is your cottage?'

'It's one of the pink ones. It's called Mulberry Cottage. We're right opposite you if you're in Squirrel Cottage. I didn't know you were there!'

'Put all the lights on it'll be easier for me to find you,' said Dr Leighton, who had been given this useful tip by Dr Hill.

Dr Leighton picked up her black bag, checked that she had her keys and realised that walking across the village green would probably be quicker than using her truck to drive around to Mrs Pettigrew's.

Ten minutes later she handed a packet of antibiotic medicine to the mother of her first night call patient. 'Give him two tea-spoonsful of this medicine now and then again every four hours. There's enough for two tea-spoonsful at a time for four doses.' She wrote and handed over a prescription as well. 'Bring this to the surgery tomorrow morning and I'll give you more of the medicine – enough for another five days.'

'Both Mr and Mrs Pettigrew were grateful and Mr Pettigrew offered to walk her back across the green to her cottage. Dr Leighton had thanked him, tactfully refraining from pointing out that after his evening playing darts, he was so unsteady on his feet that he would probably need escorting back home and, with her feet lit by a large torch, had safely made her way back across the village green.

And less than ten minutes after that, Dr Leighton was back in her own cottage. Her first night visit was over. She thought about telephoning Dr Hill to tell him that everything had gone well. But then she remembered how tired he'd sounded on the telephone. She made herself a cup of coffee and ate three chocolate digestive biscuits as a reward and a small celebration. She felt very proud of herself. She felt that this was another important step on her professional ladder. She realised that she had definitely made the correct decision in joining Dr Hill's practice and that she wanted, more than anything else, to stay in Stratford Peverell. She felt she could make a good country doctor – and, no doubt linked to that, it was something she very much wanted to do.

She sat and read until 1.30 am and then went to bed. The phone didn't ring again.

Chapter Twenty Two

The next morning, Dr Leighton was woken up by someone shouting. She lay in bed for a moment, not entirely sure whether she was still asleep and dreaming. But the longer she lay there the more it became clear that someone really was shouting. And if she concentrated hard she could make out that the man, and it clearly was a man, was shouting 'Taxi!' at the top of his voice. She looked at the clock. It was twenty past seven in the morning. She climbed out of bed, tiptoed to the window and pulled back a corner of one of the bedroom curtains.

Outside on the village green, not twenty yards from her front gate, stood a man who even at that distance seemed to be in a very bad mood. He was rather red-faced, he had both hands on his hips and every few minutes he called 'Taxi!' in a very loud voice. He was wearing a sheepskin coat and a pair of heavy brown boots (second to Wellingtons by far the most popular footwear in Stratford Peverell) and between the two items of clothing, she could see a foot or so of a pair of striped pyjama trouser. On his head he wore a brown trilby hat which was wrapped in a protective plastic cover as though it had last been worn on a rainy day. Since there were hardly ever any taxis in or around the village green (except on the rare occasion when a resident came back to Stratford Peverell from a foray into the outside world) it seemed a pretty decent bet that the man was either quite insane or having a breakdown. Dr Leighton's first thought (a city dweller's thought) was that she should telephone the police. Her next thought was that as the only immediately local representative of the medical profession she should, perhaps, try to find out what was troubling the man. Maybe, she thought, he had formerly worked in London and imagined that he was still in the city, looking for a taxi to take him to work.

Since she was on call she had her clothes laid out on a chair beside the bed. (This was another practical tip from Dr Hill. 'Keep some comfortable, easy to put on clothing beside the bed. No buttons, no press studs, nothing fiddly. You should be able to dress and get out of the house within five minutes. If the patient calling you is truly in need of help they won't give a damn whether you've put on your make-up or combed your hair'.)

Dr Leighton quickly pulled on some clothes, hurried downstairs, and was walking out through the front gate to her cottage just a minute or two later. She had a comfortable pair of shoes by the front door (and a pair of Wellington boots in the passenger side foot-well of the truck) and, expecting it to be chilly, she had slipped on the coat which, in the absence of a coat rack (an item of furniture on her shopping list) was hanging over the newel post at the bottom of the staircase.

Once outside she approached the man cautiously. She remembered to look to see if he had a plastic hospital identification band on either wrist. When she had been a medical student she'd been told that escaped mental patients who had fled enforced incarceration rarely remembered to remove the plastic wrist band which carried their name and other basic details. There was no plastic band on either wrist. She felt rather silly for looking.

'Good morning!' she said, as brightly and cheerfully as she could manage. She tried not to show any nervousness. 'Are you all right?' She suddenly realised that she recognised the man. Now that he was closer to her there was something very familiar about him: the old-fashioned moustache and the overbearing, rather aggressive manner. She couldn't quite remember where she'd met him before.

'Of course, I'm not OK,' snapped the man. 'My damned dog was scratching at the front door so I let him out. And now he's buggered off somewhere and I can't find him. You haven't seen him, have you?' He paused and then added: 'I'm Scrymgeour Wallace, the Lord of the Manor.' He didn't hold out a hand to shake.

'What does your dog look like?'

'Labrador. Chocolate Labrador.' Said the man rather briskly. 'He usually comes when I call him. The silly old bugger must have found a rabbit trail to follow. You don't have a cat, do you?'

'No, I don't have a cat. And I haven't seen any dogs this morning.'

'Fat lot of use you are,' snapped the man.

Just then a large, chocolate coloured Labrador puppy came bounding up, full of fun and apparently appearing from nowhere. The dog ran up to the man who, sighing in exasperation rubbed its head and slapped its side rather briskly. The dog seemed happy enough.

'Are you OK?' asked Dr Leighton.

'I am now,' said the man briskly. 'Problem solved.' He started to walk away.

'May I ask you one thing?' said Dr Leighton, who, despite the appearance of the dog, was still not sure that the man wasn't suffering some sort of breakdown.

'What's that?' demanded the man.

'Why were you calling for a 'Taxi!' asked Dr Leighton.

'That's the dog's name, you fool!' said the man rudely. 'I spent half my working life standing on London pavements yelling 'Taxi!' so I called my dog 'Taxi!' so that I never forget what I'm not missing.'

And with that he turned and walked away, the dog Taxi trotting obediently at his heels.

Dr Leighton, smiling to herself, headed back to her cottage, wondering what to have for breakfast.

'I say,' called the man, just as she approached her gate, 'aren't you the doctor's new gofer?'

Dr Leighton turned and retraced her steps. She suddenly remembered where she'd seen the man before. He was the rude fellow she'd met at the small party which Dr Hill had held to introduce her to a few of the villagers. But even wrapped in his thick sheepskin coat it seemed clear that he'd lost quite a lot of weight.

'I am,' she said. She introduced herself. 'I'm working with Dr Hill.'

'Oh, you're a doctor too, aren't you? In that case I need to talk to you. I've lost a bit of weight recently. No real reason for it. Been upsetting me a bit. Worried I might have some disease or other. You need to give me a check-up. Let's do it now – save me sitting in that damned waiting room for half the morning.'

'It's not really convenient at the moment,' said Dr Leighton, rather startled by this unusual request. 'I only got out of bed because I heard you calling for your dog.'

The man with the moustache and the chocolate coloured Labrador looked at his watch. 'It's twenty past seven!' he said, as though it were three in the afternoon. 'What sort of time do you get up in the morning?'

'About now, actually,' replied Dr Leighton.

'That's fine then. Anyway, you're up. Which is your cottage?'

Dr Leighton pointed to her new home. 'It's called Squirrel Cottage. The one with the truck in the driveway.'

'You've got a visitor, have you? Young farmer? Doesn't bother me. I'm as broad-minded as the next man.'

'It's my truck?' said Dr Leighton, as icily as she could manage. It seemed that every time the man spoke he managed to annoy her.

By now it was too late. The man was marching ahead of her and heading straight for her cottage, where the front door remained wide open.

Curiously, as he passed her, Dr Leighton felt sure that she could smell something that reminded her of nail varnish remover. Could it really be nail varnish remover, she wondered. Did the bossy, rude man with the moustache have a little secret? Or was there another more medical explanation for that distinctive aroma?

'Comfy little cottage, isn't it?' said the man, who had, uninvited, entered her cottage ahead of her and who was now standing in her hallway. 'Have you bought it or are you renting?'

'I'm renting.'

'They're well-built cottages,' said the man, looking around. 'They've got amazingly thick walls. An electrician tried to drill through one of my walls and gave up. His drill wasn't long enough. He had to make a hole in the window frame and poke the cable through that.' He walked into the living room and looked around as though he were a prospective buyer. Dr Leighton looked to see how much mud he was traipsing into her living room and noticed something about his boots that made her look twice.

'How much weight have you lost?' asked Dr Leighton. She didn't ask the man to sit down. She wanted to get rid of him as quickly as possible. The man's chocolate coloured Labrador ran around the room excitedly.

'Stone and a half,' replied the man. 'About that I would guess. I don't have any weighing scales but my trousers are loose. Damned embarrassing. Have to wear belt and braces. They nearly fell down the other day.'

'And have you noticed any other symptoms?'

'Nothing that I can think of?'

'Are you thirstier than usual?'

'Can't seem to stop drinking. Not alcohol. The other stuff. Cups of tea. Bottles of pop. That sort of thing. Always thirsty. Is that a symptom? I suppose it is.'

'And you have to pass urine a good deal?'

'Course I do! It's got to end up somewhere hasn't it?'

Now Dr Leighton knew what smelt like nail varnish remover. Ketones. She looked down at his shoes again. Sure enough there was another tell-tale sign there.

'Is there any diabetes in your family?' she asked him.

'On my father's side. My father was a diabetic. And his father before him. And his brother. Lots of diabetics on my father's side of the family. They all died young. Never really knew my father.'

'I suspect that might be what's wrong with you,' said Dr Leighton. 'Come along to the surgery this morning. Bring a urine sample. And I'll take some blood to test.'

'Good heavens!' said the man. 'Diabetes, eh? Don't so much mind that. You can treat that can't you? Thought I was on my last legs with some terrible wasting disease.' He nodded at Dr Leighton and waved a finger at her. 'That's not bad doctoring! Making a diagnosis just like that.'

'I need to do some tests,' said Dr Leighton quickly. 'But it's a possibility. In fact I think it is a likely explanation.'

Chapter Twenty Three

'Mr Wallace, the Lord of the Manor, was very impressed with your diagnosis,' said Dr Hill. The two doctors had both finished their morning surgeries. Dr Hill had come in to see Dr Leighton. 'And I hope you don't mind my saying so but so was I! Making a diagnosis in two minutes in your living room! It doesn't get any sharper than that. Word will get round the village in minutes.'

'Have you seen his Lordship, then?' asked Dr Leighton, managing to make the word 'Lordship' sound like an insult.

'No, but he made a point of telling Martha what a wonderful doctor you are! And he did it very loudly and in front of a waiting room full of people.'

'Oh dear,' said Dr Leighton, rather embarrassed. 'I'm sorry.' The doctors she had worked with in London did not take kindly to hearing patients praise their younger colleagues.

'What on earth are you sorry for? I'm delighted. Congratulations. But what made you think of diabetes. The weight loss could have been anything. But from what I heard you'd got the diagnosis before he told you about the drinking and the urination hadn't you?'

Dr Leighton agreed that she had been pretty sure that he had diabetes before she'd even spoken to him. 'Two things gave it away,' she admitted. 'First, he reeked of ketones.'

'Ah, the good old reek of nail varnish remover.'

'Exactly!'

'I bet you wondered what he'd been up to! Taking off the nail varnish from the night before?'

'It did cross my mind,' admitted Dr Leighton.

'And what was the other thing?'

'His boots.'

'His boots?'

'There were dried white splashes on the toes.'

'Aha! I've seen that only once in my life,' said Dr Hill nodding his understanding. 'Dr Joseph Bell of Edinburgh was the first to spot that one I think?'

'I think he was.'

Dr Bell had been one of the doctors who had trained Sir Arthur Conan Doyle, the creator of Sherlock Holmes. Doyle had based Holmes on Dr Bell and had explained that his teacher had once made a diagnosis of diabetes after spotting a white stain on a man's shoe. The man had urinated without accuracy and some of the fluid had splashed onto his shoes. When it dried it left a white mark because of the high sugar content.

'So you had the tell-tale smell of ketones and the sugar in the urine before you even tested his urine or took a blood sample.'

'Yes'.

'Marvellous!' said Dr Hill, who was genuinely pleased for the young doctor. 'That's absolutely marvellous. He smiled and nodded his quiet satisfaction. 'Maybe you'd like to try your diagnostic skills on me.'

Dr Leighton looked at him. 'What's wrong?' she asked.

'Oh, nothing very much,' said Dr Hill. 'I've been meaning to talk to Mallory. But I didn't like to burden him. He goes up and down but he's been getting a good deal better recently.'

'Do you think he'll ever practise again?' asked Dr Leighton.

'No. I don't think so. Nor does his wife. He suffers terribly from depression. Most nights he wakes up about five in the morning.'

'And he won't take anything?'

'Oh no. He won't take any drugs. I don't think he would take anything if he were dying and could only be saved by some miracle drug.'

'And he won't see anyone?'

'Definitely not. We talk about it occasionally. But he can't forgive himself. He knows it's not rational. But he can't forgive himself. I don't think it would have hit him so hard if he hadn't found them. That must have been awful. He and his twin brother were very close, you know.'

Neither of them spoke for a moment or two. The only sound was the tick-tock of the grandfather clock in the hallway. You could hear the clock in every downstairs room. Dr Leighton found it strangely reassuring.

'Tell me about your symptoms,' said Dr Leighton eventually. 'What have you noticed? What signs?'

'Tiredness. I'm tired all the time. For months now I've been getting increasingly weary. I'm not as young as I was but people don't get as tired as I feel at my age. Some days I feel as though I need a nap in the afternoon.'

'You work too hard.'

'No, I don't. I don't work hard in the way that a farm labourer works hard. I know a dozen farm workers who are older than me who work 14 hour days during the harvest season.'

'What else have you noticed?'

'I've lost a bit of weight. – just a few pounds. And I get terrible pains in my joints.'

Dr Leighton nodded, thinking. 'And what else?'

'How do you know there's a 'what else'?' smiled Dr Hill. 'Have you got a diagnosis in mind?'

Dr Leighton smiled but didn't say anything.

'I feel as weak as a kitten,' admitted Dr Hill. 'I can't carry things about without having to stop and rest. The other day I came home with a large bag of potatoes. After I took them out of the truck, I had to stop and rest three or four times before I got them into the larder.'

'Have you done any blood tests?

'No.'

'I need to.'

'I know,' said Dr Hill. He smiled wryly. 'I don't think I wanted to find out. It doesn't sound terribly good, does it?'

'Have you got any enlarged glands?'

'Not that I've been able to find.'

'I'll need to examine you.'

'Of course,' agreed Dr Hill.

'Have you noticed that you bleed more? Have you had any unexplained bruises?'

'No. No, I haven't.'

'Have you had more infections than usual? Do infections take longer to resolve?'

'No to both those.'

'Well, leukaemia doesn't seem very likely,' said Dr Leighton.

'No. It doesn't, does it? Any ideas?'

'When I was at medical school we were shown a patient with something similar,' said Dr Leighton. 'It's quite rare. And I haven't seen a patient with it since then. I'll take some blood when I've examined you. That'll give us the answer. 'She paused for a moment, struggling to remember the details of the case she'd seen. 'Do you have any Celtic blood?'

'I have some Irish blood circulating in me. My mother came from Dublin.'

'Do you have any brothers or sisters?'

'No, I was an only child.'

'Do you have any relatives with any chronic diseases? Anyone who had the same symptoms that you've got?'

'My parents died a long time ago. My father had a heart attack and my mother died of lung cancer. They both smoked very heavily.'

Dr Leighton nodded. 'Let me see if I can feel any lymph nodes. Is this a good time?'

'Never is a good time,' smiled Dr Hill, removing his jacket.

Dr Leighton put a clean sheet of paper on her examination couch and waited while Dr Hill undressed and lay down.

'You haven't been abroad recently?' she asked, as she examined him.

'Not for years,' laughed Dr Hill. 'I've not been able to get away for a long time. The last time I went abroad was in the 1980s.'

'So you are unlikely to have picked up any strange disease that isn't in the ordinary text books?'

'No, I don't think so.'

'I can't find anything wrong,' said Dr Leighton at the conclusion of her examination.

Dr Hill slid off the couch and dressed. 'What was wrong with the patient you saw at medical school?'

'Haemochromatosis,' said Dr Leighton.

'Crumbs!' said Dr Hill, buttoning up his shirt. 'I've never seen a patient with that. I've hardly heard of it, to be honest.'

'It just happened to be something I saw in the teaching hospital,' said Dr Leighton. 'It was rare so they made a big fuss of the patient. You know how teaching hospital consultants are only interested in really rare diseases!'

'I remember,' agreed Dr Hill. 'Haemochromatosis is genetically transmitted isn't it?'

'It is. I'll have to look it up but I remember it's caused by a faulty gene which affects how the body absorbs iron. It's commonest in people from Ireland, Scotland and Wales. The iron levels build up and cause exactly the sort of symptoms you've been having.'

'What's the treatment?'

'The easiest thing is to have a pint of blood taken out every now and then. How often depends upon how bad the condition is.'

'That's all?'

'They make a drug, of course. But it's easier and probably safer just to take out some blood.'

'And throw it away?'

'I'm afraid so.'

'I could put it on my roses,' said Dr Hill.

'You could – though if you win prizes for them you'd probably have to declare a secret ingredient. Before you put your jacket on let me take some blood to send to the lab.'

Chapter Twenty Four

Two days later, when Dr Hill's blood results came back and Dr Leighton's provisional diagnosis was confirmed, the young doctor's reputation as a skilful diagnostician was beyond dispute.

'I rang the consultant haematologist at the hospital,' Dr Leighton told her employer, mentor, partner and patient. 'He said I need to take blood from you once a week for a month or so, and then check your iron levels. If they're satisfactory then we'll probably need to take blood every three months.'

'For the rest of my life?'

'I'm afraid so! The haematologist said there is a drug you can take to reduce the amount of iron in your body. But I'd prefer to take blood out than to give you a drug.'

'I absolutely agree,' said Dr Hill. 'I must say that as chronic disorders go this one is pretty much on the mild side. And far less frightening than some of the diagnoses I was thinking of. I confess I never even thought of haemochromatosis.'

'Well it's fairly easily treatable. You should be feeling a good deal better quite quickly – as soon as we get some of the excess iron out of you.'

Dr Hill, like the Lord of the Manor, was quick to make sure that everyone in the village knew of young Dr Leighton's diagnostic expertise.

And then, rather suddenly and almost unexpectedly, Dr Leighton's probationary three month period was up.

'Do you realise what the day is?' asked Dr Hill one day, as Dr Leighton slid a needle into a vein in his cubital fossa and prepared to take out another pint of blood.

'No, I don't,' admitted Dr Leighton. She suddenly had an awful thought. 'It's not your birthday is it?'

'It's three months since you started work here,' said Dr Hill.

'Surely it can't be!' said Dr Leighton, who had genuinely not realised how quickly the weeks had passed by. Since she'd been living and working in the village, time seemed to have taken on a strange life of its own. For the first month it had sometimes seemed to her as though she'd been working in Stratford Peverell for no more than a day or, at most, a week.

And then suddenly, inexplicably, without her really noticing, she began to feel so much a part of her new environment that it seemed as though she'd been working there for a hundred years – maybe longer. The truth, simple, undeniable and more comforting than she could have imagined was that she had settled into her new life with a seemingly effortless ease which had surprised and delighted her.

'So, how have you enjoyed your three months?' asked Dr Hill. 'Are you going to stay?'

'I would love nothing better,' said Dr Leighton.

'I'm delighted,' said Dr Hill, who clearly was. 'And I know the patients will be pleased too.'

And that was that. Dr Hill said they thought to have something in writing, mainly so that Dr Leighton would have some rights in the practice should anything happen to him. He promised to talk to a solicitor he knew and to have a proper partnership agreement drawn up. He said he would make sure the contract didn't take up more than two sheets of paper.

'Are you going to carry on living where you are? Are you happy there?'

'I love the cottage,' replied Dr Leighton. 'There will be strawberries, gooseberries and blackcurrants to pick soon and the hedges will be full of blackberries – if the birds leave me a few. The fruit trees had plenty of blossom and I planted a small herb garden near the back door. To be honest I'd like to buy the cottage if I could. Do you know I've been renting for three months and I still haven't met my landlord – I don't even know their name. The bank pays the rent for me and the agreement was with a solicitor.'

'I'll have a word with the landlord and see what I can do,' said Dr Hill.

'You know the landlord then?'

'So do you,' said Dr Hill. 'Squirrel Cottage is owned by someone in the village – someone you know quite well. He's been letting it to holidaymakers.'

Will you have a word with them? See if they'll sell it to me.'

Dr Hill promised that he would.

Dr Leighton felt that mixture of excitement and nervousness that all prospective home owners experience when they are about to purchase their first property. For the first time in a long time, perhaps for the first time ever, she felt she was at home. She'd been brought up in a small town that was neither one thing nor the other: it didn't have the excitement of city life and nor did it have the quiet, contained, settled certainty of life in the country. Like many people, she had leapt at the chance to work in London but although she knew some people (such as her former husband) loved living there and would hate to move away, she'd found it too exhausting, dirty and aggressive for her taste. She had always been sensitive to atmosphere and there were, perhaps, too many people living in London who had been disappointed in one way or another and whose lives were now dominated by disappointment, despair and relative poverty (a pound in the countryside seemed to go an awful lot further than a pound in the city) but who could not drag themselves away from the city because to do so would be to admit defeat to themselves and everyone else, and who consoled themselves by reminding everyone they spoke to that London was the centre of glamour; that it was the place to be for first nights (which they never attended), the place for operas and concerts (which they couldn't afford), for museums and art galleries (which were always crowded with parties of noisy school children being rushed from one iconic image to another) and shops (where all they could do was watch rich tourists paying thousands of pounds for a handbag and hundreds of thousands for a watch). 'If you want the wild of the countryside there are always the parks,' they would say, defensive to the end. But who could compare the manicured efficiency of a London park to the real thing, and not be disappointed? And most of those who claimed to live in London were, in reality, marooned on suburban estates an hour or more away by a clunky, stuttering, overcrowded tube train or stuttering bus, from the London they and everyone else thought of as London. They talked of the food hall at Harrods ('you can buy absolutely anything there') but, in reality, did their grocery shopping in a local Tesco store and they talked of the shops in Bond Street but bought their own clothes and shoes from small shops located in a shopping centre precinct dominated by urine, graffiti and ever present squalor and crime. People who love London always quote Dr Johnson: 'A man who is tired of London is tired of life'. But Johnson was talking about a very different London, and Dr Leighton wondered if he would really like the city that London has become.

Dr Leighton realised that for the first time in years she was able to think of the future with a heart full of hope.

'I'm going to buy a Christmas tree,' she thought to herself. 'I've never had a tree since I left home to go to medical school but I'm going to have one. And I'm going to decorate it, and the house, with ornaments and streamers and ribbons, but not balloons because they always frighten me when they go 'bang'. And I'll invite people round for drinks and mince pies which my guests will kindly allow me to pretend I made myself. I'll have my Christmas dinner at The Jolly Roger, surrounded by friends, and we'll all eat too much and drink too much and we'll probably all pile into the kitchen to help with the washing up. On Bonfire night I'll have a huge bonfire, roast potatoes on the embers of the fire and serve hard, tooth cracking toffee that I've made myself. At Easter I'll paint eggs, hide them in the garden and invite village children in to find them. I want to become a part of the village, respected and loved and warmly thought of as something of an eccentric. And I want to carry on Dr Hill's legacy and practise medicine the same, old-fashioned way until I can no longer see or hear well enough to do my job.

And with God's blessing and a little luck, she thought, I'll never leave Stratford Peverell again.

Chapter Twenty Five

The telephone call from Jasmine came quite out of the blue.

'I haven't heard from you for ever!' complained Dr Leighton's London friend. 'Not since you wanted to know if you were allowed to drive a tractor with an ordinary car driving licence.'

'Oh yes,' said Dr Leighton, who recalled being rather embarrassed by the call, and her friend's teasing. 'I remember.'

'So are you still happily pootling round in your tractor? What is it? Have you got a good old-fashioned Massey Ferguson? Or did you splurge out and buy one of those huge Lamborghini tractors so that you can plough a ten acre field in twenty minutes and still take a ten minute tea break in the middle?'

'I'm afraid I never actually drove a tractor at all. I bought a truck instead.'

'A truck! One of those twelve wheel things that are always jack-knifing on motorways?'

'No, I think that's called a lorry. I meant a truck; a pick-up truck. You see them everywhere. They're just cars with a bigger than average boot. Inside, mine is more like a car than I'd imagined.'

'What happened to that lovely Lotus you had?'

'I've still got it. I keep it in the garage and run it round the village green a few times every fortnight to keep the engine, tyres and battery healthy.'

'I didn't think you knew about such things.'

'Well, I didn't. A man in the pub told me I needed to exercise it occasionally. Apparently, cars are like horses. If you don't exercise them regularly they don't do what you want them to do when you need them to do it.'

'Well, I'm impressed. And I can't wait to see your pick-up truck,' said Jasmine. 'I can't wait to see what you pick up in it.' She paused. 'The thing is,' she went on, more diffidently, 'I was wondering if I could come and stay for the weekend? Have you got a bed for a couple of nights?'

'Of course! I'd be delighted to see you. When would like to come?'

'Well, that's the thing, you see, I was rather hoping I could come this weekend. But if it's not convenient you must just say so.'

'That's perfect for me,' said Dr Leighton. 'It's my weekend off. I can take you round the village, pop into the pub and, if the excitement isn't too much for you, we can pop into the village shop and buy a loaf of bread and a bottle of milk.' She hesitated, remembering. 'There's a darts tournament on Saturday and I really have to go to that.'

'You play darts as well as drive a truck?'

'I do!' laughed Dr Leighton. 'The landlady and I have formed a darts doubles team. You'll like Rosemary, she's lovely. We haven't won a match yet but I'm getting better and some people stand near the dartboard these days – which they didn't do for a while. We're hoping to form a pool team too. Our big advantage is that Rosemary tends to wear very short skirts and bends over the table a good deal. The opposition can hardly see straight when it's their turn at the table.'

'You haven't acquired any tattoos have you? To go with the darts and the pool and the pick-up truck?'

'No, not yet. Rosemary says she has one and told me where it is but I haven't seen it and unless she comes to see me as a patient I don't expect I shall.'

'And now that you've got rid of that awful Peter is there a new man in your life?'

'Well, there may be,' admitted Dr Leighton.

'What does 'may be' mean?'

'It means that a rather dishy young fellow has asked me to go to the Young Farmers' Dance in a couple of weeks' time.'

'And that's it?'

'Things move slowly down here in the country! We're quietly getting to know each other though; he's asked me if I'd like to help out with the cricket club teas. Apparently that's rather like going steady down here, so in village terms we're moving ahead at breakneck speed.'

'Going steady! I haven't heard that since I was 14. What does he do?'

'He's a surgeon,' replied Dr Leighton.

'Oh, no! Not another surgeon! I'd have thought you'd had enough with Peter. Why would you want another surgeon? And where on earth did you meet a surgeon down there?'

'He's not that sort of surgeon,' laughed Dr Leighton. 'I was teasing. He's a tree surgeon. I met him a month ago in the pub. It's a bit tricky because he lives in Stratford Peverell so technically he's a patient of our practice. But he's registered with Dr Hill and I've never actually seen him as a patient so I think it's OK. He's five years younger than me but I don't care and I don't think he does.'

'You said 'our practice' rather than 'the practice' or 'the practice where I work'. Does that mean you're staying there?'

'Yes, they've invited me to be a full and permanent partner.'

'And you've accepted?'

'Of course I have. I love it here. I want to stay here forever. I'm going to buy a plot in the cemetery so that I never have to leave.'

'Tell me more about your surgeon.'

'There isn't anything much more to tell you. I'd met him in the pub, so when a branch fell off a tree and the tree needed tidying up, I asked him to come round and have a look. He dealt with the tree in no time at all and then afterwards I gave him a cup of tea and a slice of Madeira cake.'

'You're baking now as well?'

'No, I bought it from the village shop. It was home-made though.'

'I never thought of you as a pub sort of person.'

'I didn't used to be. But the pub is the only entertainment in Stratford Peverell. It's also the only restaurant – they do terrific simple, country food by the way. Oh and I've started playing skittles as well.'

'Is skittles like ten pin bowling?'

'It's what ten pin bowling grew out of, but you wouldn't recognise that when you watch a game of skittles. Our pub has a skittle alley that is probably the most dangerous place in the village. Elvis has been champion for the last three years.'

'Elvis? From the pride in your voice I suspect that Elvis is the tree surgeon?'

'He is. Except in the summer when he becomes a Punch and Judy man. Apparently there isn't much call for performing surgery on trees in the summer months so he gets out his Punch and Judy tent and puppets and tours around the bigger holiday villages for a month. He packs everything in a little trailer which he tows behind his bicycle.'

'I'm beginning to suspect that you've drifted into a parallel universe,' said Jasmine. 'And his name really is Elvis?'

'It is. And his middle name is Aaron.'

'Oh well, never mind. You can always call him something else.'

'But not within hearing of his mother. She's the original Elvis's biggest fan. She's got all his records and has been to Graceland.'

'So calling him Dirk or Cyril might not be a wise move.'

'Probably not. Besides, I like the name Elvis. It's got a good history.'

'Tell me more about the skittles.'

'Well, huge blokes with muscles, which they got from lifting up cows rather than pumping iron in a gym full of women in leotards, hurl solid wooden balls at nine wooden pins and it's a dull evening if at least one of the spectators doesn't get hit by a ball bouncing off a ninepin and out of the skittle alley or, even more alarming, one of the wooden pins leaping over the side boards and flying through the air. There's no heating in the skittle alley and the roof leaks in a dozen places but no one cares or complains. When you see a skittles match you'll realise that ten pin bowling is an incredibly sanitised form of the game – and a great deal safer. There's a lot of drinking at a skittles match and a lot of shouting and a lot of betting.'

'I think I've got my old crash helmet somewhere, from when we had a motorbike. It sounds as if I might need it. Do you remember that motorbike Oliver bought when we were students? It was far too powerful for him and I was always absolutely terrified of it.'

'Yes, I do remember it. He gave me a ride on it once and I've never been so scared in my life. The helmet is a good idea! Bring that. Is Oliver coming with you?'

'No, he's not. That's the other thing. And that's why I rang you to be honest. You remember that he's a manic depressive?'

'Yes, of course. I remember.' Jasmine's husband was also a doctor and had been in the same year at medical school. He practised as a psychiatrist in a London teaching hospital and had a small but booming private practice.

'Well he's going through one of his manic phases at the moment. He met a couple of blokes who want him to go mountaineering with them. He's never climbed anything that I know of – other than the stairs – but he's said 'yes' and so he's going climbing at the weekend. If I stay at home by myself I'll just worry all the time. Last month he stood on a stool to change a light bulb and he wobbled and fell off the stool and cracked his head on a cupboard. He refused to go to hospital because he was too embarrassed and I had to close up a long cut with five butterfly plasters. Heaven knows what will happen when he tries climbing a mountain. But I can't stop him. When he is depressed he's five foot two inches tall, a weakling and dangerously close to feeble minded, but when he's manic he's six foot six inches tall and could take on Samson with one hand while writing an opera with the other. When he's in a manic phase he won't take his tablets because he says they'll slow him down, and when he's depressed he'd take twice the dose if I didn't watch him. I love him very much and I don't know which of them is easier to live with – it's like living with two different people and it can get a trifle exhausting at times.'

'So, there will be just you?'

'Just me. I desperately need a bit of a break, Dr Leighton. A couple of days in the countryside will be wonderful. Fresh air, sunshine and pub grub. Bliss. And I can't wait to meet Elvis. Tell me more about him!'

'He's about nine feet tall, all the time, and nearly as wide. He climbs trees like a monkey, except that he can do so while carrying a chain saw that I can't lift off the ground. He's blond and has a beard which looks as if it might tickle, and even on the coldest days I've never seen him wearing anything other than jeans and one of those shirts that Canadian lumberjacks are supposed to wear.'

'Looks as if it might be ticklish?' said Jasmine, putting the emphasis on the word 'might'.

'Looks as if it might be ticklish,' said Dr Leighton firmly.

Jasmine tutted. 'Email me instructions on how to get to wherever it is that you are. Oh no you can't do that, can you because you don't have email?' laughed Jasmine. Don't worry, just give me the postcode and I'll use the Sat Nav.'

'Your Sat Nav won't work,' laughed Dr Leighton. 'Just head for Stratford Peverell and then look for The Jolly Roger. They'll give you directions to my cottage which is, for reasons lost in history, known as Squirrel Cottage. The pub landlady, who is also the barmaid and the chef and a good friend, is called Rosemary and she's a darling and always there.'

'Are you sure I won't need my passport? Any special injections I should have? Do I need to take malaria tablets?'

Quite suddenly, after Jasmine had put down the telephone, Dr Leighton realised, with something of a shock, that she now had more friends, real friends, than she'd ever had before in her whole life.

Chapter Twenty Six

Jasmine came, arriving just before lunchtime on the Friday, and brought with her three large suitcases, one of her husband's suit bags, a pair of Wellington boots in an old plastic shopping bag and an overnight bag full of make-up. She also brought with her a pack of 200 cigarettes, and two dozen miniature bottles of gin which she'd purchased at the last moment from a shop at the railway station. (They didn't have any large bottles.)

'I wasn't sure that your village shop would sell cigarettes and gin,' she whispered. 'So I thought I'd bring supplies for the weekend.'

'What on earth have you got in those suitcases?'

'Just clothes! I left my 26 volume edition of the *Encyclopaedia Britannica* behind because I felt sure you'd have something to read if I got bored. I've brought you today's paper because I assume you're always a week behind with the papers. I wasn't sure what we'd be doing with ourselves so I brought a couple of formal frocks and all the trimmings. I didn't want to let you down if you'd arranged for us to go to a country house party or a ball.'

'I don't know anyone who has a country house, let alone anyone who hosts balls or formal dinners.'

'And I put in my old riding jodhpurs, which just fit me I'm pleased to say, though I have to be honest and admit they are a little tight across the bum, in case you arranged for us to go riding.'

'I don't know anyone who has horses! Did you bring shoes you can walk in?'

'Oh yes. And a pair of jeans and my Barbour coat in case it rains. I didn't bring my golf clubs because there wasn't room in the car.'

'Splendid. There's no golf course around here and I don't play anyway. It sounds as if you've brought everything you'll need.'

After making lunch and showing Jasmine around Squirrel Cottage and the garden (Jasmine drooled about both and admitted that they more than made up for having only very intermittent internet access and no satellite television) Dr Leighton asked her friend if she'd like to take a look at the village.

'If we're trekking across fields, dodging bulls and clambering up and down vertical hills, the answer is a rather weak maybe,' she replied. 'But if we're heading straight for that lovely looking public house just down the road, the answer is a resounding 'yes'.'

'I thought we'd go to the pub,' said Dr Leighton.

Jasmine cheered. 'Do you have a hat I could borrow?'

'You don't need a hat,' said Dr Leighton. 'It isn't a church.'

'I don't want it to wear. I want it to throw up into the air as a simple sign of celebration!'

Half way to the pub the two women were halted in their tracks when they found the road blocked solid with motor cars. Some drivers were trying to park on the verge. Some were attempting to find a space on the already over-crowded village green. And some simply seemed to be abandoning their vehicles in the road, regardless of the fact that in doing so they were blocking what the locals regarded as the highway.

'I thought his was supposed to be a quiet little village!' said Jasmine, looking around. 'This is the worst traffic jam I've seen since I drove out to Isleworth by mistake one Sunday afternoon.'

The drivers and passengers who had climbed out of the cars were all male and all carrying strange looking poles, all of which had a disk shaped piece at the bottom and a harness for strapping around the owner's chest.

Dr Leighton and Jasmine threaded their way, with difficulty, through the cars and the disgorged humans and eventually arrived at the lounge bar of The Jolly Roger. The pub was full; heaving with men wearing jeans and army surplus jackets and carrying what Dr Leighton and Jasmine now recognised as metal detectors.

After introducing Jasmine to Rosemary, and vice versa, Dr Leighton asked what was happening.

'It's Jack's fault again,' said Rosemary with a sigh. 'I'm so sorry.'

'Aha!' said Dr Leighton. 'What is it this time?'

'A friend of his reportedly found three gold coins and some Roman jewellery in our field,' explained Rosemary. 'There was a picture and a story in the *Daily Mail* today. The people queuing up outside are all people who go metal detecting and treasure hunting.'

'Are they hoping to find more gold coins?'

'And jewellery.'

'Will they?'

'No they won't. First because the gold coins pictured in the paper were made of chocolate and covered in gold foil. They were left over from Christmas. And second because I've told Jack that he isn't to allow any of these people to start digging up our field. We need the grass for our cows, and both village football teams will go mad if they can't play their cup tie tomorrow afternoon. It's the semi-final of the annual Cup competition.'

'It's a vital fixture,' Dr Leighton explained to Jasmine, 'because both teams go through to the final.'

Jasmine looked puzzled, as anyone would have done, and seemed about to say something but Rosemary held up a hand to stop her. 'Please don't ask,' she said. 'Let Dr Leighton explain things to you later – preferably when you have alcohol inside you. What can I get you to drink?'

The two women each ordered a glass of white wine and found a table where they could sit and where Dr Leighton could quietly explain about Jack's trickery with the bird watchers.

'The pub took more money that weekend than they'd taken the previous month,' explained Dr Leighton. 'Looking around I'd think they're going to do it again.'

'Your village is more exciting than I thought it would be,' confessed Jasmine.

'It has its moments.'

'Apart from snuggling up to Elvis and making him endless pies and cakes, what else are you going to do in the evenings?' asked Jasmine, as they ate breakfast together on Sunday morning. 'I should imagine those long, dark nights could become a trifle tedious without a captivating hobby.'

'I'm writing a book,' said Dr Leighton.

'What on earth about?'

'Oh, I thought I'd write about the difference between practising in a smart, modern medical practice in London and practising in an old-fashioned village practice that doesn't have an appointments system.'

'An autobiography!'

'Well, yes, I suppose so. I thought putting in some personal stuff might make it a bit more interesting for the reader. But I'll write it in the third person and give the heroine another name so that no one recognises me.'

'Do you think people would read that?' asked Jasmine. 'I'm not being critical. But does enough happen?'

'I hope so. Other doctors have done it. Our travelling library has a doctor's autobiography called *Practice Makes Perfect* and there is a series of books called *The Young Country Doctor*. There must be a readership for these books.'

'Yes, I can see that might work! How true are you going to make it?'

'Oh fairly true,' I think. 'Mostly true, anyway. And I'll change everyone's name so that I don't get sued. If I find the writing too hard going I can always get a professional writer to turn my notes into a book – arrange it into chapters and so on. The writer could then put their name on the book and we'll share the royalties!'

'Don't forget to put in about the tractor and the pick-up truck! And Elvis the tree surgeon deserves at least a chapter.'

'Hmm. I'll see. You'll be in it anyway. So watch what you say!'

'From now on everything I say will be carefully edited and polished to make sure it looks good on the page. And if you need any help with your book you can always ask Jeffrey Egerton,' said Jasmine.

'I've heard of him. Didn't he write that book that won a big prize a year or two ago?'

The Lion's Pride. They turned it into a movie. I saw him speak about it at the National Theatre a couple of years ago. It was his last appearance in public. He's written a load of famous film scripts and I've got all his novels. The critics say that if he weren't a white English male he'd have won the Nobel Prize by now. His books are wonderful.'

Dr Leighton smiled and nodded, thinking Jasmine was joking. 'How on earth could I even get to meet him? And why would he be interested in helping me with my book?'

Jasmine looked puzzled, started to say something and then stopped. 'You don't know who he is, do you?'

'No, I don't.'

'I've only been to The Jolly Roger twice and I've seen him twice.'

'Who on earth…?'

'The old, scruffy looking bloke sitting next to the fire – that's Jeffrey Egerton.'

'Jeffrey? But he is just a roguish old fellow who writes salacious limericks and is the official poet of The Jolly Roger. He drinks too much, and flirts with every woman over 20 and under 100!'

'That's Jeffrey Egerton.'

'No! It can't be. He's never mentioned anything about writing books or films! He just sits by the fire and pretends to write silly poems and to bet on the horses.'

'Have you ever looked to see what he's writing?'

'No, of course not! Anyway, if people stand near the fire he always closes his notebook and stops writing. He gets a bit uppity about it sometimes.'

'I've heard that he's ever so private and hardly ever does interviews. His agent was quoted in *The Daily Telegraph*, complaining about him. He's famous for being a recluse. *The Sunday Times* ran a big feature about him but they could only interview people who used to know him. They said he was more of a mystery than that artist whatshisname…Banksy. I remember them saying that no one knew where he lived – though there was a rumour that he was living in Switzerland. But he isn't – he lives in Stratford Peverell. The BBC has been trying to make a programme about him for years but his agent says he refuses to allow anyone to film him.'

'And that's Jeffrey Egerton? Are you sure?'

'I'm absolutely certain,' said Jasmine. 'I sat four rows back at his National Theatre lecture and listened to him for three hours. Tell him that if he doesn't write a foreword to your book you'll blow his secret and tell everyone who he is!'

That wasn't the only surprise Dr Leighton had that day.

An hour after Jasmine had set off back to London, there was a knock on the front door of Squirrel Cottage. It was Dr Hill.

'I've got some good news for you,' he said. 'And so I thought I'd deliver it in person.' He was carrying a bottle of Dom Perignon champagne.

'What's the good news?'

'I spoke to your landlord. He's happy to sell you 'Squirrel Cottage'. He said he hates estate agents so he'll leave the price to you. Just pay what you think is fair.'

'Do I get to know his name?'

'Yes, of course. It's Jeffrey Egerton. He lives in the village.'

'I've just discovered that he's the chap who sits by the fire in The Jolly Roger!'

'That's the fellow. He keeps a pretty low profile but over the years he's bought quite a bit of property in the village. He says it's his pension fund. But he likes you and wants you to stay in the village so he'll sell you the cottage for what he paid for it seven years ago. He says the cottage has earned its keep for seven years and he doesn't want to make a profit out of it.'

Dr Leighton headed for the kitchen to fetch a couple of glasses added, over her shoulder: 'I'll bring some plates too. I've got some wonderful home-made coffee and walnut cake.'

Author Biography

Sunday Times bestselling author Vernon Coleman qualified as a doctor in 1970 and has worked both in hospitals and as a principal in general practice. Vernon Coleman is a multi-million selling author and since 1975, he has written over 100 books which have sold over three million copies in the UK, been in bestseller lists around the world and been translated into 26 languages. Several of his books have been on the bestseller lists and in the UK paperback editions of his books have been published by Pan, Penguin, Corgi, Arrow, Century, RKP, Mandarin and Star among many others. His novel 'Mrs Caldicot's Cabbage War' was turned into a successful, award winning movie. He has appeared on Top Gear (the motoring programme), written for a DIY magazine and contributed to a cookery video. He has presented numerous programmes on television and radio, including several series based on his best-selling book Bodypower which was voted one of the 100 most popular books.

Vernon Coleman has written columns for the Daily Star, Sun, Sunday Express, Planet on Sunday and The People (resigning from the latter when the editor refused to publish a column Vernon Coleman had written questioning the morality and legality of invading Iraq) and many other publications and has contributed over 5,000 articles, columns and reviews to 100 leading British publications including Daily Telegraph, Sunday Telegraph, Guardian, Observer, Sunday Times, Daily Mail, Mail on Sunday, Daily Express, Woman, Woman's Own, Punch and Spectator. His columns and articles have also appeared in hundreds of leading magazines and newspapers throughout the rest of the world. He edited the British Clinical Journal and founded and edited the European Medical Journal. For twenty years he wrote a column which was syndicated to over 40 leading regional newspapers in the UK and to papers all around the world. Local health officials were often so irritated by the column that they paid doctors to write competing columns without charge. Fortunately, with a few exceptions, this made little difference to the success of the column.

In the UK, Vernon Coleman was the TV AM doctor on breakfast TV and when he commented that fatty food had killed more people than Hitler, he wasn't fired until several weeks after a large food lobbyist had threatened to pull all its advertising. He was the first networked television Agony Aunt, working on the BBC. Many millions consulted his Telephone Doctor advice lines, and for six years he wrote a monthly newsletter which had subscribers in 17 countries.

In recent years Vernon has been banned from all mainstream media because his views are often at variance with those of the medical establishment. Since March 2020, the ban has been extended to include most of the internet and he is banned from using or even accessing YouTube because the videos he made contained uncomfortable truths. He made over 300 videos about the alleged covid-19 pandemic, compulsory vaccination, the murder of the elderly, digitalisation and so on, and within 6 weeks had nearly 250,000 subscribers. YouTube then removed the channel because it contained too many truths. He then moved to Brand New Tube and acquired 75,000 subscribers before the entire platform was attacked by hackers. Most of his videos are now available on www.vernoncoleman.org which is constantly attacked by hackers. He was refused admittance to Facebook, being told that he would be 'a threat to the Facebook community', expelled from LinkedIn (with no reason given) and banned from all social media. For over 30 years he has had a website (www.vernoncoleman.com and www.vernoncoleman.org) and right from the start the sites have been visited regularly by representatives of the CIA, the FBI and by members of armed forces around the world. The latest figures for www.vernoncoleman.org show that between 25 and 30 million people visit that site each month.

Vernon Coleman has a medical degree, and an honorary science doctorate. He has worked for the Open University in the UK and was an honorary Professor of Holistic Medical Sciences at the Open International University based in Sri Lanka. He worked as a general practitioner for ten years (resigning from the NHS after being fined for refusing to divulge confidential information about his patients to State bureaucrats) and has organised numerous campaigns both for people and for animals. He can ride a bicycle and swim, though not at the same time. He likes animals, cricket (before they started painting slogans on the grass), cycling, cafés and collecting cigarette cards. Vernon Coleman is a bibliophile and has a library larger than most towns. He used to enjoy cricket when it was played as a sport by gentlemen and loves log fires and making bonfires.

Since 1999 he has been very happily married to the professional artist and author, Donna Antoinette Coleman to whom he is devoted and with whom he has co-written five books. They live in the delightful if isolated village of Bilbury in Devon where they have designed for themselves a unique world to sustain and nourish them in these dark and difficult times. They rarely leave home.

Vernon Coleman: What the papers said (before March 2020):

Since the beginning of 2020, when he first exposed the `coronavirus hoax' in his first video, which was seen by millions around the world and then banned, Dr Vernon Coleman has been attacked, demonised, monstered and lied about in the mainstream media and on the internet. Below you will find what the papers said about him BEFORE March 2020 – when he first explained (accurately) how he knew that the alleged pandemic was a hoax and that the hidden agenda was compulsory vaccination, the annihilation of the elderly and the disappearance of cash.

'By the year 2020 there will be a holocaust, not caused by a plutonium plume but by greed, medical ambition and political opportunism. This is the latest vision of Vernon Coleman, an articulate and prolific medical author…this disturbing book detects diseases in the whole way we deliver health care.' – *Sunday Times* (1988)
'…the issues explores he explores are central to the health of the nation.' – *Nursing Times*
`It is not necessary to accept his conclusion to be able to savour his decidedly trenchant comments on today's medicine…a book to stimulate and to make one argue.' – *British Medical Journal*
'As a writer of medical bestsellers, Dr Vernon Coleman's aim is to shock us out of our complacency…it's impossible not to be impressed by some of his arguments.' – *Western Daily Press*
'Controversial and devastating' – *Publishing News*
'Dr Coleman produces mountains of evidence to justify his outrageous claims.' – *Edinburgh Evening News*
'Dr Coleman lays about him with an uncompromising verbal scalpel, dipped in vitriol, against all sorts of sacred medical cows.' – *Exeter*

Express and Echo
'Vernon Coleman writes brilliant books.' – *The Good Book Guide*
'No thinking person can ignore him.' – *The Ecologist*
'The calmest voice of reason comes from Dr Vernon Coleman.' – *The Observer*
'A godsend.' – *Daily Telegraph*
'Superstar.' – *Independent on Sunday*
'Brilliant!' – *The People*
'Compulsive reading.' – *The Guardian*
'His message is important.' – *The Economist*
'He's the Lone Ranger, Robin Hood and the Equalizer rolled into one.' – *Glasgow Evening Times*
'The man is a national treasure.' – *What Doctors Don't Tell You*
'His advice is optimistic and enthusiastic.' – *British Medical Journal*
'Revered guru of medicine.' – *Nursing Times*
'Gentle, kind and caring' – *Western Daily Press*
'His trademark is that he doesn't mince words. Far funnier than the usual tone of soupy piety you get from his colleagues.' – *The Guardian*
'Dr Coleman is one of our most enlightened, trenchant and sensitive dispensers of medical advice.' – *The Observer*
'Vernon Coleman is a leading medical authority and known to millions through his writing, broadcasting and bestselling books.' – *Woman's Own*
'His book Bodypower is one of the most sensible treatises on personal survival that has ever been published.' – *Yorkshire Evening Post*
'Dr Coleman is crusading for a more complete awareness of what is good and bad for our bodies. In the course of that he has made many friends and some powerful enemies.' – *Western Morning News*
'Brilliant.' – *The People*
'Dr Vernon Coleman is one of our most enlightened, trenchant and sensible dispensers of medical advice.' – *The Observer*
'The most influential medical writer in Britain. There can be little doubt that Vernon Coleman is the people's doctor.' – *Devon Life*
'The medical expert you can't ignore.' – *Sunday Independent*
'A literary genius.' – *HSL Newsletter*
'I would much rather spend an evening in his company than be trapped for five minutes in a radio commentary box with Mr

Geoffrey Boycott.' – *Peter Tinniswood, Punch*
'Hard hitting...inimitably forthright.' – *Hull Daily Mail*
'Refreshingly forthright.' – *Liverpool Daily Post*
'Outspoken and alert.' – *Sunday Express*
'The man with a mission.' – *Morning News*
'A good read...very funny and packed with interesting and useful advice.' – *The Big Issue*
'Dr Coleman gains in stature with successive books' – *Coventry Evening Telegraph*
'Dr Coleman made me think again.' – *BBC World Service*
'Marvellously succinct, refreshingly sensible.' – *The Spectator*
'Probably one of the most brilliant men alive today.' – *Irish Times*
'King of the media docs.' – *The Independent*
'Britain's leading medical author.' – *The Star*
'The only three things I always read before the programme are Andrew Rawnsley in the Observer, Peter Hitchens in the Mail and Dr Vernon Coleman in The People. Or, if I'm really up against it, just Vernon Coleman.' – *Eddie Mair, Presenter on BBC's Radio Four*
'Dr Coleman is more illuminating than the proverbial lady with the lamp' – *Company Magazine*
'Britain's leading health care campaigner.' – *The Sun*
'Perhaps the best known health writer for the general public in the world today.' – *The Therapist*
'The patient's champion. The doctor with the common touch.' – *Birmingham Post*
'A persuasive writer whose arguments, based on research and experience, are sound.' – *Nursing Standard*
'Coleman is controversial but respected and has been described in the British press as `the sharpest mind in medial journalism' and `the calmest voice of reason'. – *Animals Today*
'Vernon Coleman...rebel with a cause.' – *Belfast Newsletter*
'...presents the arguments against drug based medicine so well, and disturbs a harmful complacency so entertainingly.' – *Alternative News*
'Dr Vernon Coleman has justifiably acquired a reputation for being controversial, iconoclastic and influential.' – *General Practitioner*
'He is certainly someone whose views are impossible to ignore, with his passionate advocacy of human and animal rights.' – *International*

Journal of Alternative and Complementary Medicine
'The doctor who dares to speak his mind.' – *Oxford Mail*
'He writes lucidly and wittily.' – *Good Housekeeping*

Printed in Great Britain
by Amazon

36171844R00129